Camo Angel

CASSANDRA KIRKPATRICK

*Gloria,
Thank you for being there and loving me when I felt unlovable. Always remember to stay stronger than duct tape and sweeter than honey!
♡ C. Kirkpatrick*

Copyright @ 2014 by Cassandra Kirkpatrick

All rights reserved. No part of this publication may be reproduced, distributed, or transmitted in any form or by any means, including photocopying, recording, or other electronic or mechanical methods, without the prior written permission of the publisher, except in the case of brief quotations embodied in reviews, fan-made graphics, and certain other noncommercial uses permitted by copyright law.

Cover Model:
ALEXIS KIRKPATRICK

Cover Designer:
DYRANI CLARK

Editor:
CELESTE MARTIN

Author's Note:

The characters, names, locations and events portrayed in this book are products of the author's imagination or are used in a fictitious manner. Any similarity to real persons, living or dead, is purely coincidental and not intended by the author.

WARNING This book contains lots of emotion, graphic language, and adult situations. It is not suitable for readers under the age of 17.

Dedication:

To all those who have believed in me through the years, thank you for letting me prove you right. To all those who doubted me and told me I couldn't through the years, thank you for letting me prove you wrong. To my husband, family and friends, thank you for dreaming with me.

Table of Contents

CAMO ANGEL 1
COPYRIGHT 2
AUTHOR'S NOTE: 3
DEDICATION: 4
CHAPTER 1 7
CHAPTER 2 19
CHAPTER 3 29
CHAPTER 4 35
CHAPTER 5 45
CHAPTER 6 51
CHAPTER 7 59
CHAPTER 8 61
CHAPTER 9 67
CHAPTER 10 77
CHAPTER 11 83
CHAPTER 12 89
CHAPTER 13 97
CHAPTER 14 105
CHAPTER 15 113
CHAPTER 16 119
CHAPTER 17 123
CHAPTER 18 135
CHAPTER 19 147
CHAPTER 20 159
CHAPTER 21 169
CHAPTER 22 175
CHAPTER 23 181

CHAPTER 24 187
CHAPTER 25 201
CHAPTER 26 205
CHAPTER 27 209
CHAPTER 28 213
CHAPTER 29 223
CHAPTER 30 227
CHAPTER 31 233
CHAPTER 32 239
ACKNOWLEDGEMENTS: 242
ABOUT THE AUTHOR 243
CONTACT ME: 244

Chapter 1
ABBY

*T*oday was my big day; I was finally graduating! Liz and I were supposed to be getting ready. Well, I really was getting ready, while she was off somewhere flirting with my brother, Liam.

I slipped into a soft purple, silky, floor length dress that matched my eyes perfectly. Lynn did a great job in picking out my graduation gift. My mom zipped it up as her beautiful blue eyes began to tear up. "I can't believe you are graduating today! Seems like it was yesterday your father and I brought you home from the hospital. I love you even more than I ever thought I could love a person; you will always be my Little One," Mom whispered as she hugged me, leaving a kiss on my cheek before finally pulling away, still smiling as she watched me.

She smoothed her hands down her teal blue knee length number nervously. As she looked at herself in the mirror of the old fashioned vanity, she gently pushed her slightly graying hair behind her ear. A smile played across her lips. For having eight children, she aged very nicely and was just as beautiful as the day I was born.

A knock on my door had me instantly turning, pulling my face into a bright smile. I was 95% sure I knew who was on the other side of that door. "Come in!" My voice gave away my excitement as it pitched higher than normal. I never was a girly girl, except when I was excited.

Nudging the door gently open with his booted foot, Micah stood there dwarfing the door frame with his 6'4" muscled body. His sparkling smile could brighten up the darkest of days. "Look at you

Little One, all grown up and even more beautiful each time I see you." He smirked.

Micah had his hair cut into the typical "high and tight" I've grown used to over the years. He wore a button down charcoal gray shirt with the sleeves rolled up, showing off his sleeves of ink, jeans and his boots. He was a handsome man. Of all my brothers, he looked the toughest and most menacing. My, how looks could be so deceiving, he was the sweetest, most caring person I knew. That boy would move heaven and earth to keep me happy. *Yes, I was a bit spoiled by him.* His blue eyes glowed with pride and love as he swept me into his arms spinning me in the greatest hug a girl could get from her big brother.

I snuggled even closer as tears of joy leaked out of my eyes onto his shoulder. "Don't cry beautiful! We don't want to mess up your beautiful face, make it all blotchy and shit." Mom cleared her throat. "Sorry Mom," he responded and glanced to the ground embarrassed. Swearing wasn't allowed at the house. Micah never used to swear. Since he joined the Army, his language became more graphic. He easily forgot where he was at times, letting the curse words slip.

"It's been too long Mikey." I smiled through my tears, afraid to let go of him, afraid he might disappear. I loved being wrapped up in his strong tattooed arms. It was my safe place.

"We just saw each other on Skype last night." He beamed his smile bringing out his pair of matching dimples, softening the menacing demeanor, letting the rest of the world see the man I see.

"Seeing you in person beats Skyping with you all day, any day! You have totally made my day! Screw graduation, I'm happy enough here."

I popped up on my tip toes, planting a kiss on his cheek, leaving a perfect light pink lipstick kiss. Patting his cheek, he smiled. "I'm wearing that proudly. I plan to make you squeal like the little girl you are, in just a moment Little One. Your day is about to get even better." I knew what the surprise was even before he showed me; there were only a handful of things in this world that would make me squeal. Only one of those followed Micah through hell and back. He smiled as he pulled away from me, heading towards the door. He called out, "Get your ass in here."

His battle buddy and best friend since before they crawled out of the womb, Eli, leaned in the doorway with a smirk showing off a single dimple. He was in a pair of darker Levis, his trusted combat boots, and a navy polo shirt testing the strength of the seams. "Miss me?" His teal blue eyes danced as they met my pale purple ones, his grin deepened.

I ran over, threw my arms around his broad neck, effectively jumping into his open arms. I hugged him with all my strength. "You came!" I squealed. He might have been Micah's best friend, but he was there when the abuse first started. He was the first to believe me—we too had an unbreakable bond. He helped me through the past five years of the bruises, bumps, even through the stitches and broken bones. While I went through the hell, I was blessed to have someone who was there constantly trying to keep my spirits up. There is something to be said about angels in disguise. My angels wear camo.

Eli wanted to kill my father, but I convinced him not to when I was 15.

I just got out of the pool; it was another long practice. Regionals were tomorrow, so I busted my butt trying to cut fractions of seconds off my times. As soon as my hands hit the underwater touch pad, I glanced up at my time and smiled. Yes! I cut off .14 seconds! I got out and hit the showers before getting some clothes on. I told the girls to have a great night and headed out of the locker rooms.

I was swept into strong arms, and a very solid chest. Surprisingly, I didn't scream. He hugged me for another second. "Babe, you are kicking ass out there." He put me back on my feet and slung his arm across my shoulders.

"What are you doing here?" I looked up at him, confused but happy.

He smirked, "We came back to see you stomp your competition tomorrow. Micah is out in the truck."

Hearing that Micah here had me jumping up and down with excitement! Yay! My big brother is here! I squealed to myself.

Eli touched the bandage on my arm. He removed it and looked at the latest wound. "How the fuck did this happen?" We walked towards Micah's truck. I searched the ground while my brain searched for answers. "Babe, how'd this happen?" I could feel the concern without even looking up.

"Dad broke a beer bottle and swung it at me. It got stuck." I continued to stare at my feet.

"I'm going to kill that motherfucker!" he growled as we got to the truck.

"Hey, Little One!" Micah's smile faded when he saw the look on Eli's face. "What's going on?"

I was squeezed into the middle part of the seat, between my heroes. Happy is what they made me. They wanted to always be there to save me.

"Show him, Babe," Eli stated.

I pulled up the sleeve of my arm and showed him. "Daddy said it was an accident."

Both of the boys shook their heads in what I could only see as a mix of hatred and hostility. "We are going to do something about this," Eli stated.

"You can't kill him; think of what it would do to Mom."

"Little One, we can't just sit back and keep finding out how bad it is. You should be safe and happy, not scarred and scared." Micah kissed my forehead.

"Two years Micah, that's all I have left." I tried to reassure them, I was going to survive through all of this.

"Two seconds are too long Abs. What if instead of killing him, we hurt him?" Micah suggested.

"It's always worse after someone interferes. Sure, I get a week or two of reprieve, but then it starts up again and is usually worse than before. I will just stay in my room when no one else is home." I shrugged.

"Not happening. Mom signed the emancipation papers, right?" Micah asked

I nodded. "Dad refuses to sign. Two more years, I will come out of this scarred but stronger."

Micah's dimples activated. "You really are stronger than duct tape and sweeter than honey." He kissed the side of my head. "I still want to kill him Abs."

I shook my head. "No. It would destroy Mom. It would ruin your careers. Even if it's bad now, it will be that much worse if you did. It's only me; everyone else is safe. Promise me you won't try anything."

"We can't promise that. The only thing we could promise you is he won't die by our hands. That's all we can agree to."

As he put my feet back on the ground, I leaned back and playfully slapped his chest. "You lied! You told me you couldn't make it!"

He kissed my cheek. "Surprise Babe." He has called me that for as long as I could remember. Liz always told me it was because he forgot my real name. Honestly, I think she was just jealous of our bond.

Micah raised his eyebrow. "That's still my baby sister." He playfully punched Eli's shoulder. Mischief shined bright in his eyes, making me wonder what was going on. Making me wonder how much he knew. Did Eli really keep our secrets as he promised? Micah refocused his attention back on me, he joked, "Abs, this is your real gift from me."

Eli cocked his eyebrow in challenge. "Ahem," he failed terribly at acting offended. "This is from *both* of us." He slipped a shiny, silvery chain around my neck, clasping it in the back. When he brushed his fingers lightly over my bare shoulder, he evoked a small shiver from me. "It's platinum, Babe, not silver or white gold, only the best for you," he whispered as he kissed the top of my head.

I smiled and squealed, "Oh my gosh! It's beautiful!" I lifted the pendant up to examine the three beautiful diamonds dangling.

Micah kissed my forehead, he added, "It's not nearly as beautiful as you. Those diamonds stand for the past, the present, and forever. We will be there with you always." He hugged me tight. "Congrats Little One, I am so proud of you."

We have never planned for the future, only for forever. It was just our thing. Future means nothing if you have no plan of forever.

Mom hugged us, pulling us all in tighter for a group hug. "I'm so glad you could all be home for this. How long do you get?" I loved seeing her smile.

Micah had Mom's beautiful smile, their dimples even matched, he answered, "A week. I wish it were longer, but they could only postpone our next mission for so long." I knew they were looking forward to this next mission; though they couldn't tell me the details. I just knew they were going to rescue some damsel in distress, or maybe hack and slash their way to fame and fortune, who knew? Our camo angels were saving the unsaveables.

Liz came dancing and twirling into the room with a huge smile on her face, her normally sleek black hair slightly mussed, and her green eyes sparkling brightly. Adjusting her assets, she straightened her emerald knee length dress. "Looks like you got one hell of a graduation gift!" She wiggled her eyebrows suggestively at me.

I burst out laughing, trying to regain my composure. I couldn't help but shake my head. "You need to get ready Liz! There's no time to be running off with Liam." I turned to the boys, trying ineffectively to shoo them out. I nudged them closer to the door. "Out you go, but not too far."

Mom smiled. "Make yourselves useful and get everyone to the living room. I want pictures." She closed the door as she pushed the boys the rest of the way out of the room before she turned to help me put the finishing touches on Liz.

By the time we were dressed, and every hair on our heads was in place, we joined the massive celebration happening in the living room. The wall of pictures drew my attention, a smile snuck across my face. The wall was filled with framed pictures of our family through the years; they fit together like pieces of the puzzle. My favorite was a picture from the beach when I was about five; everyone truly looked happy.

I loved the open floor plan of our house; more people could fit comfortably. Mom could be cooking in the kitchen and still carry on a conversation with the rest of the family. My favorite place to sit was at the bar unit—I ate there, did homework, searched the internet, watched Mom cook, I even had late night chats with Mom, Micah and Eli.

My oldest sister Lynn snatched me up in a tight hug; she pulled back so I could catch her smile. She was 23 years older than I was, so I tended to see her more as a second mother figure than a big sister. Honestly, I was closer to her oldest daughter Celeste, who was older than me by a mere couple months. I loved Lynn and saw her as someone I could share my joys and sorrows with. She was one I could actually talk with and share my fears, never one to pass judgment. Celeste and LeAnn both had the Remlock hair and eyes. You could tell they were Lynn's daughters. Terence, her son, looked more like his dad but still had the Remlock striking blue eyes.

The telltale clicks of cameras began. I looked around and saw huge smiles everywhere. Flashes went off from every angle of the room, brightening it that much more.

Rob lifted me off my feet, pulling me into his side as his wife Gina shared our hug. Their five boys ranged from the twins Ben and Briar being ten, down to baby Caleb, who was only six months old. Alex was six years old, and one of my biggest fans, ever since I taught him how to swim like I do. Richard was three, and only worried about his toy cars and shiny things. I was used to having boys easily distracted by shiny things and squirrels, my brothers' attention spans rivaled that of a goldfish. I was fully engulfed in Rob's mob as we've dubbed them, it was amazing the awesome feelings I was feeling right now.

My father grumbled, "It's just a graduation from high school, not a huge achievement. Every one of our kids has done it." He kicked back in his old blue recliner and popped open the beer Pauline, his favorite spawn, handed him. The chair had been used so often by him over the years it literally had an indent where his butt sat.

Father always told me the only way he could put up with me was if he had a drink in his hand. When I came home from school, I always looked at his hand before I told him something that might upset him, which could've been anything that came out of my mouth. If he had a drink, I told him. Otherwise, I tried to cower in my room until he found a drink. Too many times I was beaten with his empty fist.

Pauline sneered in my general direction, as she usually did. I knew she hated me, having heard it too many times over the years. Just like my father, she too wished I was never born. I was the abortion that didn't take place, because Mom felt her pregnancy happened for a reason. She was against abortion no matter the reason. In Pauline's eyes, I was just an outcast. The only reason she was here was to please *Daddy*, oh and the fact she still lives at home. At least I had a direction in life, I wouldn't be almost forty and still in my parents' house, I already had a plan.

Liz pulled me away from Rob's family and deposited me between Eli and Micah while she giggled. "Say cheese!" We were laughing together while Liz continued to take candid shots. Liam snuck up behind her. He slipped his arms around her and planted a kiss on her neck. Turning the camera around, she snapped a few of the two of them.

Mom smiled proudly as she watched us all interact. Wes, Rob's twin, slipped an arm around Mom, pulling her closer to him. "You look incredible Mom! Hard to believe your baby is already graduating, any news on her college choice?"

Wes and Rob may be identical twins, but they led completely different lives. Rob was perfectly happy being a house husband with his perfectly combed hair and still in love with his high school sweetheart. Wes was a straight up player with his just got out of bed hair, which apparently according to him, 'chicks dig the messy look.' Instead of staying home, Wes worked long hours and many late nights; he just hired a maid to take care of his cooking and cleaning.

"She got accepted at USC, American University in Paris, and Columbia, among a few others. I'm letting her decide," Mom answered as she beamed at me. Her eyes were on the brim of letting tears slide down. "She's earned full rides with some and athletic scholarships with others. She's destined to do great things like you did."

I hugged Wes and replied, "It's a secret! You have to wait for the big reveal at the party tonight. Thanks for coming! Where is Beth, I think that was her name, right?" I'd only met her once on Skype, and was pretty sure it was by accident considering her state of undress.

He chuckled. "She and I were very short-lived Little One, definitely wasn't worth bringing home. I'm between *flavors*, as you call them. I wouldn't have missed this day, no matter what. I'm fine flying solo." He kissed my cheek before walking off in search of Micah and Rob.

The front door banged open as Colton and his wife of ten years, Missy, came running in. Colton smiled as his eyes met mine. "Sorry we are running late Little One. The time slipped away from us." You would think they were still newlyweds. I've never seen two people so deep in love. They loved on each other every chance they got; they barely took their hands off each other, like a couple of frisky teenagers. She was the apple of his eye. I wished one day I would have a man look at me the way he looked at her.

Mom hugged them. "So glad you are finally here. Let's get the family all together in a couple shots."

She pried my father from his chair, his frustration evident. "It's just another fucking day Karen," he sighed as he sat his beer down and continued to mumble under his breath.

She shook her head. "All our kids are home. I want a family picture."

She handed the camera to Eli and kissed his cheek. "Would you be a dear and take a few pictures for us, please?"

"Yes ma'am!" Eli smiled sweetly. The gentle giant was one hell of a teddy bear. I couldn't help but laugh at the face he made; innocence didn't suit him. I stuck my tongue out at him, earning a wink and a smirk from him.

We were situated from youngest to oldest. Mom stood proudly beside me, wrapping her arm across my shoulders as I held Liam's hand. Unsurprisingly, Dad stood beside Pauline, and as close to Lynn as he could get. When asked to take one of just him and me, he flat out refused, not even trying to cover his look of disgust. Some people would be offended, but I just shrugged it off and thought *oh well*. I wasn't surprised.

Mom even managed to get her wish and get a couple pictures of all eight of her grandkid—Lynn's three teens and Rob's five boys. She took advantage of all the free space a digital camera had to offer. The camera kept clicking, memories saved with each click. She even managed to get pictures of just Rob's family, as well as Lynn and her husband, and their three—Celeste, LeAnn, and even Terence going through a shaggy-haired emo stage.

I loved having a big family; there was more love to go around. My whole life has been full of doubt if I would ever break the surface of my father's stone cold heart. It wouldn't stop me from busting my ass to make something great of myself because I knew everyone else loved me.

The laughter, smiles, hugs, and love flowed freely through our living room. I never realized just how blessed I truly was. In the end, I was loved, and that was all that mattered. It just takes being loved by one to ease the hate showed by many.

I had to admit, although maybe with a little bias on my part, my family was beautiful. My mom was the shortest at five and a half feet, the rest of us grew from there, all the way up to Micah's 6'4" frame. Our hair, although different styles and cuts, was the same shade of dark blonde with natural lighter highlights. Everyone, but me, had the brightest, prettiest blue eyes I've ever seen. According to my father I'm defective, so my eyes only managed to get a few flecks of that blue, while the main color was a pale purple that darkened depending on my mood.

I couldn't wait to see the pictures we took!

Chapter 2
ABBY

*G*lancing at the old grandfather clock, I realized we were going to be late. "Crap Liz! We need to get going! We're going to be late!" We had to be there in five minutes, but it took ten to get there from our house.

My father had checked his watch before he snapped, "As usual, Gail is running late."

Mom started issuing out ride assignments; she was the most organized person I've ever met. "Ed, you can drive Abby and Liz, her parents are there waiting. Maybe Lee, you want to ride with them?"

"I'm riding with Daddy!" Pauline stood up and wrapped her arms around my father's arm. Of course, she wouldn't let him out of her sight.

"Good, I will sit in the backseat with these two beautiful girls," Liam responded as he slung his arms over Liz and my shoulders as we made our way out to my father's rusty old gray Chevy Celebrity.

I heard Mom asking if Eli and Micah would mind running with her to pick up my cakes. Of course, they would do absolutely anything Mom asked of them. Asking them was out of courtesy instead of necessity.

We pulled out of our gravel drive. I sat in the back and fidgeted as I tried to get my honor cords to lay just right. I ran through the speech in my head. The nerve battle had begun. I didn't like being the center of attention; I've always tried to blend in. I was an awesome swimmer because I blended in well with the water.

Taking his eyes off the road momentarily, my father eyed me in the rearview mirror. "Gail quit your damn fidgeting! Do you have your speech completely memorized?" He was the only family member ever to call me Gail, aside from Pauline. I've come to despise it as much as I did them.

I nodded and twined my fingers together to still them. "Yes sir," I responded.

"You better. You are a Remlock. I don't need you to embarrass us," he stated before he returned his focus to Pauline and the road ahead.

I muttered under my breath, "Yeah I know. You do enough embarrassing the family name for the both of us." As I rubbed the left side of my forehead, I fixed my long bangs to make sure the freshly healing scar was covered.

Liam tugged my hand into his, giving it a little squeeze. As he leaned over to swipe a stray curl behind my ear, he whispered so only I could hear, "I love you Little One. I'm blessed that I get to call you my sister, even if you do have cooties!" He laughed. "You will do awesome! Pretend it's the fifty-meter butterfly."

I laid my head against his shoulder as I struggled to keep my composure. The youngest of my brothers gave me more strength than he knew.

As we pulled up outside the auditorium, Liz and I quickly darted in through the instructed door, while Dad mentioned he would find a parking spot. Liam blew a kiss in our direction and said he'd be in there to watch us graduate.

Our balding principal, Mr. Daniels, greeted us at the door, extending his hand. "So glad you decided to join us Miss Carmichael, Miss Remlock."

I ducked my head; my cheeks reddened with embarrassment as we answered, "Sorry Sir."

The room was filled with fellow graduates. We were all lined up by our last names. I remember joking with Liz that one of us needed to change our last names, so we weren't seated so far away from each other. We were partners in crime and belonged in each other's pockets. As the two lines started moving, all the excited chatter amongst our classmates died down. The voices of our fans, families, and friends erupted into loud cheers, a deafening roar of the crowd. I looked at my fellow classmates, dressed in our matching black robes and our square graduation caps; I knew their bright smiles were mirrored on my face as well. True elation, it was finally the day we were all waiting for.

Since Liz and I were chosen as co-valedictorians, we were escorted up to the stage, instead of moving to our places in the crowd. We hugged each other tightly whispering words of love and encouragement before taking our respective seats.

Once everyone was seated, our class president gave a prayer. I was relieved he decided to give us the shortened version, instead of the ten minute one he was thinking of giving. The choir sang a beautiful rendition of Lee Ann Womack's *I Hope You Dance*, which caused more than a few teary eyes in the building. I was already emotional; I patted my pockets in hopes I had enough tissues.

Please, don't let my mascara run! I begged to the heavens.

The principal stood up and addressed the crowded auditorium, "It is my honor to introduce our first speaker. Not only has she set new records on the track, she has dedicated countless hours to the tutoring program. Her brilliant mind made her one of the brightest mathletes I have ever had the pleasure of working with. One of this year's twelve perfect GPAs, she has been offered a full ride at Columbia, which she will be starting in the fall. It is my pleasure to introduce Miss Alizabella Elise Carmichael."

Everyone, including myself, stood up to clap and cheer for her. Through the cheers, I could hear sirens go off somewhere in the distance. Of course being in Salt Lake, it was a normal occurrence, but for some reason it felt off. Being a person of faith, I sent up a prayer for the safety for those that required the emergency services as well as peace for the families involved.

Liz proudly took center stage, placing her hands on the podium in front of her. "Like every great speech starts out, I must first thank everyone for showing up and listening. So Principal Daniels, staff, fellow classmates, family and friends welcome and thank you for joining us."

She gave a breathtaking smile to the crowd then turned to me, mouthing *I love you*. Her beautiful emerald eyes were glistening with the threat of tears. I blew a kiss and whispered, "I love you more." It was all I could do to fight the urge to run up and throw my arms around her to hug her tightly to me. God couldn't have given me a better friend than the girl standing proudly in front of the crowd. She was as bold as I was shy.

"Today we are going to talk about motivation. Just like Pinky and the Brain, tonight we are taking over the world. We are about to spread our wings and fly." She smiled. "We started out all these years ago as caterpillars. Through luck and a lot of hard work, we have blossomed into beautiful butterflies ready to take flight. I know, I know, you boys don't want to be beautiful butterflies. So for you, I shall say you have battled your way up to be the handsome beasts you thought only existed in your dreams. For the duration of my speech, you get to be lions." Laughter and roars broke out.

"All right so elementary and middle school helped foster growth, change, and self-awareness. For us ladies, we were in our cocoons, gathering the strength to come out, busting out with bigger assets. While we were developing, they too went through *the change*. They didn't have a cocoon to get all awesome in, so we got to experience their voices go from squeaky mice to small growls! Most are still working on facial hair. We are still waiting to hear their *great* roars." More laughter erupted. She knew how to work the crowd.

"On a more serious note, we've all experienced hardships; we all have a flaw or two. To be honest, I've got more than my fair share of them. My best friend tells me to love the flaws you were blessed with. All our wings are different, but if we don't love ourselves and believe, we will never be able to fly. Guys, you gotta continue to work hard to become the king of your world. Just keep pretending your pack is bigger than mine, it's ok, my roar is bigger than your bite. That's my challenge to you, become the leader your pack deserves because if you follow everyone else, the view never changes. So step up, become a leader, and watch as the world changes for you. 'Why fit in when you were born to stand out?' That was the question asked by Dr. Seuss. I ask you that same question tonight." She looked out and gave the crowd one of her show-stopping smiles.

"I planned each race carefully, wearing a different motivational quote on the back of my uniform. From 'Pain is temporary, pride is forever' to 'If you are reading this, practice harder.' I even had one that said, 'It's ok, I'll wait for you at the finish line.'" She paused. "I did wait at the finish line to congratulate everyone for going the distance and completing the challenge. Don't give up, keep going! Go forth, be strong, wise kings like Mufasa. Although I know some of you will only retain the intelligence of Ed! I also know about 10% of you think differently, don't worry your nose will grow like Pinocchio's!" she smirked playfully.

"I am going to leave you with one last bit of wisdom. Of all the challenges and mountains you have to face or climb, you only have to do it once to say you've done it! After that, you are just showing off!" She turned and headed back to her onstage seat. The crowd's cheers blew the roof off the auditorium. I was so proud of my best friend.

When the cheers finally calmed back down, Principal Daniels took the podium. "Excellent speech Miss Carmichael! The choir is going to sing *Time of My Life,* now," he announced before he sat back down. The choir members stood where they were in the crowd and belted out the tear jerking song made famous by David Cook.

As they finished, Mr. Daniels took the podium; the choir took their seats. "Now it's time to introduce the other half of the Valedictorian speakers today. Our next speaker is the youngest in this year's graduating class, in a couple days, she will finally be 17. Not only has she skipped a grade or two, she managed to maintain a perfect GPA while doing so. Let's see," he paused to look down at his notes. "Ah yes! She led the swim team to multiple victories, breaking records that were once held by her brother Wesley, not just at Regionals, but at State as well. She has participated in several trips with our local mission and volunteered extra hours at the local soup kitchens. With a heart of gold, she has put others before herself time after time. Help me as I put her before you, Miss Abigail Lucille Remlock."

I blushed as the crowd cheered and clapped. I gave Mr. Daniels a hug before continuing to the podium. When the crowd calmed again, I smiled at Liz before facing my fellow classmates and an auditorium filled to the brim. "Wow! With an intro like that, what could I say to top that? I can't top it, won't even try. Liz was up here giving you motivation, so that leaves me to give you advice," I chuckled a little, me of all people, giving advice.

I looked out at the crowd; it felt so surreal standing up here with everyone willing to listen to me. My heart swelled in my chest as I swallowed down my nerves. I psyched myself up; *I got this! It's time to put on my big girl panties and get this done with.*

"I'm going to make this as short as possible. I know I'm not the only one ready to run across this stage to get a piece of paper to start our future. My advice is to count your blessings and learn from your mistakes." I smiled and turned around to head to my chair as the hoots and hollering took over.

Liz burst out laughing and managed to join in with the crowd chanting, "Abby! Abby! Abby!" They were all standing and proudly chanting my name.

I finally returned to the podium after bowing down worshipping them from where I stood. Taking the mic, I stepped away from the stand. Looking out to the crowd, I smiled. "I am not worthy. I do have a little speech prepared if you want to use this time to take a power nap while I talk, I understand. It's ok, go ahead, relax! I promise there will be no pop quiz at the end of this." I took a deep breath and started my actual speech, "First off, I want to thank Principal Daniels, the staff, coaches, family and friends for joining us on this glorious day. To my classmates and teammates alike, we did it!"

"Let me say that being the youngest of eight children, I have heard my fair share of advice. I've heard it all. From 'I wouldn't touch that if you know what's good for you' to 'Grow a pair if you want to win' and the ever famous 'I told you so.' And yes, I've even used the infamous, 'I'm telling on you' only to hear 'not if I tell on you first' or 'go ahead and tell I don't care.' Yes, everything in our house was a competition, even tattling." I glanced out to the crowd looking for my brother Rob, the pro tattler, but the lights were shining too brightly, blinding me.

"I do want to set the record straight. Principal Daniels mentioned I broke a couple swimming records originally set by my brother Wes. I didn't just break a few of his records; I shattered them, six of them to be exact, thanks to the help and support of an awesome coach and stellar teammates. It's true bubba; you got beat by a girl." The lights had moved, so I was able to see more. I smiled as I looked to where my family was supposed to be sitting, and panicked a little when I only saw Lynn, her family, and Liam sitting next to Liz's parents. Lynn's reassuring smile helped me regain focus; I had a speech to finish. Panicking would have to wait.

I had taken a couple calming breaths before I began again, "All right. I'm going to share with you a little bit of advice that my mom has always given us. As we grew up, Mom always told us to keep our heads in the clouds, our hearts full of love, and our feet firmly planted on the ground. Don't be afraid to take risks, or you may never find the greatest joys they may bring. If, along the way, you encounter sorrow, may you find peace soon after." I smiled as I thought of my mom's ability to brighten my days.

"We approach our future today with our eyes wide open and our hearts full of hope. Whether we decide to stay around here, join the military, become drunken bums, or go to a school across this great country, we will all carry this day with us for the rest of our lives. A significant milestone." I couldn't help but laugh with the crowd.

"I remember walking into kindergarten all those years ago, standing together and reciting the Pledge of Allegiance. Just for old time's sake, can we all stand one last time and recite it together?" I asked as the flag was brought front and center, bringing everyone to their feet. Some held their hands over their hearts, some saluted, but everyone joined in as we boomed the Pledge of Allegiance proudly. After the last amen had ringed out, everyone returned to their seats.

I began again. "As we step across this stage and receive our diplomas, a piece of paper representing our freedoms and accomplishments; put those freedoms to good use. And make sure to tell your family and friends how much you care about them." As I looked out, I sent love to my family in the crowd. I took a moment to scan the crowd in hopes the rest of them were sitting elsewhere. Silently praying they were all okay, and I just missed them. I glanced once more at Liam; his face glowed with love and pride as he nodded for me to continue. I swallowed back tears and carried on—I had to finish this speech.

"To my family and friends, may you always remember the love I have for you will last no matter how far away we may roam. My brother Micah has always told me, 'no matter where you go; we will go there together.' As a soldier carries pictures of loved ones in their Kevlar, or protective gear to the common man, they carry their memories in their hearts, taking loved ones with them wherever they go. That's what I ask of you, bring pictures wherever you go and remember the good times! You must also learn from the bad times as well.

"Take pictures, laugh often, and love always. Remember not only where you are going, but also where you've been. Leave your marks on the world and let them know you were here. Your next test may not be in a classroom but out in the real world. I want you all to ace it; we've been preparing for this since kindergarten. You've got this! *We've* got this!

"Down the road at our class reunions or wherever we may bump into each other, I want to hear your joys and triumphs. I also want to hear of your hardships and how you managed to overcome them. Instead of continuing to ramble on, I will leave you with this. Go forth and prosper! Congratulations to our amazing class!" I smiled. I stood up on my tiptoes; my fist pumped to the sky as I tried to emphasize my excitement.

"Enjoy this beautiful day with your family and friends! God Bless!"

While the crowd cheered, Liz and I were escorted to our seats among our fellow classmates. Never before had I hated having a last name starting with the letter 'R', nor have I hated having 350 classmates, but I did now. I sat nervously bouncing my leg and begged this slow moving circus would get the show on the road. Hurry up and be done. Dang it! What happened? Where is my family? As they called Liz's name, I stood up and cheered for her, although Liam's booming voice drowned mine out. He was awarded a special smile from her reddened face. Ugh, the names kept going on and on and on. It seemed to be an endless eternity.

Nerves were getting the best of me. A newsreel of possible things that could be keeping the rest of my family from my graduation scrolled through my brain. From our family cat got out of the house to Caleb losing his favorite pacifier, maybe the cake wasn't quite ready or Wes had a flat tire? What if Colt hit Micah? Maybe Dad's drunken ass got himself killed? Or was he just passed out in the car waiting for this all to get done? My hands started to sweat as I anxiously twisted and twined my fingers.

Finally, our row stood and moved forward. It was our turn to approach the stage. I stepped one step closer to the stage, feeling more off than normal. They finally called my name. I felt like I could dart across the stage, but settled for a quickened pace. I heard screams and cheers for me, but my eyes were on the prize. I received a friendly hug from my swim coach as she handed me a diploma. Hmm, for some reason it didn't feel as good as I imagined it would. Then I remembered something wasn't right, most of my family was missing. At home, I pictured receiving the diploma and shoving it in my father's face before I walked away from my childhood hell.

As I sat back down to wait for all the rest to be called, my thoughts went to my mom and Micah, and yes, even Eli. They wouldn't have missed this day for the world. Something must be wrong. I managed to sound the droning voice out as they continued calling one student at a time while the rest remained lined up like sheep being herded.

I managed to phase out the end of the ceremony only catching the "Congrats to this year's class!" Trying to stay in the moment, I threw my hat in the air with the rest of them. I even accepted a couple hugs on my way to Liam. Liz managed to get to me before I made it to my destination. I didn't stop, pushing my way to my family, halfway dragging her with me.

Chapter 3
ABBY

"Abs! We did it!" Her smiling face instantly dropped to one of panic. "Baby cakes, what is it? Why are you so pale?"

I couldn't focus on her, or her worrying, I was busy muttering to myself, "Gotta get to Lee and Lynn, gotta get to Lee and Lynn." I set out on a crash course through the crowd as I frantically tried to remember where they were. Full blown panic mode was setting in.

Arms wrapped around me, as I crashed into Liam's broad chest. "Great speech Little One. Congrats!" I knew he was trying to calm me, but it wasn't working, I had to know. There was no use beating around the bush with me. If I wanted sugar coating, I'd find a bakery.

Without warning, I broke down into tears. I sobbed and tried to get the words out. "Where?" I gasped trying to get a breath. "What?" Finally, I just collapsed in his arms from the emotional overload.

Lynn's motherly voice tried to calm me down as she rubbed my back. "Shh. Breathe Little One." It wasn't working; nothing was.

The grim look on Liam's face told me my day was going to take a turn for the worse. "There has been an accident. Colt called me. Dad went to them." He hugged me tighter as I felt the ground trying to swallow me whole.

"Mom? Micah? Wes? Colt?" I started listing them off, trying to get more answers as I searched Liam's face.

Liz rubbed my shoulder as we waited for answers. Finally, Lynn spoke up, "Colt and Wes are just fine. They were behind them when it happened."

Liam lifted me into his arms, he knew I was unable to move, shock evident on my face. I couldn't figure out how to put one foot in front of the other, breathing was hard enough.

I don't remember leaving the building or how we got to the hospital. The only memories I could recall were a few words of my speech and crashing into Liam's strong arms. Oh, and the panic. I remembered the panic clearly.

Liam barely slowed the car before I jumped out with Lynn right behind me. He might've said something about parking, but I was too focused on moving forward to find the rest of my family.

I walked into the waiting room filled with my family. Each of them was in different stages of shock and grief. I barely made two steps into the room when my father stepped in front of me. Effectively he stopped me in my tracks. His finger jammed into my chest, I felt positive a bruise was forming immediately. "You! This is all your fucking fault!" he yelled. Saliva shot from his lips, landing on my face.

He tried to push me towards the wall, but couldn't budge me beyond the wall of siblings standing behind me. I asked, "Daddy? What happened?"

His hand slapped me senseless, dropping me to my knees. "Don't you dare fucking *daddy* me! You are a waste of perfectly good air and don't fucking belong here."

Colton, the calm, managed to get in front of me. "It's not her fault Dad. She was just trying to make her family proud of her. She was trying to get us to notice her." He paused to look at me, giving a hint of a smile as he continued on, "Grats Little One. I am sure your speech was beautiful; although it had to pale to your natural beauty." He looked to Liam. "Find her an ice pack, please, Lee?"

Lynn smiled. "She called Wes out on all his records she smashed. It was beautiful Colt; I recorded it for everyone to watch later."

My father attempted to charge towards me again, only to be dragged back by the twins, Rob and Wes. "It's not her fault Dad. The only one at fault is the drunken jackass that hit them." Rob tried to stay calm as possible. He struggled to remain the voice of reason; there was unsettling shakiness in his voice I had never heard before.

Pauline stood beside Dad. "If it weren't for Miss Smarty Pants, she wouldn't have been graduating today. Mom wouldn't have been fucking worried about picking up a stupid cake."

Liam held the ice pack against my cheek as he replied to Pauline's comment, "And if the dog hadn't stopped to take a shit, he would've caught the rabbit. Leave her alone Polly."

A bulky security guard came into the room. "Is there a problem in here?" he asked as he looked between the members of our family.

My father thrust a finger in my direction and shouted, ".6 is our only problem." The security guard glanced at me and shrugged his shoulders before he turned to walk back out of the room.

An older man in dark gray scrubs and a white lab coat came in as the guard left. "I am looking for the family of Elijah Montgomery." He looked up from his notes.

Everyone stepped back. I heard Liam say something about Eli's mom being on her way, so I moved forward, but my father's booming voice drowned my weak one out, "No one gives a shit about Elijah. We want news on Micah and Karen Remlock."

"Sorry sir, I am working with Elijah. The other teams are working on the other passenger. I'm sorry for your pain and loss, but Karen was pronounced dead at the scene. I do believe they informed you of that earlier," his voice was filled with sympathy and concern as he responded.

"Sir, I am part of Eli's family. Can I see him, please?" I barely whispered, afraid of my own voice.

"Abigail?" the doctor asked after glancing at the papers he was holding. "Are you Abigail? He has been muttering and calling for you since he arrived." I simply nodded and followed him out of the room with Liz holding tight to my hand. Silently, I hoped I could absorb some of her strength. We were walking down the long sterile hall. It felt like I was one step closer to my heart's death. He stopped us outside the last room on the right. "It's not as bad as it looks, he was lucky. You can go in."

I thanked him and walked inside. Trying to be brave, I gave Eli a weak smile. Tears were already streaming recklessly down my cheeks as I walked across the room slowly.

"Babe, it's not as bad as it looks." He reached his hand out, beckoning me closer, "Come here. Please?"

As I closed the distance between us, I took his proffered hand and took in the damage. His left arm was in a cast, a huge gash across his forehead; there was a smaller slit on his cheek. Also, it looked like there was blood seeping into the sheet that covered his legs. I guessed there was probably another wound there too. "What happened?" I asked as I sat gingerly on the edge of the bed, afraid to jostle him.

"There was an accident," he stated and squeezed my hand. Unsure why, I hauled off and slapped his chest. I leaned forward and put my head on his chest, soaking his hospital gown with my tears. It suddenly hit me that they mentioned Mom not making it? The tears fell faster as the words began to sink in. How could Mom not have made it? He ran his hand over my hair. "Shh. Babe, it will be ok. Don't cry. Babe, please don't cry for me." He reached up and touched the spot Dad had hit. "What happened to your cheek? Where are Micah and Karen?"

"I don't know. I'm so scared. What happened?" My mind was unable to focus on a single thought. "Don't worry about me; it's nothing Daddy hasn't done before." The sporadic thoughts bounced back and forth leaving me so confused. I was trying to figure out everything he asked.

"Mom," I spit out, "Mom didn't." I needed to get it out, but I couldn't form the words, it would make it real, and I wasn't ready for that, I'd never be ready for it. My tongue was a massive boulder petrified in its place.

Liz snuck back in. "Abs, they need you a few rooms down." Her pale face and shaking hands said it all. Wasn't this supposed to be one of the greatest days of my short life? Prom, graduation, college, wedding, and all those other unforgettable days were supposed to be so amazing and happy.

I stood and gave Eli a chaste kiss on his lips. "I will be right back."

"Wait! Babe, let me go with you." Eli started to sit up, taking the pulse ox monitor off his finger.

"No. You need to get better too Eli. Relax, I will be right back." Trying to appear braver than I was, inside I was a scared little girl once again. I shivered while I followed slowly behind Liz. We headed down the hall and turned into another room. I barely got one foot into Micah's room. There was no warning; it took me by storm. When I saw the tubes and monitors, the next thing I saw was the floor coming closer, followed by complete darkness.

I came to in Liam's arm. He held me and reassured me, "It's ok, breathe Little One."

"It's not ok! I want to see him, please Lee. What happened?" I whispered to Micah, "Bubba, what happened? Talk to me!" Liam pulled a chair over and sat me next to Micah's bed. I grabbed Micah's hand. "Mikey, stay with me bubba. Don't you dare do this to me Micah!" I was half pleading, half crying. I was scared out of my mind.

He had tubes down his throat, so I didn't think he would be able to say anything, but he squeezed my fingers tightly. I looked up at his face and kissed his cheek; his eyes met mine, and I knew it was him telling me he loved me and to be stronger than duct tape. As I felt his grip loosen, I looked up at the machines as they started beeping. I cried and planted a kiss on his hand. I silently begged him to squeeze my fingers again. *Please! Just one more time! Please!*

The nurses came and pushed buttons silencing the machines. My father simply shook his head, making them turn and leave just as quickly they entered. We all knew he had a DNR (do not resuscitate), it was his wish. He signed the papers when he signed up with the Special Forces. I wasn't going to accept it. Micah never was one to give up.

Damn it! How could he do this to me?

I felt an arm around me as a kiss was planted in my hair. "Shh Babe, I've got you," Eli whispered. I started to kick out and tried to dislodge myself from his arms. But I knew whose arms were around me, and I knew he too was hurting. No matter how hard I fought against him, he held me close and continued to try to console me. I tried to pry Eli off of me, but he wasn't giving up. I knew he would never give up on me, no matter how much I hurt him.

Liz squatted in front of me and reminded me she was with me but knew I would fight any closeness. More than anything in the world, I hated pity. I saw her face riddled with pain. She wished she could pull me into her arms. I shook my head and refused any closeness; it was the only way I was going to make it through all of this.

Right now, I didn't feel stronger than duct tape.

I finally pulled away from Eli and crawled up in bed with Micah to attempt my own version of CPR. "Damn it Micah! Don't you quit on me now! You promised!" I kept pushing against his chest until I finally just collapsed against his slowly cooling body. I let my grief take over. "Mikey, please come back! I need you!" I begged.

Eli rubbed my side, tears cascading down his cheeks. "Babe, he's gone."

I slapped at him, unable to see through my tears. "Leave me alone! I want Micah back! Damn it! Bubba come back!" I screamed.

Liz pulled me off the bed and into her arms. "Abs, look at me." When I didn't turn to face her, she put her fingers under my chin. "Abigail, look at me, please." Finally, she managed to get my eyes to meet her pain-filled green eyes. "You gotta relax Babes. Let me help."

I knew she was trying to take some of my pain away, but it was my grief to deal with, not hers.

Chapter 4
ELI

I watched her walk away from me crying, being pulled out of my room and into the hall. It killed me every time I saw her cry or walk away from me. Without putting any thought into it, I ripped the IV from my arm and pulled all the cords out so I could go be with her. It hurt like hell. My body was screaming at me, but my heart needed to be closer to Abby. Who worried what I was wearing when I had a girl that needed me?

What I saw when I walked into Micah's room, I wasn't prepared for. I felt instant hurt and pain, but it wasn't physical. The love of my life was crying while holding the hand of my best friend, begging for him to come back to her. As much as I wanted to collapse, I knew she needed me.

I couldn't worry about my pain. I had a promise to keep to Micah. Abby was never supposed to feel unhappy or pain. Our last mission we told each other that on our last breaths we would protect Abby, find her the happiness she deserved, ensure her safety, and diffuse her pain.

Without any further thought, I pulled her into my arms and tried to console her best I could. Wrapping her in my arms, I tried to whisper consoling words to her. What I said I didn't know, I don't even know if it helped her, the words just spilled out of my mouth. I looked up at Micah and fell apart with her.

Momentarily, I lost my grip on her and she climbed up and loomed over him. She begged him to come back as she pushed against his chest. I couldn't bring myself to pull her off of him, I knew she was hurting. I may have just lost my best friend, but that was her brother, her protector, her hero and her closest friend.

As I watched Liz try to get her under control, I lost it. I left the room and threw my good fist into the wall. I just lost my best friend. After spending birth through our senior year together, we spent six years in the Special Forces doing multiple tours in places that had no names in our society. My battle buddy kept my ass safe and introduced me to one of the strongest, most beautiful girls I've ever met. *Why couldn't I keep him safe? Fuck! I let him down. I let his sister down.*

My best friend before birth was taken from me, but I had to be strong for the beautiful girl mourning him. He was her hero. My buddy was killed in the same place we grew up, not on foreign soil. All those missions we came home safe only for him to be killed by a drunk driver in broad daylight. After being held a prisoner of war for a month and a half, he made a full recovery. Why couldn't he recover from this?

From day one, we were inseparable. He was there through the loss of my father and joined the Special Forces because I did. He stopped me from going too far. We walked through gates of hellish places only to return together. Stronger. Without him, I felt pathetic. I couldn't be Abby's hero; I was too weak.

The next thing I knew, I was being thrown against the wall as fists flew at me. There was no use fighting it. I let my guard completely down, something I was told never to do. It was drilled into my head over and again—stick up for yourself because no one else would. It no longer mattered that I was lethal in hand-to-hand combat. I lost one of my biggest reasons to fight. "You worthless pile of shit! You killed my wife and my son! Now you are trying to move in on my fucking daughter?" he yelled as he continued to rain fists against my body.

Suddenly Abigail got between her father and me, as she screamed, "Daddy stop! Now I'm your daughter? Earlier you wanted nothing to do with me!"

He continued to swing, managing to catch Abby in the process. Seeing her get hit pulled me out of my private hell. If it weren't for Wes and Rob restraining their father, I would have taken him down. Nobody hurts Abigail in my presence. As much as I hated her father, I couldn't fight in front of her. It would hurt her more, even if she didn't fess up to it.

Her hands flew to my face, as she stuttered, "Eli, are you ok?" Never have I felt more love for this girl than right now. She didn't care that she was bruised and bleeding; she was worried about my sorry ass.

I kissed her lips. "I am ok, Babe. I need to get out of here. Come with me?"

Liam nodded. "Get her out of here. Abby, go with him. We will check in on you in a little bit, put ice on that," he told her a he kissed her head and handed keys to me. I found a pair of scrubs in one of the drawers. They would have to do because we needed to get out of here. I even managed to sign an Against Medical Advice paper, so I couldn't sue the hospital because I left on my own will. My girl was more important than my health.

We got back to my childhood home, Mom wasn't there. Relief washed through me, we needed some alone time. I got Abby into my room and held her in my arms as we lay on my old bed. The physical pain was nothing compared to the emotional wreckage ransacking our bodies. I couldn't tell who was crying more, but with Abby, I wasn't ashamed to show that I too was hurting.

Sometime later she got up and went to the bathroom, bringing back a wash cloth and some Band-Aids. "Eli, look at me. Let me clean you up." As brave as she tried to be, her shaking hands gave her away. "Please tell me what happened. Eli, please." She was begging for answers I wasn't sure I could give her. The trauma from the accident caused my memory to blur.

I pulled her hands into mine. "I don't know Babe. All I know is Micah and I were chatting with your mom, and a car came out of nowhere. Baby I'm so sorry." I tugged her into my lap.

I knew she was in shock, but I never expected to hear her say what she said. Looking into my eyes, she said, "Make me forget. Give me a temporary memory lapse. Eli, you are the only one that has the power to help me forget." She pulled away from me and stripped off her dress. Sitting on the bed beside me in just her matching cotton bra and panty set.

"Baby, are you sure? Come here, let me hold you," I tried to offer. I begged she'd let me hold her.

"No. Don't try to *baby* me. Damn it! Make me forget!" She tugged at my shirt, trying to get it off of me. "Eli, please, I need this. You need this."

I told myself that I was going to wait until she was 18. I promised myself I wouldn't act on the feelings while she was still so young. The pain she showed me tore me open and caused me to lose my resolve. Seeing her completely baring herself physically, and emotionally, stole my breath away.

Was I worried she would say I tried to force myself onto her? No, this brave girl protected her father all these damn years; she would protect me too. Wasn't I supposed to be protecting her, keeping her safe from the evils of this world? As much as I knew I would hate myself later, I couldn't deny her now.

"Will you promise to tell me if I am hurting you? I can't do it otherwise Babe." When she nodded, I shook my head. "Babe, I have to hear you say it."

She smiled nervously up at me. "I promise." I knew without a doubt she was still holding her 'V' card. I knew I had to be very careful; this wasn't just some girl, this was *THE* girl. I felt like the King of the World, Leonardo Di-Fucking-Caprio from the *Titanic*, that I was her choice to take her innocence. Except, this ship won't sink, it's about to soar out of this fucking world.

I was more nervous about having sex this time than I was the first time. In all honesty, a lot more was at stake. Taking this further could ruin our friendship, as it has to too many before us.

She looked up at me, her amethyst eyes hypnotized me. "You have to be careful because of your injuries."

I kissed her lips. "No, I have to be careful because of you Babe." My fingers snaked through her hair, passionately pulling her lips closer. I was already wishing I could tear this fucking cast off; both my hands wanted to touch her. She must've been watching my every move, because she took her hand and pulled my casted one to her side.

I slid down her body, easing her out of her pale purple bra. I had never realized she was that well endowed in the breast department, she kept them well hidden. I leaned up and kissed her lips then down her chin to the spot right below the ear, evoking the lightest, sweetest, sexiest sounding moan I had ever heard. Trust me, I've heard my fair share of moans, but this one had the power to bring me to my knees. I continued my journey further south, planting gentle kisses and swiping my tongue over her warm, soft skin. Her skin felt as though it was made of the finest silk.

When I glanced up at her, I met her eyes, darkening with desire, watching my every move. Her lips formed a beautiful smile. I couldn't help myself; I reached back up planting another soft kiss on her lips, getting another little moan from her. Using it to my advantage, I slipped my tongue in to caress her tongue. My fingers found their way to her pert breasts, working each nipple into a tight pebble. Never in my life would I have guessed she would be this reactive. Maybe I'm not the only one with feelings here?

I pulled back from her lips and sucked in one of her pebbled nipples. Her back arched as her hands pulled my head closer to her chest. I ran my tongue along the underside of her breasts, enjoying the little moans she was letting out. My attention turned to the other nipple, offering it the same appreciation. Leaning most of my weight on my left arm, my right hand continued to explore her beautiful body. Her skin soft and body arched into my calloused hand as though it craved my touch.

Trailing my fingertips lightly over her flat stomach, to her hips, I caressed her with gentle touches. I could do this for hours. I slipped a finger under the waistband of her plain cotton panties, pausing to pull back and take another appreciative look at her delicate features. She made cotton look sexier than most women could look in silks, laces, or satins. She nervously tried to cover herself as she whispered, "Sorry, it's not what you are used to."

I pried her fingers gently away, lacing them with mine, my eyes soaking up every last inch of her. "No need to feel ashamed, you are absolutely gorgeous. This is far better than I'm used to." I lightly kissed the tip of her nose. "You ok?"

She nodded with reassurance and smiled at me. Her eyes darkened with desire, looking like a starless night. I slipped her beautiful body out of her panties and planted a kiss on her hip. I cupped her bare mound, feeling the warm liquid proof of her arousal. I had to pull back and untie my pants, my steel erection screamed for freedom. She pulled my chin up so I could see her face. "Let me see, please? I want to touch it." Her fingers reached out and stroked me through my boxer briefs, nearly causing the death of me. She whispered, "Take it all the way out, please Eli?"

I stood up and let my erection spring free. Her eyes got bigger as she eyed my erection. Trying to ease her fears, I laid back down beside her. "It's ok, we will take this slow."

"How will it all fit?" Her innocence made me smile.

"You sure know how to boost a man's ego. Babe you stretch a little. If it hurts too much, I will stop. I am bigger than average, and it's not me bragging. Let's get you a little more ready sweetheart." I kissed those beautiful lips again. I was officially addicted to her. My blood was pulsing; my heart was beating out of my chest.

I slipped my tongue into her moistened slit, instantly committing her sweet taste to memory. She was my new favorite flavor, honey had nothing on her. Using my finger, I slicked it in her juices before slipping it inside her tightness.

Her breath caught, pulling my eyes back up to that beautiful mouth of hers.

"You ok Babe?" I asked before kissing her already kiss-bruised lips.

She smiled. "Better than okay." I planted another kiss, this time deepening it as my finger continued to move in and out of her.

I watched her arch up. Moving back down her body, I sucked lightly on her hardened nub. We maintained eye contact. Even if I weren't able to see those eyes watching me, I could feel the heat of passion pouring off her body. A fine layer of sweat glistened along her body. Feeling the need to be closer, to fill her just a little more, I slid a second finger in, reveling in her tightness. Her juices flowed a little more freely, I savored every last drop, pulling as much as I could out of her.

Her body started to stiffen. I knew what was coming, but sensed some hesitation on her end. She needed a little more coaxing. "It's ok Babe, I got you. Just let go, it's ok. Trust me." I sucked harder on her clit as my fingers did a "come hither" motion. Finally, she let go. Her back arched as her legs twisted and twined around my head, trapping me in a little slice of heaven. Her channel tightened around my fingers, pulling them in further. Holy hell! This was far better than I could have imagined.

Like a starving man, I lapped up every last drop of her sweet nectar. Damn she tasted so good. Her taste alone almost caused me to blow my load. Afraid of losing our forward progress, I pulled away long enough to roll a condom on. The way she watched me, made me feel like I was putting on a private show just for her. If only the fucking cast was off, it definitely wasn't helping me. It was slowing me down. Damn this girl was beautiful. MY girl was beautiful.

"Babe, this might hurt a little more than normal. You are really tight. If it's too much, tell me and we can do something else." God I hoped like hell she wouldn't tell me to stop, but I'd stop if she asked me to.

She nodded, her eyes filled with lust. I pulled a nipple between my lips as I ran my erection through her moistness. Man how I wished I was bareback right now, but I was pretty sure she wasn't on any form of birth control. This was a girl I wouldn't take risks with.

I aligned the tip at her entrance, slowly rocking back and forth. She hissed through her teeth. When I looked up at her in question, she smiled and nodded, urging me on. Her hands snaked around me and rested between my shoulder blades. I pushed in a little further as her nails bit into my back. She was tighter than I could have imagined. *Holy fuck*! I wasn't going to last long.

Normally I wasn't a fan of girls marking up my back, but this wasn't any girl, this was Abby. She could do anything she pleased. I lost all inhibitions with her. Everything felt so new and so right with this beautiful girl.

"You still ok Babe? Is it too much?" I asked as I continued to ease myself in and out of her.

"Am I in heaven? It's a blissful pain." Her hips moved up to meet mine, giving me easier access. I urged her to try to relax a little more. Her tightness could be a problem with my size. The more she relaxed, the more I nudged in, allowing her to continue to stretch around me. I was begging I didn't make this a minute man episode as my balls tightened, threatening an early release.

I pushed past the hymen, causing her to flinch a little. Not wanting to stop, I pulled out a little and pushed back in a little further. Her tightness created more friction, bringing me closer to release, much closer than I was ready for. I continued to work in and out of her, picking up my pace, unintentionally thrusting a little harder than I meant to. Her nails creating bites of tingling ache in my back. She was close again, as was I. Fuck! No! I wasn't ready for this to be over yet.

As her orgasm hit, she screamed out my name. Her tight cave milked every last drop of my orgasm out of me. I was in sheer ecstasy. Damn! I'd never felt so good afterwards. I felt like I could fly.

Pulling out and disposing of the used rubber barrier, I eyed her carefully. I was worried I might have hurt her, or pushed too far.

Her smile lit up my heart. "That felt amazing!" She tugged my navy blue comforter over her, as her eyes began to droop. "Is it normal to feel tired afterwards?"

I leaned down and kissed her. "Yes ma'am. Just means I did it right. But don't fall asleep yet Babe. I'm going to run you a bubble bath."

Heading to Mom's bathroom, I found a honeysuckle scented bubble bath, it would have to work. Starting up the water, I added the bubbly foam and made sure I had towels for her.

Chapter 5
ABBY

*H*e disappeared into the bathroom to turn on the bath. I had a little bit of pain, but it wasn't anything like I expected it to be. The tenderness left me many pleasurable memories, making it well worth everything. I'd heard my fair share of horror stories, even Liz had told me her first time hurt like hell. There was a little discomfort, but the pleasure definitely outweighed the pain. He must've been telling me the truth, *he did it right*. The gentle ache had me craving him again. Was that normal?

Eli came back in and plucked me off the bed, placing me into a bubble bath set to just the right temperature. It felt so warm and soothing. The tub was filled with perfection. I thought this stuff only happened in movies. *How'd he know the perfect temperature?* When he turned to grab a cloth off the counter, I saw the marks I left on his back. I gasped, and felt ashamed of myself, "Oh my gosh Eli, I didn't mean to leave marks."

"I am wearing these babies proudly. They are better than any war wound I've ever gotten." His eyes full of concern as he tried to mask his distress with a smirk. "Are you feeling all right, love?" He asked as he knelt down beside the tub and kissed my shoulder. Somehow he even managed to get my hair clipped up, or I did, I don't quite remember. All I remember is pure heavenly bliss.

"I was nervous, but able to relax and enjoy every moment because it was with you. My dreams came true. I felt incredibly overfull." I leaned over the edge of the tub to kiss him. "Was it as good for you as it was for me?"

He kissed me again, and smiled. "It was better."

We sat like that and chatted until I could no longer fight to keep my eyes open. Eli helped me climb out, quickly wrapping me with a fluffy green towel. He planted another kiss on my lips as the doorbell rang. Hastily he tugged on a pair of gym shorts and threw a shirt over his head as he headed down the stairs to see who it was.

When he opened the door, Liam and Liz were smiling at him. "We just wanted to stop by and check to make sure everything was ok," Liam explained. I stood at the top of the stairs listening in for a moment; I was hidden but could watch their interactions.

"Where is Abs?" Liz asked as she walked right in and began looking around the first floor.

"She was getting out of the tub when I came downstairs," Eli answered, shutting the door after they both made it inside.

Liam tossed Eli a bottle of pills. "They let me get your prescription for you, considering the circumstances. These are for pain. How is she doing?" Concern weighed heavily in his words.

"She has her ups and downs. I think she's finally worn out enough to sleep." I could hear the smile in his voice.

I walked down the stairs in one of Eli's shirts. "Hey guys! What are you doing here?" I asked cheerily as I cuddled into Eli's side, his arms wrapped around me and pulled me in front of him.

He whispered, "My shirt looks damn fine on you." I rubbed my backside against his front. Touching my hips lightly to still their movement, he kissed my neck and whispered, "Stop Babe. I know you are bare below that shirt, but we have company."

Liz smiled. "We brought you a couple changes of clothes Abs. You know, if you want, you can always stay with me."

"She's fine here. We were getting ready to crash in a few," Eli spoke for me. He glanced down and gave me a wink.

Liam gave me a concerned look. "If you need anything else, let us know Little One. We love you."

I crossed the room and hugged Liam, offered him thanks. "I know bubba, I just need a little bit to get my emotions under control. We lost our brother and Mom. One of the world's greatest best friends was taken from us today. I don't need to be alone right now, and neither does Eli." I gave him a weak, reassuring smile.

After hugging Liz again, I took my bag to Eli's room and set it next to his dresser. Sleepiness was really starting to take over. I figured it would probably be best if I waited for Eli in his bed. As I climbed in, I realized the sheets were wet. I guessed some blood mixed with our lovemaking too, but the navy sheets hid the colors. I heard about the mess that was made when the girl lost her virginity. Feeling embarrassed, I stripped the sheets off the bed. While I looked for clean sheets, I began to randomly open hall doors, peek inside and shut them back quickly. I hated not being able to find what I was looking for, it really made me feel out of place right now. Their chatter downstairs was still being heard up where I was. I was sure if I could hear them, there was a good chance they could hear me as well.

I broke down as I slammed yet another door. Tears came out of nowhere, wreaking havoc on my body. Before I knew it, I was curled up into a ball, crying my broken heart out. Eli must've heard me, because I heard his muscled frame give the stairs hell as he climbed them. He scooped me into his arms. "Babe, what's wrong?"

I felt ashamed. I knew I went in search of sheets, but I couldn't remember why I was crying. Between sobs, I tried to tell him, but couldn't find words. He kissed my forehead as he tried to reassure me that we would get through this. Grief stole my words as Eli stole my heart.

After finally taking a couple calming breaths, I asked him where some fresh sheets were. He kissed my lips. "They are in the top of my closet."

"Can I have a few minutes to myself?" I asked shyly. Suddenly I was embarrassed at my fallout.

"Of course. I'll be downstairs if you need me." He tugged my chin up so he could plant his lips on mine. "Please Babe, don't shut me out," he begged, his face was etched in pain, his eyes showed torment, fear, and concern. I knew he was asking me to stay strong and stay his. He lost his best friend. According to him, I was the only thing he had left.

I nodded, offering him a weak smile. He let me out of his hands as he headed back to our company. As I found the sheets and finished making the bed, Liz walked into the room. She plopped on the corner of the bed, blurting out, "So, did you have sex?" She never was one to beat around the bush.

My cheeks heated up as I shook my head. "We made love. It was the best feeling in the world." I beamed, sitting beside her. "I thought you said it was scary and painful?"

Liz blushed. "It was. My first time felt like I was being ripped in two. Really!? It didn't hurt?"

I shook my head and smiled. "He must not have done it right then." I let out a small laugh, trying to pretend her first time was not with my brother. "There was only a little bit of pain, but tons of pleasure. I can't wait to do it again," I admitted. We shared some of our intimate details of our first time; it was nice that I wasn't the last virgin left in Salt Lake. It was even nicer having something more in common with Liz, we both lost our virginity to our childhood crushes. I must admit that my first time was more enjoyable and perfect compared the seeming "pump and dump" that was Liz's first time. Oh my God, that was still too much information about Liam.

"He was seriously a 'one-pump dump chump.'" Liz laughed.

"The old 'stick it and zip it?'" I wiped the tears out of my eyes from laughing so hard. I needed a good laugh.

Was I suddenly bipolar? One minute I was crying missing my brother, the next I was smiling as I admitted to having mind blowing sex to my best friend. What was wrong with me? I missed Micah something fierce. Taking my mind off him for a moment felt utterly wrong to me. The pleasure I felt still doesn't completely take away the pain of losing my favorite brother.

Liam and Eli entered the room a little while later. "Little One, are you hungry?" Liam asked.

"No, thanks. I am really tired though." I looked up to Eli from where I was sitting cross-legged on the bed. "Is it ok if I crash here tonight?"

He nodded and gave me a smile. "Of course Babe. Mom is out of town until tomorrow."

I must've been really worn out. Not even waiting for them to leave, I crawled under the fresh covers and cuddled up with my head on a pillow, closing my eyes.

Liz took the hint and turned to Liam. "Come on Lee, let's let them get some rest. If they need anything, they *will* call." She kissed my cheek, and whispered, "I love you Abs."

My body relaxed as I inhaled Eli's seductive scent left behind on his pillow. I must've managed to doze off for a few seconds because my body suddenly became more alert as I felt Eli crawl in bed behind me. I rolled over so I was lying chest to chest with him. I leaned up on my elbow and smiled at him. The moonlight filtered into the room, giving Eli the appearance of a Greek God on display. He looked perfect, aside from the slashes on his face, his casted arm, and the tears slowly streaming down his cheeks. I kissed a couple of the tears away, running the back of my hand lightly over his cheek. His hands stilled my head, as his lips found mine, bruising them with such passion. I could tell he was hurting, even though he was trying his damnedest to hide his pain. Eli pulled me closer as he whispered, "I love you Babe. I don't want to ever let you go." He moved my hair back, tucking it behind my ears. Eli reached down and tilted my head up so I could see the pain in his eyes clearly. "You are the only one I have left."

I rested my cheek on his broad chest and placed my hand gently over his heart. He slid his fingers through my curly, multifaceted, blonde hair, before resting his casted hand over my hand on his chest.

I felt safe.
I felt loved.
I felt protected.

Chapter 6
ABBY

*H*e made this week of hell easier to deal with. Staying by my side through a morning breakfast with all of my family, he showed more strength than lifting up a truck. Luckily, my father and his favorite spawn, Pauline, decided not to show up for the family meeting. I couldn't handle another confrontation right now.

We were gathered around the café tables we put together to accommodate our large family, reminiscing some of our happiest moments, pretending we weren't meeting with Mom's lawyer. He introduced himself as he stood near us, "I am glad you all could join me, I apologize for the difficult circumstances. My name is Alan Williamson. I represent your mother, Mrs. Karen Remlock, and your brother, Micah Remlock."

We went around the table introducing ourselves to him as pain settled back into my heart. Eli wrapped an arm around my shoulders and kissed my temple, silently he gave me strength and love. But more than anything, he offered me understanding.

"Micah's last will and testament requested that his money from his military insurance be split equally among all of his siblings. I have a check made out to each of you."

Tears erupted from my eyes like lava spewing from a volcano. Eli's arm pulled me closer to him, kissing the top of my head. "Shh, Babe, I'm right here." His hand trailed up and down my spine offering as much comfort as he could manage. He whispered so only I could hear, "I am pretty sure you get a little more."

"I don't want money, I want Mikey back! He promised me safety and promised me he was always going to be here for me! He promised me forever!" The dam burst open. I lost it, no longer able to hold back, big, pain-filled tears escaped my eyes.

Eli held me as I soaked his t-shirt with my tears. It wasn't long before our tears and sorrows mixed together. Everyone at the table could be staring at me, but I no longer cared. I lost my safety blanket and best friend, my hero. The pain I felt was as though I was being decapitated, although maybe that would have hurt less. My heart was ripped to shreds. "I need out of here E," I whispered.

He picked me up into his arms and carried me to his truck. Once I was safely in the cab of his truck, he slid me over and climbed in the passenger side behind me. The pain showed in his face as he held me close while we remembered one of this world's greatest men. He let me pour my heart out, as I told him all about Micah, even though I'm sure he knew him just as well as I did, if not more.

My eyes finally ran out of tears, though only temporarily, before we decided to rejoin the family inside. I needed my family right now, they may not need me, but I definitely needed them. I craved the closeness of them as much as I needed Eli's comforting touch. This was the time I needed to be strong, but I couldn't be strong alone, I needed to borrow some strength. Sitting here was too hard for me to do on my own.

Stepping away from the table, Mr. Williamson pulled a group of envelopes from his briefcase.

"Each one of you will get two envelopes. One containing a check from Micah's last will and testament, the other check is from Karen's, your beautiful mother." He walked around the table and handed them out. I managed to squeak a little thank you as my tears began using my face as a slip 'n' slide. Without opening either of them, I silently passed them to Eli. He wrapped me closer to him, planting a kiss on my temple. Mr. Williamson stated, "And now I have a letter to read to you all from Karen."

Before he began, he silently nudged a box of tissues closer to me.

"To my dearest children. If you are reading this letter, something has happened and I can no longer be with you all physically, but I will never be far from you in spirit. I know growing up with your father was not easy, but I am all the more proud that you all have become such wonderful people, God couldn't have blessed me with better children. I know each and every one of you will continue to make me proud, and continue to share the love I taught you." He paused and looked at each of us, offering sympathy.

"I want you to put your heads together and put your inheritance to good use. Always remember where you came from and use it to your advantage. Each and every one of you holds a special place in my heart." He paused again before looking at Lynn. *"Lynnelle, you were the first gift God brought into my life. You have grown up tough and good-looking, use your vast knowledge to help the younger ones grow up to be as strong and beautiful as you, not just your siblings, but your beautiful children as well. You have the power to bring the world to its knees."* His attention turned to look for Pauline, continuing to read in her absence, *"Pauline, remember to put aside your hatred, and love all who love you. You are bright and intelligent. Continue to keep your chin up. Try to spend more time in love than in hate."*

Turning to face Colt, he continued to read, *"My dear Colton, you are my brave one. You have never backed down from anything that might seem scary or unknown. Continue to use your bravery to keep moving forward, don't give up! You have a beautiful wife that loves you more than one could love one's self."*

*"To my twins, Wesley and Robert, you boys have always been competitive, and never backed down, I feel proud to call you my sons. God blessed me twice when he gave you to me. Remember, you are strong, competitive, and loving. Please continue to use your skills for the good in people. Rob, your boys count on you and look to you for guidance. Continue to instill love and competition in them. I hope one day you will find a woman worthy enough to settle down

with Wes, I wish you happiness." The lawyer looked between the twins with a sad smile.

Refocusing his attention onto the letter, he started to read the part of the letter aimed for Micah and I lost it. Violently shaking my head, I begged he would stop. Without finishing Micah's part, he skipped forward. He paused to glance towards Liam. *"Liam, you are a very caring and sensitive soul. My dear son always put your family before your friends. You are the glue to our family, stay strong, and hold on—for the better days are coming. Your hard work and beautiful heart would make any mother proud to call you their own."*

The lawyer focused his attention on me. *"Abigail, you are my baby, having you made our family complete. Please remember you are loved, strong and beautiful. Anything you put your mind to will be accomplished. Your father took out most of his anger on you, even though you never deserved it. Always look to your brothers and sisters for advice, never give up on family. I expect great things for you."* Eli wrapped me up close to him, as he tried to offer a sliver of comfort.

"Remember what I've always told you—keep your heads in the clouds, your hearts full of love, and your feet planted firmly on the ground. Remember my children, you need to stick together. Never forget who you are, and you will go far. I love you my dear children, I never meant to cause you pain. Forever in my heart and in my head. Love always and forever Mom."

Once he finished reading, he offered his condolences again. "The money in the envelope from your mother is technically from your grandparents. They set aside the money while they were still living, and asked that she save it for each of you children, to give you a nest egg, to help get you on your feet."

Trying to lighten the somber mood, we began reminiscing more of our happier moments. Micah and Eli were always trying any new pranks they found out about YouTube. From Kool-aid powder on freshly showered battle buddies, to the cinnamon dare. Wes and Rob shared their funny stories from growing up with Micah, even Liam had some to share. My stories of Micah were known already, but I shared a few anyway. We were able to smile through our tears.

One of the best things that happened at that table was how we planned on keeping in touch better. We were scattered all over the world, closeness was hard to keep. Lynn and Rob had families of their own, travelling less often for visits. Thankfully there were apps like Facebook, Skype, and even email. And what girl wouldn't like to get a package once in a while, especially from across the big pond?

"So Abs, where'd you decide to go to college?" Wes asked.

"South Dakota State University." I smiled.

"What about all those other offers you had?"

"They are still there. I just didn't want to go there. With all this stuff that has happened, I need to get away and get on my own two feet."

I got up and left the table. Liz was right behind me. "I was going to ask if you were ok, but your answer would have been 'I'm fine.' What can I do for you baby cakes?"

"I want out of here. Help me get out of here. I need to find a happy-ish place."

Liz nodded in agreement.

"Ms. Remlock, I need to talk to you alone if you have a moment." I nodded and followed the lawyer into another room. "This is the other part of Micah's will I was asked to read to you in private."

I took the piece of paper and read it silently to myself.

> Abs,
> If you are reading this, I am no longer with you in body, but will always be with you in your heart, and that beautiful head too. At first I didn't believe you and that got me angry with myself. You would never lie. I need you to know that I do believe you. I have sworn to keep you

55

> safe and as happy as possible. Eli and I made a deal, he will take care of you if for some reason I no longer can.
>
> Don't feel sorry for me, and always remember you are stronger than duct tape, sweeter than honey.
>
> Remember the house we used to talk about? It's yours now little One. I promised to find a way to keep you safe if it was the last thing I ever did. The house has the highest security available, you will always be safe. You have the address written in your journal; yeah I took a peek around a bit before I wrote it on a page between the hearts and Eli's name. I want you to go there and be happy.

I couldn't continue reading; my tears blurred the lines too much. Instead of handing the letter back to Mr. Williamson, I folded it up and put it in my pocket. Looking over my shoulder, I nodded to Liz and Eli. Eli gave me a sad smile. He knew about the letter, I was pretty sure he had another one similar to it waiting in Micah's stuff to ship home. Mr. Williamson had offered his condolences one last time before he stepped out of the little café.

Liz took my arm and led me to the safety of her car. "Where to chick?"

"Anywhere but here," I sighed, touching my pocket to ensure the letter was still there. She started the car and took off out of the parking lot. I could feel her sympathetic eyes looking at me. "Just don't Liz. Please. I can't," I begged.

She nodded and drove a while longer before I realized where she was taking us—an old play house we used to sneak away to, our hideout. We ate many chocolate bars and all the junk food we managed to sneak out of our houses. I remember dreaming about Eli while she was busy daydreaming about Liam. In a way, we each got a slice of happy-ish ever after.

A smile snuck across my face. "Our slice of heaven, where chocolate and chips were the ideal meat and potatoes, and calories don't count."

"The one place where we can go and not give a shit what anyone else thinks! It's our home away from home." Liz smiled as she pulled me into a hug. She pulled back and grabbed her purse. After digging around in the abyss that is her purse, she pulled out a CD. "We are going to a happy place baby cakes."

I wiped my tears away from my face as I eyed the CD she was holding. I asked, "Liz? Is that the mixed CD?"

She smiled. "Oh hell yeah it is!" She popped it into the old disc player we managed to score when I was ten, benefits of being Micah's favorite sister.

When the first song came on, I burst out laughing. Liz smiled as she did her attempt at getting her boogie on, she belted out, *"She's a brick house, she's mighty mighty! And she's lettin' it all hang out and she's a brick house!"*

I couldn't help but join in, it always had been one of my all time favorites, *"And like lady's stacked and that's the fact. Ain't holding nothing back she's a brick house! Yeah she's the one, the only one built like an Amazon!"* We finished our jam session by plopping back onto the rickety old futon we conned the boys into dragging in here for us, laughing with tears in our eyes.

"Abs, look what else I have." She pulled out a King-sized Reese's peanut butter cup. "Calories don't count in here! Swim and track seasons are over!" She opened it and dropped two onto my lap. "Cheers, Chick!"

I looked at her and smiled. "You really do know how to cheer a girl up," I mumbled in between nibbles around the outer edge. "Oh. My. Gosh! You even froze them for me!" She knew how I loved to enjoy the chocolate first before savoring the peanut butter center.

I missed my brother like crazy, but this girl was trying her damnedest to help me through this rough time. When my cell phone rang, she answered, "She's busy savoring the deliciousness I have to offer. Her moaning is so cute, you should hear it!" She blasted her smile my way. "Oh wait, that's right you've probably heard your share of moans."

My eyes nearly popped out of their sockets as my face turned to match her red shirt. I stole the phone from her. "Eli?"

"Hey Babe, just checking on you. Everything all right?" he asked.

"Yep, considering the circumstances." I leaned against Liz's shoulder. The CD skipped to Red Hot Chili Pepper's *Love Rollercoaster*.

Eli laughed his deep rumble. "Babe, is that what I think it is? Please tell me you aren't listening to that mixed CD still. When did you make it, like ten years ago?"

Liz stole the phone and told Eli. "Still a classic. Don't hate, don't hate." She hung up for me, returning her attention to me, she asked, "Abs, really? You realize you are still considered jailbait for him."

"I know Liz, but it felt so good, so right." I swooned, "It's been love for so long Liz, sex is the next natural thing. You said it yourself a couple years ago about you and Liam." I laid my head on her lap. "I'm not jealous anymore. I finally got to experience the feel of making love to one of the best friends I've ever had."

I knew the next few days would be hell. I wasn't in any hurry to leave our piece of paradise. At least here, it was easier to pretend all was right with the world.

Chapter 7
PAULINE

*D*addy sent me to follow the family nuisance. I was even promised that new outfit I've been wanting, but only if I found out anything we could use to destroy her. It's just giving her something she deserved for destroying Daddy and my family. First it was her birth, then growing up always pissing Daddy off, bringing out his mean side. I'm just glad all his anger went to her, not me. She's the one that deserved it. The final straw was when she managed to get Mom and Micah killed worrying about her stupid cake.

It was bad enough she ruined my chance of a future. I dropped out of school to help Daddy put up with her colic, and other health issues, and never went back. So, I still live in the house I grew up in. Abby took away all our money and most of my happiness. It's time for paybacks. I want to ruin her future for her. It's only fair.

So here I am sneaking around in the bushes outside the small rundown hut she liked to hide out with the annoying neighbor girl, Liz, who was the apple of Liam's eye. Honestly, I didn't mind her. I just didn't understand why she hung out with Gail. Personally, I thought Gail was the world's biggest mistake. Yeah, she might've been a record breaking swimmer, but Daddy and I never wasted our time watching her play in the pool. She was a huge waste of space, what did everyone see in that spoiled little brat?

Once again she was having a heart to heart with Liz. What the fuck was that music they were listening to? Seriously, please tell me that was not *Insane in the Membrane*. Ugh. They were talking, but the music was drowning out most of their childish chatter.

Wait! What did she just say? She made love with him? Why in the hell would he settle for her when he could have me? Who cared I'm 13 years his senior, most men love older women. I was so much better than that worthless whiner. I could admit I've had a few fantasies in which he's played a key role.

Holy shit! Eli had sex with *that*? My mind was blown! I was suddenly green with envy, the evil green monster taking control of my mind. Why wouldn't he give me the time of day? Over the years, I have thrown myself at many of my brothers' friends, but I didn't pursue any of them as much as I tried to seduce Eli. I quickly returned to my car, I had to report back to Daddy.

"Polly? What'd you find out?" He was drunk and stuttering, slurring his speech. It was Gail's fault he hasn't stopped drinking since the fight in the hospital.

"Daddy! They did it! He had sex with her!" I was practically jumping up and down.

"Thank you baby girl," he responded, his words slurred together. I could hear him gulp down more of what I could only guess was his favorite honeyed whiskey. His favorite drink was whiskey and coke, hold the coke. He hung up on me without another word. I better get that outfit he promised me!

On my drive back home, I pondered what Daddy was planning to do. Instead of waiting for him to give me details, I headed back to the house. I couldn't wait to see Eli's face when Daddy told him he knew what was going on behind those closed doors.

By the time I was pulling into the drive, Eli was spraying rocks, peeling out like a bat out of hell. Eli was pissed. Damn it, I missed it! Guess I am too late. Daddy was swaying on the porch; I knew I had to go take care of him instead of going out to comfort Eli.

Chapter 8
ELI

I was dropping Liam at the house when Ed cornered me. "So I hear you like having sex with little girls. What are you? A fucking pervert is what you are." I could smell liquor pouring off him.

My mind began racing to find a response, as it also tried to figure out why Abby would say anything to him, of all people. She wouldn't have betrayed me like that. Not my Abby, she's all I have left to live for. "Sir, what are you saying?"

"You raped my daughter!" he yelled, pointing his finger into my chest. "You stole her innocence." He tried to get even closer, but I took a step back. "If you touch her again, I am going to file statutory rape charges against you. A restraining order will also be put in place. Think about how well it will look on your military record," he slurred.

Fuck! How the fuck was I going to get through this shit? Any sort of police record would fuck my military career up, but I was more worried about Abby. She needed me now more than ever, but Ed was finding a way to fuck us over again. Him and his fucking upper hand, one day I would find a way to one up him. "Imagine what the state of Utah would think if they found her medical records?"

My phone started singing Uncle Cracker's *Smile*—Abby's ringtone. I knew I couldn't answer it with Ed here, so I clicked the end button to silence the ringer. We could talk later. I tried not to let my expression change to avoid Ed realizing it was his beautiful daughter. The same one he didn't give two shits about, except when he had a chance to ruin her.

Ed laid down the law and always managed to maintain the upper hand, but this time I didn't hold my tongue. The one thing I knew? I had to get out of there before I laid his ass out. Racing back to my truck, I quickly threw it in gear and kicked up rocks, getting the hell away from him. After a couple calming minutes, I called her back.

"Eli! Glad you could call me back." I could hear the smile in her voice.

"Sorry, about earlier love, I was dropping Lee back at the house. What's up, Babe?" Hearing her voice always found a way to brighten my mood. I kept her father's words from her; there was no reason to let him ruin another day in my girl's life.

"I was letting you know I'm crashing at Liz's tonight. Is that all right?"

"Of course, Mom wanted to spend time with me and hang out. I will be by first thing in the morning to ride to the funeral together." No matter her father's threat, I couldn't back out on her there. I didn't know who needed who more. The only thing I knew was we just needed each other.

"All right, I love you Eli. See you in the morning."

I ended the call, but not before letting her know I loved her. As I got into the house, I took the steps by two and three. Closing my bedroom door, I laid across my bed to savor the scents Abby left behind on the sheets and pillows. Maybe I was a sick bastard, but the heart decides who and when it will love someone. *Fuck!* With everything happening, I almost forgot tomorrow was Abby's birthday. Pulling Micah's suitcase out of my closet, I dug out her gift, the deed to the safe house in South Dakota. I folded it up and placed it into the card he picked out for her. I swept my hand across my face as the tears got to me. This was supposed to be a happy time, instead of celebrating her birthday, we were attending Micah's funeral.

I had to call Bo to get him to bring my uniform when he came. He had everything packed and ready, willing to drop everything and show up tonight if needed. Our platoon was due in at nine in the morning. Tomorrow we bury one of our own brothers. My heart hurt more than any other wound I'd ever gotten. My heart shattered and nearly stole my last breath at the thought of laying Micah in the ground.

That night was hell, sleep did not happen, I was too strung out. Ed's words replayed over and over in my head. Every time I closed my eyes, I saw Micah's face. I spent 24 years at his side, now I'm left with many memories, not all bad, not all good. Abby texted back and forth with me most of the night, that's the only thing that helped me through, she kept my mind occupied. She was saving me once again. I could only hope I helped her as much as she did me.

I gave her a call at midnight. "Happy birthday Babe!"

"You remembered?" she asked. It sounded as though she had been crying.

"You ok love?" I asked. "What's Liz doing?"

"She fell asleep a couple hours ago. This day is going to be hell," she admitted.

"Want me to come over?" I offered.

"No. Your mom is home, I don't want to intrude on your time with her."

"I will swing by in a few Babe. We can go to the truck stop, get some coffee and talk." I was talking to her as Lee texted to see if he could chill with me, I let him know we'd be by to pick him up in a little bit.

"Lynn asked if she could join us," she admitted, "we just got off the phone a couple minutes ago. She knows I'm really struggling." After a pause, she continued, "E, I'm not strong enough for this."

I agreed to pick her up and grabbed my keys, kicking up gravel on the way out of my drive. I couldn't stay away from her no matter how hard I tried, even with Ed's warning on repeat in my head. I hoped it was nothing but an empty threat, and he'd forget about it by the time morning comes. My bet is he would be too busy with his hangover. Abby was waiting on the porch as I turned off my lights and pulled into Liz's driveway. She darted in and rested her head on my shoulder. I couldn't resist tipping her chin up and giving her a soul scorching kiss. We picked up Liam, pushing her closer to me. My hand resting on her knee, with her fingers laced with mine, it felt so good and oh so right.

"Happy birthday, Little One." Liam kissed her cheek. "Liz still sleeping?"

"Yep, snoring away," she answered. The lights from the oncoming traffic reflected on the tears sliding down her face. I wanted to pull over and comfort her, but knew she was fighting to be strong. Giving her knee a gentle squeeze, I leaned over and kissed her cheek, whispering my feelings of love to her. She nodded and twined her fingers of her other hand in with Liam's. This beautiful girl was hurting, but trying to be strong for us. She was more focused on our pain than her own. My beautiful girl deserves the best, not this hell.

We got to the truck stop and chatted until Abby dozed off on my shoulder while I held her tight. Right now she really needed closeness, and I needed her.

Lynn kept making sure she was okay until she finally realized I was trying hard to comfort Abby and give her silent strength. I wanted to let her pretend she was strong enough to get through this without breaking down. If she were to break down, I was going to be right there to pick her back up. She was trying to mask her pain, but I saw through the facade easily. Lynn thanked me for taking care of her over all these years. She didn't know just how good Abby had taken care of me all this time. Lynn admitted she didn't understand our relationship, but she saw just how much we mattered to each other. The seven-year gap seemed to weigh heavily in her mind, but she realized we didn't care if it were four days or thirty years.

We dropped her at Liz's, tucking her into the couch. After dropping Liam off, I stopped by and picked up a beautiful arrangement of roses and lilies in a vase. Sitting it on Liz's front step, I knew she would know who it was from—Micah and me.

I ended up crashing in my truck, without leaving Liz's driveway. It hurt too much being far away from her when I knew she was hurting worse than me. Not to mention, I wanted to be there to see the look on her face when she sees the flowers. If Liz's parents wouldn't have been home, I would have snuck in and cuddled with Abby on the couch. It was probably best not to cause a scene right now.

God, I can't imagine how that little girl is going to feel today. Her graduation should have been one of her happiest days; instead she lost two very significant people. Her seventeenth birthday should've been another exciting day, only it wouldn't be. Today instead of blowing out candles and making wishes, she would be burying those two bright lives. My precious angel has now fallen into the eleventh ring of hell. Her fucking father has used her as a punching bag instead of offering her the protection she needed. Thank God she had Micah and me to offer her a chance to grow up halfway happy.

Fuck! It's down to me, and her father has just issued me an ultimatum. I'd be willing to turn my military career to shit to stay close to her. Knowing that little angel, she'd be destroyed to know I gave it all up for her. She's all I have left; I swore to protect her until my last breath. Maybe I was a pervert, but I've never seen her as just a little sister. I've always saw her as mine.

Chapter 9
ABBY

*A*fter crying myself to sleep, I was up with the first light of a new day of hell. Happy sweet seventeen to me, the biggest mistake the Remlock family made. Climbing off the couch, I quickly folded the blankets I used and went in search of Liz. She was still curled up in a ball moaning something about Liam. *Eww! Blech!* That made me puke in my mouth just a little bit.

I changed into my running shorts and tank top, maybe a morning run would clear my head. Lacing up my sneakers, I was stopped on the front porch by a beautiful bouquet of lilies and roses. I smiled and looked at the truck sitting in the driveway. Had he been out there all night? I jogged over and fell into his arms as he climbed out of the truck.

"Happy birthday, Babe." He kissed me hard on the mouth. "Mind if I join you on your run?" His beautiful smile revealed his single dimple.

"You think you can keep up?" I taunted him. Stealing a kiss, I darted off with him hot on my trail. We jogged for about a half hour to the playhouse and gave it a whole different meaning of play. As we came back down, we talked for awhile before heading back on our run. We smiled through the tears that fell as we shared the good and bad memories of Micah. As we strode up Liz's drive, she was leaned up against one of the pillars, smiling at us.

"You ran without me. And I guess these flowers aren't for me either?" she commented as she pulled me into a hug. "Happy birthday, baby cakes."

"You were busy moaning Liam's name, figured I shouldn't wake you." I gave her a shy smile. "I gotta shower. It's time to get ready for hell."

Eli kissed my cheek, and said, "I got to pick up the boys before I shower and change. I will be back as soon as I can Babe." Lowering his voice, I felt his breath against my ear as he whispered, "Duct tape and honey, I love you forever." After planting one last kiss on my lips, he retreated back to his truck.

"Lynn stopped by and left an outfit for you." Liz offered a weak smile and pulled me in for another hug. "I'm going to be right there beside you."

I struggled to accept her comfort. I can't let people see my weakness, I can't cry. *I'm stronger than duct tape*, I told myself over and over again.

It was too hard to say anything, so I nodded before she tried to speak again. I pulled away and ran up to her bathroom, barely getting the door locked behind me as the sobs tore out of my chest. To drown out the sounds, I turned the shower on. I climbed in and let the water take my tears and sweat, washing them down the drain as I tried to collect my thoughts. There was no way I was going to survive this day.

Not sure how I got out of the shower or into the knee-length black wrap dress, I wasn't feeling, simply moving via autopilot. Thankfully Liz was there to help me fix the unruly curls of my hair into something more fitting for the occasion.

By the time I finally got ready, a scary calm had taken over. A form of self-preservation replaced my emotions. How long would it last? As I've learned over all these years, numbness only brings pain. Eventually.

Eli was escorting me out to his truck when I realized he had showered, shaved, and dressed in his class A's. His truck was scrubbed clean, gleaming in the sunlight, like his freshly polished shoes. If it was any other moment, I would have thought *damn he looks amazing.* Instead, now the only thought I had was *Micah would be proud.*

Slowly, I moved one foot in front of the other, one breath closer to Micah. Mom took my angel with her, why couldn't Mom take me with her too. No one was left to be strong for me. It's time to be strong for myself; who knew how long Eli would hang around with Micah gone. A day? A week? I gave myself a little pep talk. *Come on Abby, it's time to turn the page, it's time to help Mom and Micah find the peace they deserve. This is about them, not you.* I wiped a stray tear as I climbed into Eli's truck. It was time to man up and turn these feelings off.

When we pulled up in front of the church, another tear escaped. I begged for someone to please let me wake up from this nightmare. *This has to be a bad dream, someone's version of a cruel joke, they can't be really gone.*

My family was dressed in solid black, from LeAnn's hair bow to Wesley's tie, from the frame of Rob's glasses to Lynn's heels. A rebellious set of tears streaked down my cheeks, it was becoming more real by the second. Who was I kidding when I thought I'd get through this event without shedding tears?

I hugged my niece Celeste, as Lynn wrapped her motherly arms around the both of us. I felt wrapped in love. For reasons unknown, I finally realized I wasn't alone. All these years, I had felt the only ones who saw me were Micah and Eli. Right now, it felt like we were a real family.

Things took a huge turn for the worse when Daddy and Polly walked in and sneered at me. Suddenly I no longer felt welcome. Wes must've noticed a change in my posture, because he leaned in and whispered, "Relax Little One, you belong here with us." He squeezed my shoulders gently. It didn't stop Pauline from casting evil glances or shooting daggers my way, but it did stop me from letting it bother me as much.

I felt like I had entered the tenth dimension of hell. As much as I wanted to get out of here, I didn't want to let them win. *Duct tape and honey, I got this.* They were my lost loved ones as well, I deserved to be here with the rest of them. I took a seat between Wes and Lynn. I ignored how much Daddy despised me as I sat there proudly by my siblings and honored two great people. As I glanced over my shoulder, I saw Liam sitting between Eli and Liz.

The front row held Daddy, Pauline, Lynn, Wes, me, Colton and his wife, Missy. Rob's family as well as Liam, Liz, and Eli took up the next row. The entire church was filled with family and friends; I even recognized some of my classmates. If only I were able to relay exactly how blessed they made me feel. Instead, I choked on all my tears. Liz leaned forward and kissed my cheek, before she softly whispered, "Celebrate their lives, they wouldn't want you to grieve their loss." I nodded, trying to believe it was that simple.

As the minister opened up with a prayer, peace and strength were sought after. I closed my eyes and laced my fingers into Wes's hand. Gently he gave me a reassuring squeeze. LeAnn took the stage and sang her beautiful version of Michael Jackson's *You Are Not Alone*. It was my only request for Micah, it was the song he told me he wanted sang at his funeral. I never wanted to hear it played, but I wouldn't break the promise I gave him. My tears filled tissues as well as the shoulder of Lynn's dress.

Eli's hand patted my shoulder. When I turned to look at him, he whispered softly, "I love you." That hand offered more than silent strength, and comfort, it offered understanding too. I wasn't the only one that lost someone special.

I knew if Liam were to lean forward and say anything, he would tell me that we would get through this, just like everything else. Scarred but stronger. As much as Daddy made sure I knew I was hated, Micah made sure I knew I was loved. I learned early on, it only took one person's love to outweigh the hate of many. Mom had told each and every one of us how much she loved us, every night before she went to bed. How I will miss her nightly admissions of love, and her strength, but most of all, that beautiful smile. Even on her worst days, that smile was always there.

They read through Micah's eulogy first. They told the crowd about his six years in the Special Forces. Micah, Eli and the other six boys were their very own *Band of Brothers*. Continuing to share of how he led multiple successful missions, earned bronze stars and made a name for his family and this great country. As they continued to tell everyone about the greatness I already knew, tears flowed recklessly down my face. I silently added he was a one-of-a-kind brother and best friend with a heart of gold bigger than Texas. He was a born protector and caring young man with a bright future ahead of him. My brother was taken from us way too soon. I missed him so much already.

The church's choir sang *Wind Beneath My Wings*, my mother's most favorite hymn of all times. Mom's eulogy spoke of her commitment, not only family, but the community as well. They told about how her smile could light up the darkest night. Mom was a devoted wife and brilliant mother to eight remarkable children, and loving grandmother to eight beautiful grandkids.

The biggest coincidence was she worked hours on end every week as a grief counselor. Where was she when I needed help through all this grief? *Mommy, I need you!* A fresh bout of sobs escaped as I realized I had never needed anything more than I needed Micah and Mom back.

The one wish I grew up with was the wish she would've protected me from my father's abuse. But as I thought back, she was a good soul and I never wanted her to be put at risk. I silently thanked Mom. Living through that hell made me stronger, more independent, and more able to deal with the hardships I have and will continue to face. *Thank you Mom, you turned me into a survivor.*

We joined together and sang *Amazing Grace*; my voice was thick with sobs as I tried to participate. As the final prayer was said, we lined up and followed the deceased to the hearses. My father made sure to inform me I was not welcome to ride with him. I nodded and turned away. I rode with Liam, Liz, and Eli. Being wrapped tightly in Liz's arms helped me restore a sense of calm. She offered me a sad smile that touched my heart more than ever. As we followed the procession, the sound of the hazard's blinking sounded more like the loud, steady beat of a drum. Aside from our breathing, it was the only sound I heard.

We pulled to a stop in the old cemetery, near where Grammy and Papa were buried. Colt helped me out and hugged me close. I realized he looked as tore up as I felt. He found it necessary to let me know he was going to try harder to be a better brother. "I may not have been the best brother, but I want you to know, no matter what, no matter where, I am here for you Little One." Trying to find an answer, my voice seemed to desert me; the only response I could give was a simple, solemn nod.

Mom's casket was carried by her two brothers, and her four remaining sons. Since Micah was military, his coffin was draped with a flag and escorted by seven sharply dressed soldiers, including Eli, to the burial location. Micah was honored with a standard twenty-one gun salute. "Ready. Aim. Fire," one directed them as the loud shots caused me to jump. As Lynn remained in salute, she held tight to my hand. The second round went off shortly after, ending with a third and final volley. Each shot broke my heart a little more. It made this nightmare real. Lynn gave my shoulder a comforting squeeze as 'Taps' began to play.

My heart was officially shattered as I took my seat with the rest of the family.

This can't be happening, I screamed on the inside. *There was no way this could be real. Wake me up now, please! Nothing but a mistake, that is what this was. They must've gotten Mom and Micah mixed up with someone else. Micah can't be in that shiny black casket, just as Mom couldn't be lying in the pearlescent white one.*

As they folded the flag, the floodgates of tears broke open. My heart was ripped open and bleeding. It was on display for the whole world to see. Each time the flag became a little smaller, my sobs grew louder. The soldier gave the triangle shaped flag a final inspection before passing it on to Eli. Once he inspected it, he marched towards me. I wasn't prepared when he knelt before me. *Who was I kidding?* I wasn't prepared for any of this. How do you prepare for a day in hell? He gently placed the flag into my quaking arms.

He stated, with tears in his eyes, "This flag is offered on behalf of a grateful nation and the United States Army as a token of gratitude and appreciation for Micah David Remlock's honorable and faithful service. He was one of the most respectable men I have ever had the pleasure growing up and serving in the Special Forces with. He was my best friend, and he loved you to the moon and beyond. God Bless you and this family, and God Bless these United States of America." He dropped a kiss on the top of my head before turning and marching away with his fellow soldiers.

I was left shaking and clenching the flag to my body, wishing it was Micah I was holding instead.

More prayers of peace and strength were given, before finally they turned the ceremony over to our family. Kind words were said. Comforting words were given. Loving words were cherished. This world had just lost two bright stars. Our family had just lost two bright stars. They may be gone but will never be forgotten.

The funeral completed and each of us stepped forward, placing a token of remembrance on each of the closed caskets. I couldn't focus on what everyone else placed on them or I definitely wouldn't make it through. Since we went from oldest to youngest, I was the last child to go. By the time I stepped forward to Mom's beautiful casket, there were roses and notes, even a couple of pictures. I placed a peach rose symbolizing appreciation and gratitude, and a red rose beside it, to remind her she was loved, beautiful, and respected. The star pendant I laid over the dove engraving was to remind her she will always be a bright spot in my life. I knelt down, placing a kiss on the cold casket, wishing instead it were her warm, loving cheek. As I stood on my shaking legs, I wiped away the trail of tears.

Stepping to the side, I bowed before Micah's shiny black coffin. I couldn't help but think of how it would match his shoes if I were to check. I placed some forget-me-nots and a white lily, freshly kissed, atop his casket. The lily was our version of love, understanding, and belief in one another that we will always find peace. I loved him and wished that he would find the peace he deserved. Never would I forget the greatest blessings God gave to this earth.

Our family stood together and released a dove. May *we* find peace. May *they* find peace.

The other six men who assisted in the folding of the flag stepped forward with Eli. They circled Micah's casket, together they each dropped a slip of paper in the open grave. Eli pulled out a coin, kissed it, then gave it to the guy on his left who kissed it and passed it to the next guy. Once the last of them kissed it, it was placed on Micah's coffin. It was then that I was able to recognize those were the brothers he served with. A wave of sadness washed over me, they too had just lost one of their brothers I thought as fresh tears fell for them.

As a group, they moved through each of my family members, offering their condolences before moving on to the next. They circled around me and pulled me into a massive group hug.

Eli kissed my forehead and pulled me closer to him. "Babe, these are the rest of our boys. They've been alongside Micah and me all along. Normally we don't do funerals, but we bury our own, it's the greatest respect we could give a fallen brother." When he said that, I remembered their faces from the pictures I was shown. Some of the guys even stopped in during our video chats. They looked so much different in person, so much different in uniform.

"We've heard so much about Micah's princess, we are honored to be your brothers." One reached out and patted my arm. "We've chosen to take you in as one of our own. Our only concerns are your happiness and safety. I am Ryland. That is Bo, Trevor, Carl, Dirk and Christian." He pointed to each of them. At the mention of their names, each man bowed his head slightly.

I glanced at each of them, before landing back on Eli, asking him, "What did you drop in there, if you don't mind me asking?"

"The coin was our unit coin, in hopes he finds all the riches in the afterlife that he deserves," the man Ryland referred to as Dirk stated.

Bo smiled weakly. "The paper was our oath to continue to protect and love you. As an honor for our fallen brother, we have dubbed you as our platoon princess. We will keep you safe until our last breaths."

Eli offered me support as he led me away from the crowd. I collapsed into his chest, panic clear in my eyes. "I'm scared, what do I do now E?"

He kissed my temple, and told me, "No matter what, we are always going to be here for you. You aren't alone, you are my forever."

"You!" My father thrust his finger in my face, causing me to step back. I felt Celeste's arms wrap around my waist as my father continued, "I want you out of here. You don't belong!" His voice continued to rise. "You are dead to me! I wish you were the one to die in that car accident. Better yet, I wish we aborted you, like I wanted to!" he spat at me. I noticed his tear stained cheeks before he turned heel and walked away.

I glanced around praying no one else heard. Everyone's eyes were on me. Some were worried, some looked shocked, and others just felt sorry for me. I wanted to disappear at that moment. I hated pity.

I knew he was hurting. As much as he hated me, he loved Mom that much more. Dad's eyes held pain, his body appeared weaker than normal. The way he coped was to blame it all on the mistake of a daughter. If it weren't for me, he'd be happy. Mom and Micah would still be alive. It was my fault *he* was hurting. It was my fault *I* was hurting.

Knowing me as well as he does, Eli swept me into his arms and walked us straight to his truck. Gently putting me in the passenger's seat, then he darted into the driver's seat. Quickly, he took me away.

Chapter 10
ABBY

I was devastated. I knew I wasn't his favorite child, and I knew he was hurting, but those words struck me harder than a fist to the face. It wasn't just the words; it was the embarrassment of having everyone staring at me, feeling sorry for me. Eli got me home, but I wouldn't let him console me, and I wouldn't let him follow me inside. As much as I craved the comfort of his arms, I needed space.

"I'm fine Eli. I just need a little bit of time alone." I kissed his cheek and ran inside. I knew he was going to wait around for me, but prayed he would leave before I finished packing. Darting up the stairs, I pulled out my backpack and one of the stray old duffel bags out of the closet. Dumping out the remnants of my high school career, I loaded my laptop, kindle, journal, and cell phone in my bag. Before I zipped it up, I dumped my savings account information and ID in. Any electrical cords that might be necessary were thrown into the duffel. Pulling clothes off hangers and out of drawers, I shoved them wherever they would fit. I even managed to toss in a throw blanket. I stepped out of my dress, leaving it on the floor, and pulled on a pair of sweats, tank top, a hoody, and topping off my head with one of Micah's old hats. Glancing out the window, I noticed Eli was still in the driveway. Quickly, I slipped on some socks and my old tennis shoes. I felt terrible, but I was making a run for it. Carrying what little I owned on my back, I snuck out the back door and jogged the three blocks to the bank.

The only money I had was my college fund. I withdrew a thousand to get me through whatever I was going to do. I wasn't sure if I got the money from Mom and Micah's will deposited yet. Either way, I wasn't going to spend that. Unsure what else I should do, I made it to the bus station and hopped on the first bus out of town. My brain was frantic to figure out what I was going to do next. I just needed to get away. Far, far away.

As the bus pulled into the next station, I read through the list of departures. Looking at the long list of locations, I tried to remember where that house was that Micah was building. What did that letter say? I was pretty sure he said he wrote it in my journal. Oh yeah, he said it was on a page with Eli's name and hearts on it. *Way to make this easy Mikey, too many pages of my journal involved Eli's name and hearts.* Taking the seat nearest me, I pulled out my journal and quickly scanned for the page with the address. With the address, Micah wrote a little note. *Abs, if something happens, let Eli take care of you. Let Eli love you. Be safe my little One. You are my happy place. Duct tape and Honey. love you always and forever -Micah*

Crap! No! Not Here! A tear escaped from my eye. *I can't cry here.* I shoved the journal back into my bag and made my way to the ticket counter. My hat was pulled down over my eyes. "One ticket to Mitchell, South Dakota, please."

Without so much as a sideways glance, the ticket was passed to me. "Bus leaves in thirty minutes, you just made the cut off."

I followed the boarding passengers onto the bus and took a seat towards the back. Even though I was sure I was sticking out like a sore thumb, my goal was to blend in with the scenery. I settled back into an uncomfortable cloth seat and tucked my legs under me. Through the first leg of the trip, I managed to maintain a bit of space. I didn't have to share my row with anyone, thankfully. When I changed busses, it was loud and crowded. I glanced up and down the rows, looking for space to sit somewhere halfway safe. Figuring the little old lady sitting by herself seemed safe enough, so I plopped down beside her.

"You look awfully young to be travelling all by yourself." She eyed me.

"I'm going to spend the summer with my grandma. It's a family tradition." I offered a weak smile as I pulled the bill of my hat further down. My cheeks and eyes were probably still swollen and red from all the tears that have fallen.

She continued to try to converse, but I was not in the mood to talk. After not getting answers, she finally caught the hint and left me alone. *Thank God.* I pulled out my journal and rehashed my horrid day. It was so much easier ignoring what was going on around me when I was writing.

My phone went off, indicating a text message.

Are you ok Babe?

Damn it, I had forgotten the real reasons I had left town. Trying to keep them from worrying, or finding out I was gone, I responded.

I'm fine. Taking a few moments to clear my head.

Here if you need me Babe.

I know, thanks. I tried to sound better than I was feeling.

I buried my phone into the bottom of my bag. It kept vibrating, but I knew if I reached in to shut it off, it would end up being the *If You Give a Mouse a Cookie* scenario. I'd check text messages, I'd check voicemail, and then I'd have to let them know I'm ok, then one would ask where I was. See the dilemma?

Finally, I reached down into my bag and turned it off, before attempting to doze off. I couldn't sleep, my father's words kept ricocheting back to the forefront of my head. All the bad things that had happened to me reverberated in my head. Tears managed to escape, swiping angrily, I tried to tell myself, *you are fine, damn it! Abby you are all right. Duct tape and honey, duct tape and honey.*

The bus ride through South Dakota showed cornfields, wheat fields, and what I'd have to guess as being soybeans. Cows! I remember grandma always saying cattle farms smelled like money to her. It sure didn't smell anything like the money I knew.

By the time I got to Mitchell, I hadn't thought of how I was going to get to the address Micah had written in my journal. The thought of all the pain that I left behind was my primary thought.

The bus pulled up beside some shady motel with a giant bull statue out front. The brown and white paint was chipping. Why was I focused on the freaking fading bull when I really needed to find a ride? *Oh look, a buffalo statue too! Wait?* The motel was named after a corn palace? Where in the world did Micah send me? I stepped inside the motel and found a 'Welcome to Mitchell' flyer of all the tourist traps. They really do have a Corn Palace referred to as the world's biggest bird feeder, wow I really am out in the sticks!

Focus Abigail! I scolded myself. I needed to find a ride. Of course, this place has to be safe, there is no one here. Looking around, I saw a scary looking Goth chick wearing more black than I owned. "Excuse me. Do you know where I can get a cab?"

She rolled her eyes and walked away. *Great! Another difficult one.* A twenty-something clean cut man touched my shoulder. "Hey beautiful, do you need a ride somewhere?" Wasn't this how horror movies started out? Guy meets girl at the bus station and she was never seen again?

I could feel Mom turning in her fresh grave as I decided to start a conversation with this golden-eyed stranger. "Sir, could you give me a ride to my brother's house?" *Come on Abby,* I told myself, *think of a good reason why your brother wouldn't be here if he knew you were coming and make it sound believable.* My wheels spun, *come on hamster a little faster, please.* "He had to pull a double shift." Giving him a once over, I made sure he didn't have 'serial killer' tattooed on his forehead. He had to be safe, right?

"It would be my pleasure." He offered me a sincere smile, showing off a mouth full of shiny white teeth.

I got my bags loaded into the back of his truck. As I climbed into the passenger side, I recited the address out loud.

"Oh, that's just down the road a bit from me, down by my buddy Heath's place," he continued rattling off more and more, but I managed to block it out.

I groaned inwardly and rolled my eyes, just a little further. If I made it this far on the bus next to that rambling elderly lady, I could handle this chatty chump. He threw on his cowboy hat as he threw his truck in gear, tearing off down the road. If I hadn't grown up around all the boys, I might have been a little frightened at his driving skills. Placing a hand on the dash, I reached into my backpack and pulled out my phone. I turned my phone on and scanned through some of the old messages from Micah, looking for the one with the alarm code. This was where he was going to move me as soon as I got my diploma. I was to walk off that stage into the front door of the new place. That was the plan. That was what I was doing right now, but the circumstances were so much more different. I wiped away a stray tear when I thought how much, and how quickly, our plans were changed.

"You staying here long sweetheart?" His hand poked at my shoulder, trying to get my attention. "You ok over there?"

"Not sure yet." I tried to pull my body away without seeming hostile. As he pulled into the driveway, I saw the house that I've only seen in pictures and over video chat. The house I heard about every step of the way when it was getting built. From the first nail to the last coat of paint. This is what freedom looked like.

He barely got the truck into park before I was jumping out the door thanking him. He offered to help carry my stuff to the door, but I managed to get him to believe me when I said I got it, "I'm a big girl, I got this."

He tipped his hat. "The name's Dale. If you need anything, just give me a holler."

I marched up the stairs and entered the code on the panel by the door, got inside and quickly locked up behind me. An instant safe feeling washed over me. I watched out the window, waiting until the guy left. He seemed to want to stay for a while, I saw him messing with something which I guessed to be his phone. I begged silently he would hurry up and leave. With a sigh of relief, I turned my focus to my vibrating phone.

Glad you made it to the safe house Babe.

How'd you know?

Tracking device Babe. I will give you space, but remember I will ALWAYS come for you. Love you.

Love you too Eli.

I tossed my phone on the center island in the kitchen. Taking a tour of the place caused me to tear up. Micah was everywhere. The black sofa and recliner contrasted with the stark white walls. Dark wood end tables, and, of course, a huge TV dominating the wall, yep, Micah was all over this place. He loved the contrast of colors and the bigger and flashier the electronics the better. As I continued through the house, I opened doors and checked out every room as well as the closets.

The last door on the left was the door to my room, it had to be, the other rooms were too masculine, except the one that was left with a white bed in the middle of the white room which I could only assume to be a guest room. I opened the door up and instantly knew for sure it was my room. The comforter on the queen sized bed was a royal purple, with pale violet flowers on it. *Wait, flowers really? Who decided that?*

The walls were plastered with famous quotes, painted in what appeared to be Eli's elegant hand. My favorite quote was the one above my bed, *Stronger than Duct Tape. Sweeter than Honey*. The quote they always repeated when something bad happened to me, which was more times than I wanted to count. Between losing random swim meets, the abuse of my father, and coming home with something other than a perfect score on my tests—that quote gave me reassurance.

Heading back to the kitchen in search of food, I was in love with the oversized stainless steel appliances, and the dark wood cabinets. The dark marble gleamed brightly when hit by the lights overhead. However, the cabinets were empty of food except for a box of stale crackers. *Dishes! Yay!* They had a brand new set of pots and pans fresh out of the box. Opening more cabinets, I found enough place settings for about eight people. The fridge was bare, guess it was time to head out in search of something.

Chapter 11
ELI

I knew she made it safe. The relief I felt should have been great, but I wasn't with her. My heart was heavy without her by my side. The house security alarm was reset, Dirk's younger brother made sure she was safely inside before he left. Sure would've been easier if I could just get a signature verifying her delivery, as the postal service has. But for some reason they looked down on human trafficking, something about it being illegal.

Yes, as soon as I figured out from her GPS tracker on her phone she was heading to the safe house, I called up some of the guys to find a connection to ensure she got all the way there. Yes, I may be a psycho stalker when it came to the girl that was everything to me, even if she doesn't know the full extent of my love for her.

Putting my phone on my bed, I started packing up my bags. Mom had taken me out for lunch before she had to fly out for another important meeting. My flight was scheduled to leave at o'dark thirty tomorrow morning; I had a training mission waiting for me. I had to focus, I couldn't keep worrying about Abigail, she was safe for now, and my heart was too.

Fuck! Tomorrow was going to be hard! My first time on a plane without Micah, going back to the base without Micah, getting back to our room without Micah, standing in formation without Micah, preparing for our next mission without Micah. Having to continue our routine without my battle buddy, my wingman, my right arm, and my best friend was going to take some time to get used to. I don't have to be strong for Abby tomorrow. I have to be strong for myself. I couldn't help but feel a big chunk of me was buried with Micah.

Abby was the only thing I had left to live for. She's my reason for trying to be a better man. It's time to man the fuck up. Words from Carl came to mind. *It's time to nut up or shut up.*

I flung myself onto my bed, overcome with tears. Pulling the pillow where she last laid her beautiful head to my face, I inhaled her scent. It brought me peace, I couldn't explain it, and I won't even try. It'd make me sound like an even bigger pansy than I already felt. Closing my eyes, I let exhaustion take over.

As I climbed on the plane, everything hit me again; the fears, the pain, the loss. As I buckled my seat belt, I took a deep breath. Trying to calm the plethora of thoughts and feelings than ran through my head was easier said than done. This is the first time I have ever felt so alone and my first time going anywhere without Micah.

I had wanted to join the Army for as long as I could remember.

I was lying on the threadbare beige carpet playing with the little green army men, GI Joes, and tanks for hours on end. I remember looking up to see Mom watching me and smiling, she asked, "Sweetie, what do you want to be when you grow up?"

I smiled at her. "That's easy Momma, I wanna be just like these guys. I wanna be in the Army and help fight the good fight to help people that need help. I want to be in the Speckle Forces just like Daddy was. You know before he went to heaven to be an angel."

It made me laugh, it took forever before I could call it the Special Forces, now we sometimes joked around and call ourselves the Speckle Forces. The ongoing joke started out between Micah and me, but our brothers in the platoon soon joined in with us.

I crawled up into her lap and she hugged me tight into her arms. "I love you Momma. I'm gonna protect you. I promised Daddy I would."

My mom smiled at me with tears in her eyes. "I love you too baby. God blessed me when he gave me an angel like you."

My mind went to something else. Lately, it's where it always seemed to go. Abigail. I hated having feelings for her, she's fucking 16 years old, well now 17, but it's still criminal territory. Literally. To think what Micah would have done if he knew the inappropriate thoughts I was having about his baby sister. I would have been hung up by my balls, my dick fed to me for morning chow.

Now that I can get some space, I am going to put these feelings aside, one way or another, I thought determinedly. I can admit to myself that I'm nervous about this next mission, it's going to be my first mission without Micah protecting my back. I know I can rely on my other "brothers," but none of them were Micah. Micah and I have been through everything together. Kindergarten, we walked through those doors and owned that shit. We took touch football to a whole new level and joined the Varsity team while still in middle school. The girls flocked to us and they loved his baby sister. I admit I used Abby to get me a couple dates when we were in high school. *Damn it*, as usual, she popped back up to the front of my brain.

I needed to get shit faced, or into a good sparring match. Anything to keep my mind clear, I needed something to distract my thoughts from the little girl who stole my heart.

Damn it! I shouldn't have given in to my desires to make her mine. She needed a protector, she needed closeness, but I couldn't help it. Did she push me away? No, but I should've known better, she's just a child. Her first time shouldn't have been when she was in emotional distress. Instead, it should have been in pure happiness, bliss.

We were so excited about our first trip to Ft. Drum. I searched the internet to find out as much about our new base as I could. Micah was busy enjoying the barracks bunnies hopping from one room to the next. Don't get me wrong, I indulged in my fair share as well, but Micah had a rep for being a ladies' man.

He was balls deep in some bottle blonde's mouth last time I glanced into his side of the room. "Dude, Abby is supposed to be calling in fifteen." We never got too busy around the time Abby called. We didn't want her to think any negative thoughts about what we do in our free time.

Micah threw one of his boots towards me. "Don't worry, I'll be done by then."

Abby called early, so I turned the video chat option on so we could catch up while Micah was busy getting his rocks off.

"Hey boys!" Abby's face popped up on the computer screen.

"It's just me right now Babe. Micah should be done in a few. What happened?" I'd called her Babe for as long as I'd known her. I noticed her tear stained cheeks, which worried me; she never was one to cry easily. She was one of the strongest girls I knew.

She used her hair as a shield. "I will be ok. Duct tape and honey, remember? What did you guys find out? Where will you be stationed next?" She worked hard to keep up with our military career, tried to live vicariously through us.

"Babe, he do it again? Let me see." Hearing the concern in my voice, Micah finished quickly and popped over by the computer, fastening his pants. Abby stood up, raising her shirt, showing fresh bruises all over her ribs.

"Who the fuck did that Little One?" Micah traced the bruises on the screen, as if she were right there instead of halfway across the country. I'd seen Micah pissed off, but what he was showing right now was way beyond that.

"Daddy. I was five minutes late from school, because I couldn't find a ride. Swim practice ran over." Abby pulled her shirt back down. "Lee had a job interview today," she stated as a way to change the subject. "He got the job!"

"See, I fucking told you about that shit Micah, you finally going to believe me now?" I was livid, this wasn't the first time. As much as I prayed, I knew it probably wouldn't be the last time either.

"I didn't know it was that bad. Fuck!" Micah confessed. I guess he thought the abuse would end when he walked out the door and joined the Army. He was always her protector from their father, he took multiple hits for her, and I knew he would gladly take more if *necessary to keep Abby safe. His face turned to stone as he growled, "We will find a way to get you to somewhere safe Little One. Hold on tight, duct tape and honey, Little One. Love you!" His fist left a dent in the wall.*

My fist had left plenty of dents in that same wall; hate to see the repair bill. I had been trying to tell Micah for almost six months now. I was glad he finally realized I wasn't making that shit up.

"I had to get seven stitches in my forehead, but makeup and my hair covers it up. They told me I'm not allowed to swim for a couple days, but there is a big meet coming up I can't miss." She held her bangs back so I could see the freshly sutured wound. Abby was twelve, soon to be thirteen. She asked excitedly, "Where is your next duty station, you found out today, right?"

"We leave out to Ft Drum, New York in a couple weeks. We should be home in a couple days though."

"I will put Dad in his place Little One. I will find a way for you to be safe and happy if it's the last thing I do." Micah blew her a kiss and headed towards the door. "Let's go E. I need to beat some shit up."

"You guys can't do anything, it will only end up worse for me Mikey, please don't worry about it," she tried to plead, but Micah was already gone.

"See you later Babe." With that, I signed off. We ran and did sparring, and ran some more. All our training had been about combat, we chose to focus on the hand-to-hand shit. Our hands were lethal when we sparred; we exhausted ourselves with running first.

When we made it back home, we confronted Ed, their father. Had Karen not been around, we would have put the ultimate hurt on him. We had bulked up since we were last home and no longer afraid of anything. Never were we the kind to back down. I couldn't go anywhere near Abby alone due to Ed's threat of filing a police report against me. It would have been worth it to me but would have destroyed Abby. Her father always managed to get the upper hand. Fucking bastard!

For her thirteenth birthday, we took her out and treated her like a princess. Liz and Liam spent the entire day with us shopping. We finally got to see Abby smile, relax, and enjoy herself. Still concerned with her safety, we bought her a cell phone, so she could always get in touch. We laughed and joked about calling her a princess, to this day our boys still refer to her as "our platoon princess."

The day we left, left an uncomfortable feeling with us. To keep my mind from wondering what could possibly be happening while we were in the air, I chose to check out the scenery. Watching the clouds go by. The Adirondack Mountains came into view, the peaks were snow capped. I snapped a picture with plans to send it to Abby the moment it was safe to use my phone. We crossed what I thought had to be the Great Lakes, according to the research. I really hope my girl stayed safe.

I was not looking forward to the brutal winters we were soon to be facing. "Ugh! I hate the cold," I groaned. Growing up in Utah, I should've been used to it, but I never enjoyed the cold. I wanted to share the excitement of the view with Micah, but he was busy grunting and groaning in his sleep, I muttered, "Dude you can sleep anywhere."

I thought back to that and figured maybe he had the right idea; my eyes remained closed for the rest of the plane ride. I don't need to think about what they were planning for me now. I knew I wasn't here to enjoy the 107,000 acres that Drum had to offer. I would be packing up Micah's shit and putting it aside, before I embarked on the next mission with the original group, minus my best friend.

Who would be put on the duty of watching my back? Whoever it was would never be Micah.

Chapter 12
ELI

*I*t was late on Sunday night by the time the plane finally touched down. I grabbed my bags from baggage claim and threw them in the back of my big, black, jacked-up truck. No one would ever take the country out of this boy. I climbed in behind the wheel tightening and loosening my grip on the steering wheel, waiting for Micah to get in. *Fuck!* It had taken a good five minutes before I relived placing that folded flag in Abby's tiny trembling hands. This adjustment was going to be one hell of a struggle.

After I had flashed my ID at the gate, I made my way to the barracks. Slamming my truck door, I hauled my bags up the stairs. I could've used the elevator, but my body was full of pent up energy. When I unlocked my door, I opened it just barely wide enough to throw my bags in, quickly shutting it after. I couldn't go in there, not yet. I still needed to sign in, so I had another reason to stay away from my room. On my way through the halls, I banged on Dirk's door.

He answered wearing a pair of track shorts, no shirt. He was the scrawniest 'mo fo' I'd ever seen, I still wouldn't want to mess with him. Get on the wrong end of his gun, and poof you were gone. That fucker never, ever missed. "How're you holding up Monty?"

"Feel numb. Feel like shit," I admitted.

"Let me know if you need anything man." His golden eyes met mine. "I mean it."

I nodded, "I gotta go sign in. See you at morning formation." I turned and headed down to sign in. On the way back to my room, I stopped by some of the rest of my battle buddies' rooms letting them know I made it back. I was stalling. I wasn't ready to return to our room. It was the last place I wanted to be. Maybe I could just go in there without looking at his side of the room and crash. Yeah right, after 24 years spent together, it's not that easy. It's not like changing clothes; this was trying to live without the other part of me. He was the one who managed to keep my anger under control. Micah was the one to take the bottle away when I've had too much to drink. He was the one who had my back no matter what. He would have taken a bullet for me. Why couldn't it have been me lying in that fresh grave?

I unlocked our room and stepped inside, my feet suddenly felt too heavy to move me any further. My heart was full of hurt, my head full of regrets. With one look at his unmade bed, I felt the tears fall down. As I poured me a glass of water, instead of the whiskey I wanted, I tried to regain a sense of control. The only other time I had felt this emotionally overloaded was with Abby, *our first time, her first time*. I wondered how she was doing now. I hadn't heard anything since she hit the safe house. She was so strong, much stronger than my pansy ass right now. Damn I was supposed to protect her; instead I let her run off.

I swore right there at that moment that I would protect that beautiful girl from all the evils in the world until my final exhale, even if it meant keeping her from me. I am nowhere near a saint.

I kicked off my shoes, reached up to the back collar of my shirt, and pulled it over my head. Turning to the mirror, I peeked over my shoulder, yep still a few red scratches intermingled with the tattoo that spanned across my broad shoulders. Micah and I got our last names inked across our backs the first night at Ft. Drum. I smiled at the memories scrolling through my head like the bottom of a news channel.

Everything we did, we did together. From playing on playgrounds to battling bullies to top secret missions, we were together. We went from throwing footballs to tossing grenades. We used to wrestle on mats until we joined the military, then we focused on hand-to-hand combat on any surface necessary.

Stripping down, I hopped in the shower in an attempt to clear my mind. Abby's face of pure ecstasy came into focus. Fuck! My soldier stood at attention, waiting for my hand to give it an honorable discharge. My hand palmed my length as I thought back to our playhouse rendezvous.

We made it inside. She quickly locked the door behind us. Her eyes were feral and full of lust. She maintained eye contact as she lowered herself to her knees mere inches from me. I was instantly at full attention, no half mast for this girl. Question in her eyes as she reached out and ran her fingers over the bulge in my shorts, my throat dried up as I nodded to her. Her eyes had me mesmerized as she slid my shorts off. I was half expecting a "BOING!" noise when my erection sprang free. Her eyes got bigger as she knelt face to face with my erection. Then, those lips slipped over the tip.

FUCK! Just thinking of that moment had me stroking myself harder and faster.

I battled the urge to tilt my head back in pleasure, but my eyes were drawn to her amazing mouth. As she sucked me in just a little farther, her tongue massaged the steel of my erection. I couldn't help but push my fingers through her hair, and pull her head closer, helping her to suck me in deeper. Those violet eyes watched my face; almost as if unsure she was doing it right.

I smiled at her, pulling her to her feet. The sudden panic in her eyes began to fade as soon as I placed my lips on hers. "Are you trying to kill me Babe?" My forehead touched hers as I slipped my hands under the back of her shirt and pulled her against me. She was closer than a shadow could have been.

"Was I doing it wrong?" she asked, placing her hands on my cheeks to search my face.

I couldn't help but smile at her naïve response and kiss the tip of her nose. "No Babe, you were doing it more than right. You are spoiling me. I want you to share the pleasure." I kissed her deeply as

I backed us to the couch. We broke the kiss only to rip our shirts off, it deepened again as I slipped her clothes off her slender bottom half. Disconnecting our lips, I repositioned her on the futon and slid my tongue into that sweet V of hers.

Just remembering her sweet taste caused one hell of a mess in my shower. Shit, I needed to clean up. Formation was in three hours; I should have been unpacking and hitting the sack. Instead, I was reliving my perverted fantasies of my best friend's baby sister.

Five thirty came too fast. I crawled out of bed and into my PTs, I laced up my shoes and buckled the required reflective strip on as I headed out of my room. I really needed to keep busy to keep my mind from going to the dark place. I pounded some pavement with the boys, being a part of a group again was something I needed. Without crying and talking to Abby, this was the only way I would pull through this. I had to rely on my brothers. I had to learn to turn to them, shutting them out was not an option. Taking my frustrations out on the heavy punching bag helped, especially when I pictured Ed's face taking the pounding he deserved.

"Shower, chow, and report for duty at 0800 Monty. Good to have you back. Sorry, for your loss," Commander Collins directed and patted my shoulder as we walked out of the gym.

Following the laid out orders helped. I was able to focus on moving forward, as long as I only thought of the next task ahead of me. I was doing fine until I sat down at my desk in the office. Looking at the next desk over brought a tear to my eye. Crying in my room was acceptable, those tears needed to stay at bay while in public. *What the fuck? They cleaned his desk off? Already?* I looked up at the clock. Damn, I've only been here a half hour and I'm already breaking down. Right there beside the clock was Micah's face staring back at me. *Fuck!* This was harder than I thought it would be.

Pulling to my feet, I swept my arms across my desk. Everything came crashing down, just like my life.

Bo caught my hand just before the wall met its' match. "Montgomery, walk it off."

"I can't do this shit without Micah." I swiped my hands over my head angrily.

"Did they bury your balls with him?" Carl cornered me. "I know you are hurting dude but we have a fucking training exercise on Friday, you better get your shit together."

Dirk's eyes met mine. "We need you Monty. We need your head in the game."

Commander Collins chose that moment to walk in. "What is going on in here?" He looked at the mess near my desk. "Montgomery, get this shit cleaned up and take a day. You need to get your shit straight yesterday."

"Yes sir." I saluted and set about cleaning up the mess, if only straightening my thoughts was that simple.

Tossing my patrol cap on my bed, I threw on a t-shirt and shorts. The gym was calling my name. Before heading out of my room, I checked my phone and found texts from Abby asking about my day. Just seeing her picture on my phone brought a smile to my face.

I dialed her number back and slipped down the wall until my ass hit the cold tile of our floor.

"Hey Eli! I didn't mean to bug you. Just wanted to make sure you made it back and everything." She seemed nervous. I could picture her pacing the living room floor of the house as she chewed on her bottom lip.

Her voice pulled the corners of my mouth up. "Hey Babe. It's all right. I got in late last night."

"You at work?"

"No Babe. I melted down. They cleaned Micah's desk out. I threw everything off my desk, when I saw it. Collins told me to clean my shit up and take a day." I had no problems admitting my weaknesses to her.

"Oh my gosh! I couldn't imagine how horrible that would be." Her voice broke. My sweet angel worried about me, cried for my loss.

"Babe, it just caught me off guard. What are you doing up so early?" I asked as I picked myself off the floor and headed towards the door, I needed to be at the gym.

"Couldn't sleep. I was up most of the night thinking about Mikey and Mom. I even worried about you. It's too quiet here."

"Take the car to town Babe, drive around. Try to find something to do."

"I saw what vehicle you left for me here. *Really*? Could you get an uglier green?" she squealed like a little girl, it made me smile and forget for a moment what she was talking about. I had to pause to remember what we were talking about, the factory green Maverick we left in the garage. I couldn't help but smile as she ranted a little longer about the car.

"I need to get those pictures off the camera. Yes, I stole Mom's camera, the rebel in me. You should have the pictures in your email, I sent a few." I could hear a smile forming on her lips. "Oh, if Liz or anyone else for that matter asks, I am with you. That's ok, isn't it? I can't deal with them right now, it's all too much. I just need some time."

"Of course love. Let me know if you need anything. I'm heading to the gym, I love you."

"I love you too Eli. I know I said I needed some time and space, but I am here for you. I even have a brand new roll of duct tape and even a few packets of honey," she hinted at her way to fix even the most broken of things before she hung up the phone.

I sat for a moment to pull up my email. Opening up the one sent from Abby. I smiled at the first one. It was of me hugging her tight, a smile on both of our faces. *Hmm, Micah must've taken that one.* I wiped a couple tears from my eyes as I came across a candid one of Micah and myself. I glanced at his side of the room, smiling as I caught his unmade bed. Not wanting to torture myself any longer right now, I figured I would look through the rest later.

As I clutched my phone, I realized I didn't hurt as much. She was the salve for my pains. I got a better high from her than any drug I've ever tried. I shoved my phone in my pocket and took off on the treadmill, getting nowhere fast. As each foot pounded, my resolve to keep moving forward strengthened. I had a promise to keep to Micah, and a beautiful little girl in South Dakota to make proud and keep safe.

I gave the weights hell, wishing I was as emotionally strong as I was physically. When I couldn't lift one more time, I decided it was time to take a break. By the time I got back to my room, I had crashed from pure exhaustion.

Good thing I set my alarm or I would've slept through morning PT. Wiping the sleep from my eyes, I crawled out of my bed and prayed for a better day. I managed to make it through most of the day focusing on reviewing our next mission's details. That's the only way I made it through most of the week. I saved the crying until I was alone in our room, which usually happened after I attempted to break myself in the gym.

Wednesday night I cut my cast off my left arm, I didn't want to miss my training mission. The commander told me I wasn't going to be able to participate if I had the cast on, so I took my Gerber multi-tool out and cut the thing to pieces. I was going on this mission. I knew Friday's mission was crucial, I needed to have my head on straight as possible, and I didn't need any physical hindrances. I had to put Abby aside as well. I told myself she was safe. It was time to focus on the mission.

As we geared up, I said a silent prayer that I could put my emotions on the back burner and stay focused on the task at hand. These guys depended on me doing my part. It took all of us being on the same page to make our mission successful. *I can't let my brothers down. I can't let Micah down, again.*

We stood together and sent up a little prayer before receiving our safety brief. They dropped us off about a mile from the area we were to be infiltrating. Our mission was simple: infiltrate, capture villain, win.

We approached with caution. As we closed in on the area, I took the lead and started calling out positions over our helmet mics, "Red One move to flank. Red Two cover rear. Remlock cover me for the tower. On Three. Three. Two."

"Red Four! Negative! Remlock's not a go!" Someone was telling me to focus, I couldn't figure out whose voice it was.

Commandnet came live, before we could move further. "Index! Index! Index!" the commander yelled over the radio. Our training mission was over, unsuccessfully. I screwed it up. As soon as we got back for our brief, I knew I needed to prepare for the verbal lashing about to take place. I took my time so I made sure I was the last one in the room. Take it all at once instead of phases.

All hell broke loose when I walked in. The guys jumped in my face. "What the fuck Montgomery?" Carl blasted at me first.

Dirk pulled me to the side, trying to maintain a voice of reason. "He's not here. You ok man?"

"Do I fucking look all right? I don't fucking know what happened. It happened out of habit. He's always been there, I've never had to stop and think about him not being the next person on the list." I threw my Kevlar to the ground as I told myself, *this just keeps getting worse.* I had a pretty good idea what was about to happen. As soon as Collins walked in, I would have a new asshole to shit out of.

Commander Collins walked in and stopped right in front of me. "Montgomery. We got called up for this mission, you are staying back. Red Two you are Red Four. We will get a replacement from Bravo. Montgomery, you are dismissed. Red team suit up, we will repeat the exercise in one hour." He turned and walked out. Instead of chewing me out, he dismissed me. I didn't know which was worse.

I gathered my shit and headed to my truck. After kicking the tire, I tossed my bag in the bed and climbed in. I slammed my hands on the steering wheel. *Fuck! I have never failed a mission!*

Abby deserves something better than the failure I am.

Chapter 13
ABBY

I needed some food. I climbed into the old Maverick that they had sitting in the garage. Yep, those boys sure do love their old vehicles. Badass, that's how I felt behind the wheel. I went to town in search of a few groceries. As much as I hated the baby food pea green factory paint job, I loved the rumble of the engine. Realizing they left the tank almost empty, I figured the first stop should be a gas station.

Pulling up to the pump, I got out and began trying to locate which side of the car the gas cap was on. I walked around the car a couple times, huffing at the fact I couldn't figure out where the gas goes in at.

Dale pulled up at the next pump over, leaning against his truck as it filled with gas. Watching me, his lips curled into a smile. Clearing his throat, he smirked. "If it isn't Princess Abby, having problems ma'am?"

"Can't figure out where to put it in," I admitted with a blush of embarrassment.

Dale struggled to hold his laughter in. "Has it been that long for you?" I shrugged, so he continued talking, "I can put it in for you."

I let out a sigh of relief as his laughter grew. He walked to the back of the car, twisted that damn bullhead logo, quickly he revealed where the gas nozzle was supposed to go. I shrugged. "I'm not used to putting it in the rear."

"Give it time. It takes a little gettin' used to, but the more you do it, the easier it gets." Dale smirked. He tipped his hat my way then jumped in his truck and sped off. His laughter could be heard through his open windows.

I paid for my gas and climbed in the Maverick. Suddenly everything he said dawned on me. *Oh My. Gosh. Did I really just keep digging myself deeper? Man, I could be so slow sometimes.* I drove to Wal-Mart and picked up some of my necessities: soap, shampoo, food, even a few changes of clothes. Today was not a day to be driving through this little rinky-dink town, today was a day to relax. I would eventually turn tourist for a day and see "The World's Largest Bird Feeder" and maybe see what the Prehistoric Indian Village had to offer. Right now, I was interested in getting home, relaxing and showering before calling it an early night.

As I pulled the car into the garage, I grabbed as many bags as I could, trying to get them all in at once. Once all the groceries were put away, I slipped into a pair of boxers and a tank top and grabbed my kindle. It was a beautiful day, so I sat on the front porch reading about someone else's awesome fantasy life. As the sun started setting, a cool breeze picked up. I stood up and stretched. It was time to go inside, I was starting to shiver. I hated being cold. I turned to pull open the front door, when I saw a sticky note attached to it. Dale must've been by here and left his phone number. I posted the sticky note on the fridge and sat my kindle on the center island.

It was time to make something to eat. I had barely thought about food since before my graduation. Digging out a pot, I filled it with water and set it on the stove to boil. Tonight I was making spaghetti, something nice, simple and full of carbs. As I waited for the water to boil, I dug through the boys' rooms to find a hoody, settling on Eli's high school football hoody. I savored my meal before cleaning up.

Those boys really love me. They gave me a Jacuzzi tub in my bathroom. I turned on the water and watched it fill slowly. The warmth of the water was relaxing and comforting. It was like a warm, love-filled hug. My muscles loosened up and I closed my eyes, relaxing even more. I soaked until my fingers were wrinkly. The water lost its heat, so I grabbed the purple silk robe hanging on the hook, and indulged in the softness. I slipped under the blankets in the softest bed I have ever felt. That night I slept like a rock as I floated on a cloud.

The days and nights began to blend together. If I wasn't sleeping, I was crying, reading, or swimming. Most of my days consisted of staying in my pajamas, only changing for my swims. For the first time, I got to be lazy and I loved not having the rigid schedule from my school years. With no routine, I just kind of did what I felt like when I wanted to and avoided whatever it was I didn't want to do.

As lonely as I was, the pool once again beckoned me. It was the one place I couldn't resist. I went to the local recreation center and swam laps until I was no longer able to move. Then, I would drag myself out of the pool and go back to the house. By the time I would get back to the safe house, I would grab my kindle and soak in the hot tub. Each night before I dozed off, I prayed and whispered my love to each family member, even Dad and Pauline, I was following Mom's traditions.

My sleeping was usually interrupted by nightmares and flashbacks. I would wake up drenched in sweat, struggling to catch my breath, my heart racing out of my chest. I broke down crying, wishing it weren't true. Micah and Mom are still alive, the mangled cars were a myth, and Dad was my guardian angel. We didn't bury anybody. Then I truly woke up. *Yep, that wasn't a nightmare, it was reality.*

Exercise was what I turned to: sit-ups, push-ups, lunges, squats, and any other workout that would wear me out. That was how I coped. When I was too tired to lift any part of my body, I rinsed off and attempted to get more sleep.

If I was restless during the daylight hours, and not in the mood to swim, I ran up and down the gravel roads surrounding me. My body stayed in shape, but my mind was all over the place. The more I tried to think, the harder I pushed myself. At this moment, exhaustion was the key to my survival. Thinking was optional and too painful at times. I avoided more than I dealt with.

I had made it through a little over a month at the safe house before I started to get a little stir crazy. It was time to go for a short ride, see something else for a change. Instead of driving towards town, I took a right out of the driveway. Living ten minutes out of town was nice. It was peaceful, quiet, and private. It was also slightly boring and lonely.

The safe house was just that—*safe*. It kept me safe from my enemies, safe from my family. The downside, it wasn't safe from my memories or the grief that played a constant role in my life. I heard there were five stages of grief, so far I've only been depressed and angry, maybe a little bargaining has been attempted too. I guess that meant I had two more stages to progress through.

A drive could be just what I needed to clear my head, or it could make the thinking worse. Out here, I stayed lost, everything looks the same. This proved to be a problem for the geographically challenged, let's just say I spent more time taking the scenic route than I did driving the correct directions. A ten minute drive ended up being closer to twenty minutes.

I took turns randomly, exploring the area. The fields looked the same, just like the roads. The only thing I knew for sure was I was taking a break from the house. After another turn, I crossed over a small bridge. I slowed down and looked out over the water. In the distance, I saw an old train bridge that was nearly falling apart. In some cases, rust seems to destroy things. But it seemed the rust was the one thing holding the rickety old bridge together. Turning around, I pulled up beside the barricades and killed the engine. Looking around as I climbed out, I noticed a small worn foot trail. Having nothing better to do, I started down the trail. I was on a mission to clear my head.

An old tree stump sat at the end of the trail. The sun was shining through the thick branches, illuminating the stump, beckoning me to it. It appeared like a mystical light through the darkness of the surrounding trees, it was a place where fairytales began. The petrified seat was a good spot long forgotten.

As I sat down, I felt a sense of peace wash over me. The steady sound of the moving water had a calming effect over my emotions. While sitting there, I started talking to Mom and Micah. I asked them questions and silently waited for responses. And then I did what most normal teenage girls do, I started talking nonstop and didn't care who listened. I could sit out here all day. I was surrounded by serenity. This was my new happy place, this was where I could sit and pretend I will get my happily ever after promised to me at the end of every fairytale.

The sun started to hide behind the clouds, causing a chill to enter my body. Feeling a few breaths lighter, I walked back up to the Maverick; I really hoped I could find this place again. I would have saved it in my phone's GPS, but I remembered I left it on the counter after getting frustrated about not hearing from Eli. By the time I got home, the sun was almost completely hidden behind the distant hills. After I got the car in park, I hustled into the house and turned on the fireplace in the front room. Grabbing the throw blanket off the back of the couch, I curled up on the floor in front of the fire. I tried to absorb all the heat I could. I could have stayed curled up there forever, I love being warm and cuddled, it's one of the best feelings in the world.

In town, I bought a test, but couldn't find the courage to take it. When I went inside, I left it on the seat, afraid to even look at it. So much weighed on my mind, not just the *what ifs*, but also the *whys*.

When I returned to my little slice of fairytale land the next day after an exhausting swim, I sat on an old stump and pondered the pros and cons of what I might find out when I took the test.

What if I were pregnant? I'm too young to even remotely be ready for it. Maybe if I were pregnant, it could fix the brokenness between Eli and me. But what if Eli saw it as me trying to trap him in to something he didn't want, or saw it as a way for me to manipulate him to stay in my life.

I could always have a piece of Eli with me, even if I had to do it on my own. It would be hard, but after a childhood with my father, I was strong enough to try anything. It could either merge us together or rip us apart. Would it help fill the void left behind from Micah and Mom? It saddened me that they would never get to meet my baby, when or if I ever had one. Something beautiful after such a tragedy could be a blessing in disguise, or yet another tragedy.

My emotions were as sporadic as my thoughts. Emotions tore my heart apart. I trudged through highs and lows. One minute I was fine, the next I was bawling for reasons unknown. Was I an emotional wreck because I was still coping? Or maybe I was destroyed by the way my life turned out? I not only lost Micah and Mom, but Eli as well. I alienated myself from my family and friends, as my way of coping. Instead, I felt abandoned and all alone with no one to share my joys and pains with. I wept until I could weep no longer.

I exhausted myself easily. Some days it was to the point of passing out as soon as I hit my bed. Was the exhaustion from swimming too hard, the emotional distress, or something else? Not having a schedule, I found I slept a little more than I used to, or at least I attempted to.

My appetite never returned to normal after burying Mom and Micah. When I was in training mode during my school years, I never had much of an appetite. I was swimming more and more, so I ate less and less. Opening the fridge, and going through the cabinets, I found nothing that looked appetizing, so I crawled into my bed and curled up with my kindle.

What if I wasn't pregnant, what could be wrong with me? If I were, would Eli be ok with it or would he feel trapped? How much trouble would he get into if they found out he slept with a minor. I can't even imagine what it would do to his military career.

What would my family think? Would they be happy for me? Would they think he took unnecessary risks with me, or maybe they would think he didn't treat me right? Would it really matter what they thought if I had Eli on my side?

If I ever had children, I would do everything in my power to raise them and treat them better than I was growing up. I would make sure there was no doubt in their mind that they were loved more than breathing. Not only would it build a bond between us, I would be able to prove that I can love someone unconditionally.

I really needed someone to love right about now, whether it was an unexpected baby or a reunion with Eli.

Finally, I felt brave enough to take the pregnancy test I got while I was in town earlier. It was time to eliminate the possibility of pregnancy; I needed to know for sure. Even though we used protection, there was always a chance it could happen. My hands were trembling from the pent up nerves as I peed on the stick. It slipped out of my hands as I read the results.

Chapter 14
ABBY

I continued to retreat to my little slice of fairytale land each day after swimming. Might I add, I managed to find it much easier the second time around than I did the first time. Each time I left my little fairytale, I felt lighter, a little more at peace. I found a slice of heaven, *MY* slice of heaven.

About two weeks had passed since I first found the place; it had also been almost six weeks since I heard from Eli. Depressed wasn't a strong enough word to cover how I was feeling. I was feeling less like me. I had cut myself off from all my family and friends. The one person I needed had cut himself off from me.

Each time I returned to the house, I checked my phone for sign of contact from Eli. Every time I checked, there was nothing new from him, casting me further into depression. Another part of me had died off. This wasn't an innocent childhood crush turn wrong, this was an unseen divorce where he took everything and my heart.

I went down to my little place to feel a little more at peace, but today I felt as though I had done everything wrong. Had my escape from reality meant I forgot a vital piece of the people that Mom and Micah were?

As I sat on my stump, I cried an ugly cry for everything I've lost. I cried for Mom. I cried for Micah. I even cried for Eli. The aching in my heart was almost too much. I remember hearing somewhere that death leaves a heartache that no one can heal, but love leaves the memories that no one can steal. It felt like someone had tainted all my memories with more and more pain. Just when I thought things were going well, my thoughts caught up with me. I was ready to find an exit from this life. If I didn't have them, I didn't have forever. What was the point of staying? I was so focused on all that was going wrong in my life that I didn't hear the old man approach.

"Need a pole?" He smiled a near toothless smile at me. I gave him a shrug and tried to wipe away my tears. "Ain't no problem in the world bad enough that fishin' can't fix," he assured me. I didn't do anything except nod my head slightly. The old man gave me a bigger grin. "Atta girl." He walked down the bank of the river a little ways before plopping onto an old bucket.

I chose a nearby rock to settle my body onto. "Thank you for saving me from my thoughts. Just going through a rough patch, I guess." I offered a weak smile.

"Shh! Down here we fish. Fish don't like all that jabberin'." He lifted his old John Deere hat to scratch his balding head, before he replaced it cover his head from the bright sun. "I ain't a big fan neither. I listened to Betsy jabber nonstop for 58 years 'til the good Lord gave her back her wings. Now, I fish."

"Sorry, Sir."

The old man gave a tell tale sign of military experience when he responded, "Don't *sir* me. I worked hard for a living." The way he carried himself also relayed more indication of a soldier. He may be old, but he stood proudly and kept going. "For 10 years I come down here. Fish don't bite, I don't talk. We get along great."

I simply nodded and watched as he cast an empty line into the water. He handed me the other pole. Without putting any thought into it, I followed his lead, casting out my empty line.

"See how much easier it is when you don't think 'bout it?" The old man was right, thinking caused more pain and problems than not.

"It has just been rough," I admitted.

"Life ain't 'sposed to be easy. Yer still alive ain't ya?" After I had nodded, he continued, "God still has a plan for you."

"Can I ask you a question?"

"I reckon yer gonna do it anyways."

The response caught me off guard and left my mouth gaping like a fish. I quickly shut it again. "How am I supposed to carry on when I lost two very significant people in my life?"

"They ain't lost. There ain't no lost and found. The only way they get lost is nobody 'members them." He sighed, warring with continuing the conversation or returning to silently enjoy fishing. Finally, he decided to continue the discussion, the look on his face said it all—damn women. "They're prolly keepin' my Betsy company. That woman is prolly talkin' their poor ears off."

I smiled.

"You ain't gonna forget them, if that's what yer 'fraid of." He paused and waited until I nodded before he continued, "tell me 'bout 'em."

"My mom was a grief counselor and cared deeply for all of us. She never missed a chance to tell us she loved us, every night she said *I love you* to each of us. She also said a prayer every night before tucking herself in." I smiled through my tears. These were tears of happy memories, not painful ones.

The old man smiled as I continued, "Micah was my favorite brother, my best friend. He spent six years in the Special Forces, disappearing on multiple unnamed missions. He was my protector and safety net. Micah was my hero. His smile could brighten my darkest days."

"See, ya ain't gonna forget them." He patted my shoulder. "Let their memories inspire you. Live a life that'll make 'em proud. You got a whole future 'head of you." He paused and looked over the water. "Yer too young to give up. Don't give up, just fish."

The silence stretched on for a while as we watched our lines move with the water. By the time I decided to head home, I felt a renewed sense of confidence. "Thank you for the company. I gotta go home and try to fix things."

"Ain't nobody telling me it's time to go home for ten years." He chuckled as I started to walk away.

"What's your name?" I felt the need to know.

"Names ain't important. Just call me Trout, my favorite kind of fish." He gave me one last grin as I turned and headed to the Maverick.

By the time I got home, I was relaxed, refreshed. I decided to finally break the silence and call Liz. It was time to start living my life again.

"Oh my gosh! It's about time you get back with me," she nearly shrieked at me.

"Liz, please don't give me that, or I will hang up fast," I begged.

"Sorry. I've just missed you. How is it going?" With a sigh, she changed the direction of the call.

"I'm ok. Sorry I've been absent in our friendship. You deserve better. I just needed a break from the world."

"I understand. I'm still here for you, no matter what. You don't have to be alone," she stated.

I attempted to lie, but she caught me. She knew Eli hadn't been with me for a while. He stopped touching base with them a month ago. According to her, Dirk was checking in and trying to get a hold of me. As I tried to figure out why he would want to talk to me, she knew me well enough to know where my thoughts were.

"He needs someone to talk sense into Eli. You are his best hope. Eli listens to you, sometimes." She sighed.

"Great, just what I wanted to hear," I stated sarcastically. "What's Dirk's number?" I asked as I plopped into the recliner. After writing his number down, we chatted for a little bit before I finally decided to tell her the real reason I called.

"I'm scared. Eli hasn't talked to me or returned any of my texts for six weeks. I don't even know why." I swiped a tear from my eyes. "I'm scared Liz."

"Come to Chicago, we have cake! Let me take care of you. There's nothing to be afraid of, I got your back," Liz offered.

"I have to save Eli first. I promise to try to keep in touch better. I love you like my own sister."

"Love you too Abs. Thanks for calling, I've really missed you." I could hear the smile in her voice.

After hanging up, I took a deep breath and dialed Dirk's number.

"Princess Abigail! You finally called back!" He paused. "How are you holding up?"

"I'm all right. I have been going through a rough patch lately. Took a break from reality and had an old fisherman tell me I needed to keep going." I took a deep breath. "I finally decided to touch base again."

"That would explain why you haven't answered the calls or texts I've sent the past couple weeks."

"My phone has been sitting on the table. I stopped looking at it a couple weeks ago," I admitted.

"I need your help," he stated.

"What's going on? Is this about Eli? Liz told me you were trying to get in touch with me."

"Yes. He's gone off and screwed himself up. He hasn't been the same since Micah's funeral. After he failed the first training exercise since being back, he's gotten worse. He needs help and won't let any of us do it. I hope you don't mind me stealing your number from his phone."

"How can I help? He and I haven't talked for over six weeks now," I admitted nervously.

"I need you to fly out here ASAP. I can pay for your plane ticket."

"I can do that."

"I will book a flight for you now. You are still in South Dakota, right?"

"Yep, I'm an hour from the nearest airport in Sioux Falls." I paused. "How long will I be gone? Is my car just going to be sitting in storage?"

"You remember the guy that picked you up from the bus stop? His name is Dale, he's my younger brother. He will take you to the airport."

We chatted for a little bit while he was booking my flight, keeping our conversation light. It felt like I was talking to an old friend.

Oh, so that's how he knew where I was. It finally clicked. As I listened to Dirk talk again, I nodded along, adding a few *uh-huhs* and *okays* when I felt it was necessary. By the time I hung up, I had plane tickets for a flight leaving out at o'dark thirty in the morning. I also had a ride to the airport, someone picking me up, and I knew I would finally see Eli again. We had never gone more than a week without talking unless they were on some top secret mission. Dirk's words rang in my ears. *You are the only one who can save him. You are the only one he will listen to.*

Needless to say, I didn't get a wink of sleep that night. I packed my bag, I paced the floors, and I showered. Trying to figure out how I was going to try to fix him after all this time, had me shaking. Yeah, I didn't know if I could do that. Why did they wait so long before they called me? How far gone was he? I was afraid of what shape I would find Eli in. My mind bounced from one scenario to the next, instead of drifting into dreamland the way I would have preferred it to.

Dale pulled up in the driveway and honked. Way to pick up a girl, huh? I finished locking up and grabbed my bag before joining him in his truck. "Is the princess ready to go?" I nodded and smiled. He smirked and threw his truck into gear. His radio blasted country music as he adjusted his cowboy hat, and sang along—way off tune. I couldn't help but smile at his easy going attitude.

We chatted easily as we traveled down I-90. He managed to keep me laughing and my mind off the confrontation waiting for me in New York. His advice-'don't worry about what might happen, worry about what is happening right now.' Dale was a riot who had stories that had my side splitting from all the laughter. Apparently

Dale and Dirk were pranksters that easily rivaled the antics of Eli and Micah; a couple even made my boys' pranks seem juvenile. I could easily see us being friends. He may be a prankster, an off key singer, and a country boy, but he had a heart of gold and eyes to match.

He was a bit bigger and built stronger than I remembered Dirk being. I could see the family resemblance, they had the same face. He even had the golden eyes a girl could easily get lost in. I felt at ease with him, he seemed like one of my brothers.

He parked in the long-term parking and grabbed my bag. I gave him a confused look. I didn't realize we both were going to New York. "Yes, I'm going too. Come on princess, you have a prince to save, or a frog to kiss." He smirked.

"I can carry my own bag. I'm a big girl!"

"And risk my ass being kicked by Dirk? Yeah, no thanks. I got this." He followed me up to the check-in station. "Dale Stinson and Abigail Remlock," he stated.

"Wait. Why are you coming?" I still couldn't figure out why I was being escorted to New York. When I was younger I used to fly to New Mexico to spend a month with my grandma, all by myself.

"I'm making sure you get there safely, and going to visit my brother. I can only stay a couple days, it's almost harvest time," he answered and finished checking us in.

Getting through security had me laughing. I breezed through quickly. Dale had to keep going back and forth through the scanner. Each time he had to take something else off. First his boots and his cowboy hat, then the coins from his pockets, yep the scanner still dinged. Finally, he had to remove his huge, shiny, belt buckle before the machine gave him the all clear.

I was laughing. "Damn country boys and their belt buckles."

"The bigger the buckle, the bigger something else sweetheart." He winked as he laced his belt back through the loops.

"Yup, the bigger the tires are on your truck," I playfully responded as I slugged his arm.

He just shook his head and stood by the wall of windows, he couldn't help but smile. I stood beside him and watched planes land and takeoff. My mind shifted to Eli and his big black truck.

"Princess, it'll be all right. You can whip that boy into shape, I have no doubt. If you need, you can even use my belt."

I couldn't help but smile at him as I nodded. I felt at ease with Dale.

The plane ride was uneventful. It took us up in the air, flattened out for a while, then landed safely in New York. I even managed to doze off for a few minutes, resting my head on Dale's shoulder.

Dirk met us at the gate, wearing a huge smile and holding a piece of white paper with "Princess Abigail" written. I couldn't help but laugh at him. He wrapped his arms around me hugging me to him.

"Thank you for coming Abby," he whispered before throwing an arm across Dale's shoulder. "Good to see you too, man."

They both reached to carry my bag once we retrieved it from baggage claim. Finally, Dale won out with a huge smile and carried it to Dirk's SUV.

I teased him, "What? No truck?" I climbed into the back seat.

"Nah. I'm an SUV kind of guy." He smiled.

"How are we going to do this Dirk? What's the plan?" I asked. It was getting close to game time, my nerves were jittery.

He threw the vehicle in drive and admitted, "I don't really know. I was hoping you might have a plan. I know if he sees you, it will help him a lot though."

"I'm not so sure Dirk. He stopped texting and calling a while ago."

"Seeing you will help put things into perspective. Seeing what he might have hurt or lost." Dale added his opinion, "I know when I saw you, my day brightened. It'll work Abs. Have faith."

"Is there a coffee shop or something on or near post? I need a pick me up. I'm running on 'E' right now."

"What if we drop you off at a coffee house? I can leave Dale with you while I go pick up Eli."

"Sure," I agreed.

Chapter 15
ABBY

I was nervous. I managed to convince Dale to go with Dirk, I needed a little alone time to prepare myself. Scenarios played out in my head with all sorts of possible outcomes. He could be mad, feel betrayed by his buddies for calling me behind his back, or maybe he would be ecstatic and overjoyed with such a wonderful surprise. Maybe he will be pissed or happy. This could go about a hundred different ways. I just hope he still cares about me and won't beg me to leave.

Ordering a highly caffeinated glass of cold, caramelized goodness, I took a seat on the empty couch in the corner. I patiently watched as people came and went through the door. Each time the doorbell chimed, my eyes searched for Eli.

I didn't have to hear the chime to know he walked in, my body gave it away. My heart started beating faster as a smile snuck across my face. His back was to me as he walked up to the counter. I couldn't help but eye his backside up and down. *Damn, he's bulked up and he looked mighty fine*! The gym must have been where he coped. I enjoyed the eye candy that was a side effect of working out, a buffed up Eli. I took my eyes off long enough to glance around the shop. All the girls were eyeing him like a nice, thick, juicy steak. Jealousy shot through me, I wanted to shout, *he's mine get your eyes off him*, but I didn't. I wasn't sure if he really was still mine, but I knew I would always belong to him.

He was standing at the counter, shifting his weight back and forth between legs. His fingers were tapping restlessly on the counter as he gave the girl behind the register a long and complicated drink order. What had him so antsy?

I stood and walked closer, drawn to him like a moth to a flame. The poor girl behind the counter was trying to relay his drink order. I overheard him telling her to pick up the pace, mentioning something about her being slower than a turtle. Knowing Eli as I do, I felt sorry for the girl. Now was my chance, I took a deep breath. Here goes.

I stepped up closer, and slipped my arms around his trim waist, putting my front on his back. "Eli, give the poor girl a break." My voice came out barely more than a whisper.

He pulled me around to the front of him. "Babe!" *Oh, hearing him say that was music to my ears!* He trailed his hands along my sides. "What're you doing here?" Instantly he relaxed.

I wiped a tear and smiled before responding, "Saving Bekah from your wrath." Thankfully I remembered her name from when I ordered my drink. I cuddled in closer to him. *Oh, how I've missed this man.*

He hugged me tight, then leaned down and kissed my lips. My body melted into his. It felt better than home wrapped in his arms. "Damn, I've missed you Babe."

"What's got you so worked up and antsy?" I asked as I tried to pull back enough to search his face. He looked put together on the outside, but his eyes showed he was broken down inside. *My poor lost soldier.* Of course, I could never call him that out loud, but it went through my head. I'm sure he thinks I'm still the naïve little girl that is jailbait.

"There's a lot on my plate. I was getting ready to go back to the gym when Dirk stopped by." He pulled me closer. "God, I've missed you!"

"Take it out on the gym, or me, but give poor Bekah a break." I reached up on my tip toes and kissed his lips again. I've missed them so much.

Bekah handed Eli his drink with shaking hands. "Here you go sir. Sorry for the delay."

I knew I was the only female that could intimidate Eli enough to get him to do as I wished, even his mom is a pushover. I looked into his face with my eyebrows raised, challenging him. He's got to be close to six and a half feet, and packing over 200 pounds of pure muscle. With his dark blonde hair cut into a "high and tight," he looked more menacing than he actually was. He finally took the hint. "Thank you Bekah. Sorry, for the attitude." He even managed to offer her his trademark one dimpled smirk.

Once he returned his attention back to me, he rolled his striking turquoise eyes. "Need more?" he asked as he kissed my forehead, noticing my nearly empty glass.

"Nope! I'm good. Let's grab a seat." I tried to pull away to lead him towards the couch I was on earlier. I could have used another pick me up, but if I had too much caffeine, it would make me jittery.

He followed me as close as he could, closer than my own breath. He sat down and pulled me into his lap. His hand continued to travel up and down my back, the other hand holding my hand, while his lips planted little kisses on my face and neck. It was almost as if he was afraid I'd vanish or maybe I was just a dream; a desert oasis.

Laying my head on his shoulder, I laced my fingers through his. He kept whispering words of love and astonishment that I was really there. Hugging me closer than my next breath, I was in the arms of my man, and he had no intentions to let me go.

"What the fuck are you doing with my man?" a petite brunette raised her voice, jabbing a finger in my direction.

Eli glanced up. "You were a one night gone wrong. What was your name? Oh, that's right I didn't care then. I still don't." His hand continued to rub up and down my back, his attention returned solely to me.

"Oh. My. God! That's her, isn't it? That's Abby! Ain't it? She's the girl you were thinking about while screwing me? The only reason you could get it up? The Abby you screamed out?"

Eli nuzzled my neck, ignoring the brunette. I finally looked at her, after sizing her up, I knew I could take her out. "I am indeed Abby. You can leave now," I smiled and returned my focus to Eli. A smile crept across my face as I imagined him screaming out my name with his release. As much as it hurt knowing he was with another girl, it turned me on knowing he was thinking of me while messing with her.

Eli stood up after setting me on my feet. Taking my hand, he led us out to his truck. Opening the driver's door, he allowed me to slide into the middle, refusing to let go of my hand as he slid in right behind me. He turned the truck on and put it in gear. My legs were on either side of the gear shift, his arm rested across my leg as he kept his hand on the shifter.

"We need to talk Eli," I finally stated as I ran my nails up and down the underside of his arm. The play of his muscles under my nails had me imagining what was lying under his clothes. He must've added extra muscles to the already prominent muscles apparent the last time we were together. Even his muscles had muscles.

"We will Babe, but first I gotta get you back to my room. It's been too long," he stated as he stopped at a red light.

I figured now was as good as any. Before I stopped myself, I blurted, "Eli. I'm pregnant."

He continued looking forward. His permanent smile remained in place while he stayed quiet. I almost doubted he heard me. He finally turned to look at me once he threw the truck into park. It was almost as if what I said finally registered. "Is it mine?" he asked.

I gasped in shock, barely refraining from slapping him. That was really his response? "I've only ever been with you." I swiped a tear from my cheek.

He climbed out of the truck, pulling me with him. Out of the truck, straight into his arms. "You have made me a very happy man." He kissed me hard on the lips. "Let's get married."

I was still in shock. I nodded my head in agreement, trying to get my world to slow down. He wrapped his arm firmly around my waist and led me through the barracks. As we rode the elevator up, he stood behind me, wrapping his arms around my front. I laid my head back on his shoulder, he was my home. I was home. "I can't get married without Liz, or she would go all ninja monkey on me."

"Then she better get here quick. I'm not waiting much longer Babe." He kissed up and down my neck. "You brought your emancipation papers, right?"

I nodded as I took out my phone. "Eli, it's really hard for me to focus when you are doing that."

He smiled and nipped the spot just below my ear. "That's the point."

I managed to get a text off to Liz, as well as to Lynn. They knew to keep it on the down low. Lynn told me she approved of him and go get him. Liz's message had all sorts of exclamation points and capitalized words that made me laugh. Yep, she'd be here in the morning with Liam. I turned in Eli's arms. "Can you wait until tomorrow morning? That's the fastest Liz and Liam can get here." I slipped my fingers under the t-shirt that was stretched to its limits across his shoulders, trailing my nails along his bare flesh.

He nodded and picked me up and carried me out of the elevator to his room, like the bride I was soon to be. We barely made it in the room before he was trying to tear my clothes off. By the time I hit his bed, I was naked. He paused and let his eyes travel over my naked body. "Is it safe Babe?"

"It's not safe to keep me waiting." I smirked as the rest of his clothes hit the floor. He took me slow and carefully, afraid I would break. He took his time, ensuring every inch of my body was touched or kissed. His eyes never left mine. I felt like the most important girl in the world.

After our reuniting, Eli began to dig around in his bedside stand. He pulled out a small blue box. My heart picked up its pace, thrumming out of my chest, I knew what was in that box. His body was now lying along my side as I rolled onto my back. Leaning up on his elbow, he kissed my forehead and smiled. "I had plans to wait until you were 18. Micah knew my intentions and was on my side, as long as I waited until you were of age. Since we have a little one on the way, and since you are back in my arms where you belong, I see no reason to wait any longer." He pulled a beautiful amethyst ring out of the box. "I know most people choose diamonds, but I chose amethyst because it reminded me of your beautiful eyes. I'm not asking you to marry me. I'm telling you to marry me!"

"Wow, that is the sweetest thing a guy could ever say to me," I teased him. "I don't need to be asked or even told. Just put the ring on my finger dang it." I reached up and kissed his lips as he slipped the ring on my finger.

He deepened the kiss, his hands sliding down my body. Finally he pulled back and smiled. "I. Love. You. More. Than. My. Next. Breath," he said, punctuating each word with a kiss. His fingers danced across my bare abdomen, as he leaned down and planted a kiss just above my navel. "I can't wait to meet our little one." The smile on his face brought tears to my eyes. I knew he was genuine, not saying it to try to please me. This was my Eli, the one that I thought I lost, the one I fell for so many years ago.

I placed my hands on either side of his head, and pulled his mouth back up to mine. He kissed a couple of the tears that snuck out of my eyes. Placing his body between my legs so his lips could capture mine, he continued to kiss every part of my face. He lined himself up at my entrance, his eyes watching mine intimately as he slowly inched himself in. As I stretched a little further, he moved in a little further. He made it seem like I was glass. "Eli, I'm not glass, I won't break. *Duct tape and honey*, remember?" I smirked as he thrust further in, nearly sheathing himself completely inside me.

Chapter 16
LIZ

I can't believe she was getting married in 24 hours. I know I told her to go get her man, I just didn't figure she would jump into marriage. She was the one that always thought things through, I was the spontaneous one. When I got the text, I knew she needed my support. There were enough naysayers in the world. This was her shot at heaven. She really was getting her forever.

Liam was reading over my shoulder as the text came in. "She deserves her happy ever after."

"She really does. I got mine." I smiled and cuddled into Liam's arms.

"We will be there," he stated, as if there was any question in my mind.

I smiled. "I know." I climbed out of bed and looked at my closet. Nothing of mine would fit her. I needed to pick something for her to wear. I glanced at Liam, who was watching me walk naked around the room. "Quit looking at me like that. I need to go pick something for her to wear."

As I slipped into some clothes, Liam frowned, reaching out towards me as I remained just beyond his reach. "I like you naked."

I smiled as I thought back to the last few days.

I was so relieved when she finally called me. I wanted to jump down her throat for leaving me hanging for over a month, but I knew she was trying to find herself and recover as much as one could; especially when they lose vital parts of their life.

Later that night, she called to catch me up on the details of their pending nuptials and her reuniting with Eli. Then, she told me she had a secret to share with me. I was not prepared for the extra news, the real reason they were having a spur of the moment wedding.

When she told me she was pregnant, I stumbled over the words to respond. How can you be happy for someone when it's something they've dreamed of, but the one thing you fear with every last breath of your being? Honestly, I was happy for her, but that wasn't something for me. Lee and I already discussed that, he knew my mind wouldn't change. We had a pregnancy scare. I almost bled to death on the table when I had a miscarriage. I mourned the loss I never knew I wanted. Abby stayed by my side as did Liam. It nearly destroyed me. It was kept secret.

I never wanted another child, but even if I did, I could no longer get pregnant. Since there was no longer a chance of pregnancy, there was no reason for a wedding. At least, that's how I lived my life. Abby still thinks I need a wedding to finish my fairytale.

I tugged Liam out of bed telling him to get dressed. Yes, I was making him go shopping with me, for a dress nonetheless. I wished Abby and I could be the same size; it would've saved so much time. Instead, I was barely over five foot tall and she was closer to six. I tied my nearly waist length black hair into a ponytail, I wished I had the pretty natural blonde curly hair that Abby had. I missed my friend so much. We were so much alike, yet so different, opposites are supposed to attract, right?

"You know Aliza that could be us getting married." He wrapped his arms around me from behind. As he nuzzled into my neck, I could feel his lips smile.

"Keep dreaming big boy. Remember we decided no marriage, no kids. We have our forever love. We don't need to prove it to anyone other than us." I smiled and leaned back into his arms, this was my happy ever after and I was living it. Fairytales don't have shit on us.

We managed to leave our little Chicago apartment that we moved into shortly after I graduated. A pretty big step, but we had been ready for this for quite a while. It felt good to be on our own in a different city. No rules, just us. No more time spent sneaking around, two years was long enough.

We headed downtown to find a dress that would suit my best friend. It had taken only an hour and two different shops before I found one that literally called Abby's name. Liam smiled broadly when I held the dress up. "Yep that's definitely the one for her." It was a beautiful light yellow, knee length dress. She was one of the only people I knew who could pull off yellow like a rock star. I snapped a picture and sent it off to her. In return, I got a picture of her ring.

"Lee he went with amethyst instead of diamonds!" I smiled as I paid for the dress and watched the lady carefully fold it into a bag.

I knew that meant nothing to Liam, but he still managed to give me a smile. "He could have given her a lump of coal. That doesn't mean shit. The only things that matter are how he treats her and of course, her happiness."

Deep down, I knew Liam was nervous. This was his baby sister after all. He was worried about the seven, almost eight, year gap and the fact he seemed to have his glory days with Micah. She was fresh out of high school, fresh out of a life of swimming and studying. He didn't know the secrets Eli and Abby shared, or the kisses behind closed doors and over the computers. "Lee, she is happy." As much as I wanted to share her news with him, I promised her I would keep it quiet. "This is her happy-ish ever after. She wasn't a damsel in distress. She's a freaking princess that rescued her dark knight!" I laughed as we headed back to our apartment.

"She is a spoiled brat," Liam answered as he linked our fingers together.

Our plane was scheduled to take off first thing in the morning. It has been too long since I last saw my bestie. I know it wouldn't be enough time together, but we had to cherish the time we had. We had a lot to discuss, but more than anything I wanted her to be as happy as she deserves. She's always been there when I needed someone, and I wanted to be there for her, instead of having her close herself off from everyone and their mother. She was stronger than she gave herself credit for, but sometimes I wish she'd lean on me the way I lean on her.

    Micah had always told her she was stronger than duct tape and sweeter than honey, and he couldn't have been more right. I would stick to her better than gorilla glue. She's stuck with me for life.

Chapter 17
ABBY

*O*ur wedding was simple. I had my handsome prince pronouncing his love proudly in the courthouse to me in front of Liz and Liam, his battle buddies, as well as the Justice of the Peace. We didn't need anything fancy, we had each other. The yellow dress was beyond perfect. My best friend knew me so well. Eli dressed in his *good* jeans and a charcoal gray button down. A passion filled kiss from Eli at the announcement of us as husband and wife. *He really did kiss his bride.* As we left the courthouse, I cuddled close to Eli, while a mix CD filled with random older love songs played on repeat. Eli serenaded me with the Dan Seals song *One Friend* word for word, over and over. My heart was floating on something better than cloud nine. Some people went their whole life searching for the kind of love we have without ever finding it. We don't just have love though, we have forever.

After grabbing a bite to eat and seeing Liz and Liam off at the airport, we went to a beautiful suite. Eli carried me into the room and laid me on the bed before turning on the water to fill the Jacuzzi tub. He slowly tugged me up to my feet, humming softly as we swayed together wrapped tightly in each other's arms. My head rested on his shoulder, his lips planted kisses in my hair and on the top of my head. I opened my eyes and glanced at the tub. "Eli, the tub is going to overflow." I looked up at him. His eyes were still closed, he continued to hum and sway us. This is what love looks and feels like.

I pulled out of his arms and shut off the water. His hands slid down the length of my dress and tugged at the hem. He dropped to his knees in front of me, slowly lifting my dress, and kissing where there was once cloth. "You aren't wearing panties? Mmhmm, Mrs. Montgomery you are a naughty one." He planted a kiss at the top of my thighs. "Bath first. Then, I will have you screaming my name."

We lived in wedded bliss. Though most of our honeymoon was spent in the barracks, we were together and left alone for the most part. Each morning he went to PT while I used that time to get some extra sleep. After PT, he came home to shower, which I often joined. I loved being wrapped in his arms, with him buried deep inside of me. He wrapped a towel around us and carried me to bed. He loved bringing breakfast to me while I lounged in bed. I felt spoiled, I felt loved.

Today, he came home from PT and popped into the shower while I was still trying to wake up. I was lying in bed naked, our favorite way to sleep. I watched him draw closer, drops of water still rolling down his chest. "Come cuddle with me." I reached a hand out towards him.

He slipped into bed with me, lying on his back. I placed my body across his chest. There wasn't much space in our twin sized bed. "We are done with work today. I was wondering if you wanted to go for a little drive," he mumbled as he trailed his fingers along my spine, holding me close. So this is what heaven feels like?

I trailed my nails along his ribs, tracing the tattoo he got in Micah's honor. The beautiful tribal design was swirled in and around Micah's birth date and date of death. I leaned up and watched him as I batted my eyelashes. "Wouldn't you rather stay here in bed naked?"

"I got a four-day weekend, let's go to a place Micah and I spent many weekends. I promise you won't be wearing clothes for long." He tugged my head down to kiss me hard on the mouth. After he rolled me onto my back, he kissed my lips and trailed his lips down to my belly. "Come on Babe."

"My clothes are starting to not fit that well," I pouted.

He pulled my lower lip lightly using his teeth. "I have an old pair of sweats that you can wear. What's mine is yours, Mrs. Montgomery." I could tell he liked hearing the title.

I knew he was excited about showing me something, especially if my nakedness wasn't keeping him in bed with me. He jumped up and rifled through his drawers before finally tossing me a pair of old sweat pants. I whined, "I'm getting fat."

"And you are glowing. It's just more of you to love Babe." He slipped the pants up my legs, planting kisses as he went. "I love you. And I love our little one to be." He finished as he planted an extra kiss on my belly.

"Keep it up and we won't be going anywhere Mr. Montgomery," I teased as I tugged his nipple rings to bring his lips down to mine, and kissed him deeply. "These are quite useful love." I smiled.

"You were trying to convince me to take them out a couple months ago."

"They are growing on me. Maybe I will let you keep them." I winked.

"You will let me, huh?" he asked as he kissed me again.

"You did promise to love and obey." I smirked as I slipped on a bra and tank. Ugh, my breasts were tender. I quickly lost my smirk as I tried to adjust my top trying to get situated comfortably.

"I can see how well you will obey later Babe." He leaned back on the bed with his mouth in his normal smirk. His eyes were filled with lust. "Having troubles?" Leaning over he placed a kiss on my overflowing chest. He pulled a t-shirt on and slipped into his jeans and black work boots. "Come on let's go!" He tugged me out the door. Our fingers were laced together. I was enjoying toying with his wedding band. This man is *mine, ALL mine.*

We climbed into his truck, me in the middle, with his arm laying across my leg, hand on the shifter. He was my badass soldier whose heart I managed to lasso. He adjusted his worn ball cap, then gave me a full-on, deep dimpled smirk, he asked, "What's going through that pretty head of yours?"

"I was just wondering the same about you." I kissed his neck as my hand slipped up his thigh squeezing.

"I'm just imagining you naked," he smiled and squeezed my knee. "All mine with no one to hear your screams." His blue-green eyes twinkled with mischief.

"I'm not a screamer and you know it."

"Oh, but you will be." He took his hat off and plopped it on my head. "Trust me, Babe, you won't be disappointed."

I nodded and leaned into him. I was running my nails up and down his thigh while resting my head on his shoulder. Closing my eyes, I enjoyed the moment. I couldn't fight the need to doze off. Who knew such strength could be so comfortable?

"Get some rest Babe. You're going to need it." He kissed the side of my head before I rotated and laid my head on his lap, my legs curled across the seat. He trailed his hand up and down my side, sending me off to dreamland. This man spoiled me.

Before I knew it, I was being jostled awake and out of the stopped truck. I looked around. "Why are we at the airport?"

"Means to an end." He tugged me hurriedly towards check in. At the counter, he proudly stated our names, "Tickets for Abigail and Elijah Montgomery, please?" They handed over two first-class tickets to Sioux Falls.

"We are going to South Dakota? I just came from there," I questioned him. Of all the places we could go, we wound up returning to B.F.E.

"I promise you there is so much you haven't done there." His smirk hinted he was having impure thoughts. Quirking his eyebrow, he added, "At least you better not have."

"I went fishing, I visited Wal-Mart and Cabela's, I even swung by the Corn Palace. Not much left to do there." I tried to check off the list of things to do in the little town as we walked through the airport.

He whispered in my ear, "Sex in the Maverick while staring at the corn growing, sex in that huge Jacuzzi tub, and cuddling on the couch. We have a whole house to christen." His tongue toyed with my ear, turning me on.

My cheeks blushed brightly as my body filled with heat. He kept murmuring all the different ways we could christen the safe house. I savored his animalistic instincts to protect, respect and love me like I was his queen. This man with me was sex on legs. I may not be worthy of him, but there was no way I was letting him get away.

"I promised to keep you naked, and you promised to obey me." His hands wrapped around my waist, pulling me snugly against him, rubbing his erection against my spine.

"Eli, we are in public. People are looking at us," I whispered as I wrapped my hands around his.

"Let them be jealous. We are newlyweds Babe." He turned me around in his arms. His lips finding mine, whispering right before his lips touched mine, "I want the world to know you are mine. You are my first, my last, my everything, my forever."

My heart was thrumming out of my chest, suddenly everyone else in that crowded airport disappeared. When we finally pulled away, I laid my head on his broad chest, his arms wrapped tightly around me as I hummed a few lines of one of our favorite songs. I loved being nestled in his arms, in here nothing else mattered and nothing could touch us.

My hands slipped down his waist, and moved between us, running my fingers over his erection. I hoped the denim of his jeans wouldn't split. I couldn't help but tease him a little more. "Babe, I'm struggling here," he whispered as he drew my fingers away from his erection. "I don't have much control when it comes to you, please don't test me." He kissed my fingers. "When we get back to that beautiful Maverick, or to our house, you get free reign."

He helped buckle me into my seat, and held my hand tight as the plane rattled down the runway. I was nervous flying still. He moved the armrest up between our seats, allowing me to be closer. He held me like I was more precious than the finest jewels. Tracing his hand up and down my arm, he managed to calm me as I dozed off for most of the flight.

We were greeted at the baggage claim by Dale. Engulfing me in a hug, twirling me around like a long lost sister. "So good to see you again Misss Abigail! And you brought your prince back too!" Teasing Eli, he leaned over to give Eli a friendly slap on the shoulder, "You are looking better man. What'd it take to save him? A paddle? A whip? A belt?" He smirked in my direction.

"Thanks for watching out for my girl. Thanks for picking us up." Eli smirked, choosing to ignore the end of Dale's comments.

We grabbed Eli's duffel bag and walked to Dale's truck. They managed to shove me in the middle. Throughout the hour trip, the boys shared stories. Of course, Dale had to bring up my gas station fiasco causing Eli to laugh so hard tears slid out of his eyes. I swatted his chest, and whined, "It wasn't funny butthead! You should've told me."

"Really Abs? Butthead? Are we suddenly twelve again?" Dale asked as he turned into our driveway.

"Close enough." I smirked.

"Go get countrified Princess. We have some place to be when dusk sets in," Dale stated as Eli and I climbed out of the truck.

"Where are we going?" I asked although I knew he wouldn't tell me anything.

"It's a surprise, but don't worry, I picked you up your very own cowboy hat." He leaned against the side of his truck holding out a bag. "This is your wedding gift, even though you invited Dirk, but not me."

Eli raised his eyebrows, and smirked. "Your invite must've gotten lost in the mail."

I glanced inside the bag. "Aww! It's so purty!" drawling it out to mock Dale. I smiled as I took out a light blue sundress and a white cowboy hat embellished with a shiny, plastic dress-up tiara attached. "Wait! Something's missing."

Dale shook his head, chuckling. "Trust me little girl, you can't handle the belt buckle."

Eli kissed my neck. "We can meet you there, I got to hit the shower and get changed before we head over there."

"Yeah, yeah, sure, sure. I have to go pick up my girl anyways, see you in a few man." Dale climbed into his truck pulling off.

Eli swept me up in his arms, punched the code into the security system, and carried me like his bride. He kissed me before locking up behind us, not letting me out of his hands. Not a breath of air between us. Our clothes were stripped off between the front door and my bathroom, a trail of clothes tossed haphazardly along the floor, a mixture of his and mine. After he turned the shower on, he deepened our kiss. His hands heated up my skin, caressing me as he trailed them along my sides. He continued over the curves of my backside, and up over the curves of my breasts.

As the water of the shower coursed over our bodies, we continued to kiss and touch and enjoy one another. Afraid to allow an inch of our bodies' space, our bodies molded together, becoming one.

He helped me dry off and placed me on his bed. "I've got to have you Babe." He trailed kisses along my neck as his hands removed my towel. Tipping back on his heels, he traced his eyes over my body. "God, you are beautiful."

We made love—long, slow, amazing love. We took our time, we were in no rush. It was so sweet and filled with pure emotion. I love this man more than I ever guessed I could love someone.

As we came down off the high of post-coital bliss, Eli glanced at his watch. "Damn Babe, we need to get ready."

"I don't want to move," I admitted, running my nails over his back.

He pulled back, withdrawing from me. "Stay right there." He kissed my forehead and walked out of the room. I admired the sight of his naked backside. When he came back into the room, he had a towel wrapped around his waist. Using a damp cloth he retrieved from the bathroom, he cleaned me up. It was so sweet and very intimate. A kiss was planted on my nose, followed by a smile. "You need to get dressed Babe. We are already running a little behind."

I stood and headed to find some underclothes in my room that I left behind from the last time I was here. After slipping on a strapless bra and a pair of pink, lacy, bikini panties, I tugged on the blue sundress that Dale gave me. I decided since they wanted me to be countrified, I would pull my hair into two braids that lay on either side of my neck and plop the hat on.

Eli emerged from his room, looking good enough to eat. He'd slipped on a pair of Levis and his cowboy boots, topping it off with a navy blue polo leaving the buttons undone. The sleeves of his shirt only helped to accent his muscles that much more. "Babe, stop looking at me like that, or we won't be leaving the house." He leaned down and planted a kiss on my lips.

"That's fine with me. We have a lot of making up to do, as well as plenty of areas that are in *dire* need of christening," I smiled, stealing another kiss from him. After I slipped on a pair of flats, I followed Eli to the Maverick. He opened the driver's door allowing me to slip into my spot in the middle. He slid behind the wheel.

Main Street was lit up with flood lights. A local band was playing live, drawing people out to dance in the middle of the street. A huge celebration was going on. We couldn't wait to join in. Eli managed to park close to Dale's old blue Ford truck. Holding my hand tightly, he led us towards the action. We saw Dale leaning against the panels of the corral. We drew his attention, and he came to where we had to enter at. His smile broadening as we got closer. As we joined the other humans being corralled in like a bunch of animals, I couldn't help but laugh at the irony.

Dale hugged me. "Looking as beautiful as ever." He smiled and kissed my cheek.

A girl was hanging on his arm, watching us with interest. I reached my hand out for her to shake. "Abby Rem err Montgomery." I could see Eli laughing and shaking his head as his arm tugged me so my backside was attached to his front.

"Jen, Dale's fiancée." She smiled and shook my hand seeming to relax as Eli staked further claim on me by planting a kiss on my neck.

"Let's get you guys a drink or two." Dale smiled as the four of us walked towards the picnic tables.

"I'm pregnant and seventeen. Looks like I get to play DD tonight." I stuck out my bottom lip in a fake pout.

"I will have a beer, but then I plan to see my girl swaying with me to the music." Eli smirked, leaning so his lips touched my ear. "I love you."

"I love you too." I smiled. The band started up their version of *Fishin' in the Dark* and I couldn't help but tug Eli closer to the music. As we danced and swayed, I rubbed my back along his front. I laid my head back against his shoulder, smiling as I felt his erection straining to get out. His hands locked on my hips to direct them which way to go. It wasn't as much a dance as it was a swaying seduction.

As an unfamiliar song came on, we turned to find Dale and Jen. Eli attempted to adjust himself before walking with me to the table they commandeered in our absence. We spent most of the night alternating between talking and dancing.

Jen and I sat at the table chatting while the guys went in search of drinks. Even though I really could use some water right now, I had no intentions of moving.

I watched Eli from across the street, my eyes stayed glued to him. Jen asked, "You ever get tired of having all those girls drooling over your man?"

I turned my focus to her. "Huh? What do you mean?" I watched as she pointed out different girls in the crowd ogling Eli's goodies. They were devouring my man candy with their eyes. "Ugh. I can't take him anywhere, I guess. Honestly, I can't keep them from looking, I just know that he's mine and the longer they stare the more jealous they will be when he leaves here with me." I smiled, feeling more confident than normal.

Jen smiled and started talking about my pregnancy, her upcoming wedding, random bits about her life on her family's farm, and also asked questions regarding our relationship, "Is it weird that he is so much older than you? He was your brother's best friend, isn't that awkward?" She continued to pour out the questions, her mouth loosening with all her alcohol intake.

I smiled and answered most of them truthfully. The age difference wasn't weird. It's not awkward, it's awesome. I feel like it keeps me close to Micah. Yet I chose to ignore a few of them that were still too touchy. In return, she shared with me that she wanted to have three kids and stay close to Dirk's family farm.

A perky little redhead came over and sat at our table, she looked me up and down. I smiled and waved then turned my attention back to Jen. I noticed redhead's attention kept returning to me, almost as though she was sizing me up as competition. I was able to ignore her as I laughed and enjoyed the randomness spewing out Jen's mouth. Occasionally I searched the crowd for Eli, but didn't see him. *No reason to panic,* I told myself, *he probably had to go drain the lizard, or was wondering around aimlessly with Dale, meeting all his buddies.*

It didn't take a rocket scientist to know Eli was nearby, the redhead's face lit up like a Christmas tree. A couple seconds later, hands rested on my shoulders, massaging gently. Instantly I relaxed, even though I still could still feel her watching us. My head leaned back against his body and I looked up towards his face. Jen looked at us and then the redhead. "Hey you, get lost. That's her man."

She looked at us. "He might want an older woman."

Eli leaned down and kissed my neck. "This is the only woman I will ever want. Let's go, Babe."

The redhead smirked. "The old get 'em while they are young, train 'em right?"

I met her eyes. "Yep! I'm training him right."

Eli shook his head with a huge smile on his face. Dale started laughing. "Ain't that the truth. Maybe you are ready for your very own belt buckle."

I stood and let Eli fully engulf me in his arms. I wasn't ready to end this night with Jen and Dale, so I invited them over to our place for a nice soak in the hot tub. "You guys want to go back to our place? The hot tub on the back patio needs company," I smiled.

"Actually I was about to head home; it's a long day tomorrow," Jen responded, "maybe after work tomorrow?"

"Sounds good." Eli smiled as the four of us headed towards our vehicles. Long since his one beer, Eli took the wheel.

Feeling the need to bring a little more excitement to the night, I toyed with the waistband of his jeans. My hand slid inside, I let my fingers toy with his manhood. We didn't go straight home, we ended up parked in a field entrance, corn in front of us, stars shining brightly above us. According to Eli, I wasn't officially a South Dakota woman until I've experienced it.

Most of our four-day weekend was spent in bed, or at least in the house. Instead of perusing the outside world, we chose to explore each other's bodies. We skipped clothes; there was no reason to hide our bodies. We already knew each other inside and out.

I learned the reason my bedspread had flowers on it was because they were the closest Micah could find to go with my eyes. I took him down and showed him my fairytale spot and told him about Trout. We cuddled. We made love. We were us and enjoyed every single minute of it.

When it was time to head back to New York, we were relaxed and happier than ever. Every moment of together was a moment of forever. Eli spoiled me and treated me like royalty. He even held me as I cried from a random Micah or Mom memory appearing, catching me off guard. He helped me smile. He helped me to remember them the way they would have wanted me to remember them, and helped me to laugh through the tears.

I was blessed. I was cherished. He knew me inside and out, I didn't just have my soul mate, I had my forever.

Chapter 18
ABBY

*A*fter spending most of the days laying around in Eli's bed and the small barracks room, I began to find ways to entertain myself while he was gone. I spent time cleaning and rearranging his stuff. It had taken a couple weeks before I ventured over to Micah's side of the room. Of course, the first thing I did was make his bed. Unmade beds drove me crazy, unless someone's in it.

Opening Micah's closet, I hung his clothes neatly. I even folded his t-shirts and boxers. The room looked nice by the time Eli got back from work.

"Babe, you got bored today?" he asked as he kissed my lips. He stripped off his ACU top.

"Yeah, I figured I would straighten up a little." I smiled as I watched him peel off his beige t-shirt. I could stare at him all day. His six pack was so well defined, his pecs begged me to touch them.

"Like what you see Babe?" His eyebrows raised as a devious smile crawled across his face.

"Yep, I especially like that it is all mine." I tugged his nipple rings until we were chest to chest. "I'm hungry. Can we go grab something to eat?"

"Leave the rings alone or we won't get out of this room anytime soon." He nipped my shoulder. "Have I told you how much I love you?"

"Maybe, but I don't mind hearing it again." I smiled.

"I love you Babe, more than my truck." He kissed my lips and wrapped me tight in his arms. I felt safe. People talk about how their mates smell musky and dark, spicy. Eli smells like home, no not sugar cookies and Pine-sol, just safe and love. Can safe have a smell? Does love have a smell?

"You and that truck." I shook my head as a smile snuck across my face.

"That was a great night," he stated as he opened his closet to dig for a shirt. I slipped my hands around his waist and helped unbutton his pants. I slipped my hands into his boxer briefs to enjoy how quickly he hardened in my hands. I stroked him while he was trying to focus on finding clothes. "Abby, we aren't leaving if you keep this up."

I kissed between his shoulder blades. "Maybe I want my itch scratched first?"

He spun in my arms. One hand rubbed over my belly, the other on my back pushing my front closer to his. "You are getting a little belly. I like it." He kissed my lips. "Get naked and in bed. Now!" He tried to sound serious, but the smirk on his face gave him away.

I untied my light blue wrap dress, letting it fall to the floor, all the while keeping eye contact, I dared him to look away. I stepped backwards until my legs hit the edge of the bed. As I crawled up onto the bed, and lay on my back, his eyes were on mine. Eli's eyes darkened to a deep navy blue as they traveled the length of my body. "Like what you see Mr. Montgomery?" I asked.

He slipped his clothes off as he crossed the room. Using his legs, he nudged mine apart. Smiling down he slid a finger into my moistness. "You are always so wet for me. This time might be a little hard and fast. My control is gone." He placed his lower head at the entrance. As he watched my eyes, he thrust his full length in. His kiss stole my moan. "You ok Babe?"

I nodded. I knew he was giving me a little time to stretch around his hardness. The question in his eyes as to if I was ready had me nodding again. He inched out and thrust hard back in. A little gasp snuck out. He kissed me hard as he continued the deep thrusts in and out. "Oh God! E! I'm about there," I panted as I climbed higher and higher, closer to my release.

"Hold on Babe, just a little longer." He slowed down as my body began to tighten up, preparing for my release. He gave another hard thrust as my body let go. Waves of release crashed over me as I milked his release from him.

He collapsed on the bed beside me. I worked to catch my breath, watching the rise and fall of Eli's chest as he struggled to catch his. "Maybe we should just order in, I don't want to leave this bed. Clothes are definitely overrated." My nails continued to trail up and down his spine.

"I brought strawberries home at lunch."

I smiled. "There aren't any left."

"You ate all of them?" He propped himself up on his elbow, lazily trailing his fingers over my body. "What does my love want to eat?"

Smiling, I replied, "More of you?"

"We have an appointment in the morning to see the little one and how it is progressing." He kissed my lips. "I don't want to wear you out."

"How about we go to dinner and a movie?" I offered.

He nuzzled into my neck. "Join me in the shower? Then we can go out."

I nodded. Climbing into the shower right behind him, we washed each other up. He couldn't keep his lips, or his hands, off my belly. "You aren't going to love my body when I'm huge."

I didn't realize I said it out loud until Eli responded, "Is that what you think? I will love you more. You are mine to shower with love." He turned the water off and helped wrap me in a towel before tending to himself. He treated me with care, more care than the museums take for their precious works of art—I was priceless to him, just like he was to me.

By the time we were dressed and ready to go, I was slightly worn out. Not wanting to ruin the night, I pulled my lips up into a smile as he led us to the truck.

"You are worn out. You want to go back and relax?" he asked as we neared his truck. Sometimes I hated how well he knew me.

"I'm ok. I'm hungry. I may fall asleep if we go to a movie though." I rested my head on his shoulder as he threw his truck in gear.

"Are you sure, we don't have to go anywhere?"

"Yes I am. You know sex with you wears me down, leaves me relaxed and not wanting to get dressed. I love having your nakedness beside me, inside me, under me, over me, any way I can get you." I leaned up and nuzzled his neck. "You do that to me."

I could tell I was feeding his ego, as if it weren't big enough. My hand slipped onto his thigh. His body was so addictive, I couldn't get enough. He changed gears and squeezed my knee. "You aren't the only one that feels that way, Babe."

"Oh, so who is she?" I asked teasingly.

"You've ruined the thought of other women for me. You are the only one I can think about, the only one I love, and the only one in my bed." He kissed the top of my head.

I smirked. "That's a good thing. I don't think anyone else can fit." The twin sized bed was barely big enough for Eli and me.

He took me to a local Italian restaurant, keeping our conversation light along the way. I enjoyed every last piece of pasta they plated for me, so glad the nausea has been at bay. He truly was my happy place. I couldn't help but smile with him near me.

"So, have you been thinking of names for our little one?" Eli asked over our shared dessert.

"Something after Micah. Not really been putting much thought into it, been too busy resting or enjoying your body." I smiled.

He nodded, his smirk drawing out his dimple. "Of course love, I'm game for whatever you choose."

As we finished, he paid the bill and helped me in the truck. I almost fell asleep on the way to our barracks home. I barely made it into the room before I crashed on the bed. Eli stripped my clothes off and got naked himself before joining me. I cuddled into him and apologized for my lack of drive, "Sorry Eli, I'm exhausted tonight."

"Shh Babe, get some sleep." He rolled me onto my stomach and lightly massaged my back as I entered dreamland.

When I woke up the next morning, he was already gone. After a shower, I pulled on a pair of sweats and a tank top. Glancing at the clock, I saw it was almost time for Eli to be in from PT. I couldn't help but smile at how domestic it felt knowing he was coming *home* soon.

He walked in, drenched with sweat. "Babe, I got to get a quick shower before we have to go to your appointment. As much as I'd love to take it easy today, it's a busy day at work." He kissed my lips and headed straight to the bathroom for his shower.

I poured some orange juice and popped some toast in for him. We really needed to find a bigger place to live. He came out in a towel hanging dangerously low. He kissed my neck as he reached from behind me to grab a slice of buttered toast, munching on it while he got dressed. Once in his uniform, we headed to the clinic. On the ride over, Boyz II Men came on the radio, singing *It's so Hard to Say Goodbye to Yesterday*. I wiped tears away silently. I missed my brother, and my mom.

Eli rubbed my leg, comforting me with his strength and love. He went to change stations, but I stopped him. "I want to hear it. These are tears of happiness and remembrance."

He nodded and kissed my head. Our fingers stayed laced together tightly. I fingered the dangling diamonds of the pendant, with my free hand. This was what forever was going to be like without Micah. The downside of loving someone forever is when they're gone, your forever is lonely.

At the clinic, they gave me a pile of papers to fill out. Eli smiled and rubbed my shoulder while I worked my way through the paperwork. He even managed to laugh when I wrote my last name as Remlock. "Nope, you spelled it wrong Mrs. Montgomery." He kissed my shoulder before shaking his head and returning his attention back to his smart phone.

"Give me a break." I elbowed him.

When I turned in the mini book filled with my life history, they took me back to get my vitals. Eli tucked his phone away and turned his full attention to me with a proud smile in place. The nurse smiled. "We want to do an ultrasound to see if the baby is progressing normally. You are about twelve weeks, right?"

I nodded. She let us know she would be right back with the equipment. I smiled up at Eli's bright smile. "We get to see our baby!" He nodded and leaned down planting a sweet kiss on my lips.

The doctor came in and introduced himself before starting the ultrasound. I don't know what I was expecting to get out of it, but I couldn't stop smiling, even when the cold gel was put on my stomach. The doctor smiled. "Well, well, this is your little bundle of joy." He pointed at the screen and clicked buttons and began taking measurements.

A gasp escaped as tears slid down my cheeks, Eli kissed a couple of them away. "We are definitely blessed." He kissed my lips and whispered, "I love you."

I wrapped my hand behind his head and pulled his mouth to mine again, the salt of my tears mixed with the softness of our kisses. "I love you too."

"Everything seems to be going normal. We are looking at a March first due date. Congratulations Mr. and Mrs. Montgomery!" he smiled as he printed off some pictures for us. I was smiling at being called Mrs. Montgomery, I was too used to being a Remlock. As he went through a list of things to do and watch for, I couldn't keep my eyes off of Eli's face. I don't think I've ever seen him this happy, not even when I gave him my virginity.

We thanked him and left with our pictures of our little one. I snapped a picture with my phone, so Liz and Lynn could meet their newest family member. Walking out of the office, Eli wrapped his arms protectively around me. "You have always been my forever, but now we have our future." He kissed my shoulder and patted my stomach lightly.

Eli had to get back to work, so he dropped me back at the room. I laid down and tried to take a nap, but my body was too keyed up. Micah's dresser beckoned me. I knew I had a few drawers left to go through. Maybe I would find some clothes that would fit me. He was smaller than Eli but still much bigger than me.

In the bottom drawer, I found one of his favorite hoodies. I pulled it out and put it on, taking a moment to inhale the faint scent left behind by Micah. God, I miss my brother. Feeling something hard in the front pocket, I pulled out a small hard-covered green notebook. I took it over and sat on our bed. Glancing at the first page, I saw Micah's handwriting. I couldn't help but smile at this small piece of Micah.

In the inside of the front cover, Micah wrote:

This is the only way I can come to terms with all I've done and all I've seen. We were told these things were for our country, but that doesn't make them right. May God please have mercy on my soul.

I was confused when I read it. My brother would never do something less than honorable. He was the purest soul I've ever known. As I opened the book to a random page, my smile quickly faded. What I read brought tears to my eyes as the words began to blur together. Scanning through the journal, I read of them setting fires to encampments and homes, taking hostages, kicking doors in, and much worse. They even managed to steal from some of the evilest men in the world. I was able to understand that was part of their job, but when I came upon a page filled with their interrogation tactics, or persuasive questioning as they put it, and how much the other teammates found pleasure in causing so much unnecessary pain. Finding out Eli and Micah did nothing to stop it made me really start to question who they really were.

.......Carl held him off the ground while Ryland bent his fingers back. Each wrong answer, another broken finger. Dirk had the male's shoes off, holding a lighter to each of his toes, hoping the heat sparked the male's memories. That fucker was either stupid or knew nothing, our guys continued a while longer. No reason to stop them, they knew what they were doing....

If I were to come under question, how far would they be willing to go to get the answers they seek? Even if I were innocent, would I be forced to agree with whatever the thoughts were in their heads? Would I be badgered or degraded? If I were to be caught doing something wrong, how far would they take it?

....They knew nothing about who we were. The questions we asked needed answers. No one answered, so one by one they were killed. One shot, one kill. Fifteen shots, fifteen kills....

I was crushed, confused, nauseated, and completely devastated. The rug had been yanked from under my feet. I had to get out of here if that's the kinds of things they did. How could I trust them? My mind was officially blown. They did all this while giving us the impression of serving honorably for our country and upholding the values of the Special Forces. The brother I thought walked on water was suddenly a fraud. The man I trusted and loved more than anything in the world was a part of this too. I had my life flipped upside down and inside out once again.

How was I supposed to feel safe? It wasn't just me anymore, the baby was more important than I am. I'm carrying the baby of a man I thought I knew, I can't believe how fooled I was. Maybe I was as naïve as he thought. How did they manage to sugar coat what really happened? *Am I really not worth the truth?*

I wanted to confront him, but I wanted to get as far away from him as possible. I felt my heart shatter once again. I wiped angrily at the tears falling down. *Were they worth these tears?* I loved these men to the moon and beyond, I can't change how I feel about them, no matter how much it hurts. I will never stop loving either of them. I just couldn't trust them anymore.

I threw Micah's journal on the bed after ripping a few empty pages out of the back. Tearing off Micah's sweatshirt like it suddenly burned me; I let it drop to the floor. Quickly I found my feet and headed out of the room, looking for a safe place. A place I won't be seen by Eli, or any of his boys. I ended up on the second floor at the far end of the building, in a little alcove.

I wrote a letter to Eli. My hands shook as the tears cascaded recklessly down my cheeks, leaving wet spots on the paper. I poured all my emotions out in the letter, questioning him about everything.

As soon as I signed my name, I walked back up to the room I've shared with him for the past six weeks. Opening the door, I tossed my key onto the counter, there was no use keeping it. As I got closer to the bed we shared, I took off my necklace and left it on top of Micah's open journal. If *this* was how they paid for my graduation necklace, I didn't want to be part of it. I kissed the letter and left it on our pillow, along with the wedding rings he gave to me.

I hurriedly packed a few items and headed away from the room, away from the building, away from everything. I couldn't get away fast enough. The tears have long since stopped, but the tiredness was kicking in. Somehow, I managed to find a cab to take me off the post to the bus station. I hated that I was weak and running. But I couldn't be around *him*. I needed to get away to clear my mind and see if I really could overlook what went on behind closed doors, or in this case, on secret missions. Never would I have guessed Eli could be a two-faced monster.

At the bus station, I chose to go to New York City. It should be a busy enough place to help me disappear. I had to wait two hours until the bus departed. I nervously paced the station, feeling as though I was being watched. I was too keyed up to sit. Needing something to do, I stepped out of the station and saw a store. I had time to go in and find a dark color to dye my hair, which is what I did in the bus station bathroom. Hoping this change was enough to help me blend in. I was less likely to be found. Keeping my hair color and showing off my pale purple eyes would get me noticed too quickly. I couldn't bring myself to cut my hair—so blackened hair and dark sunglasses would have to do. Not able to commit to the dark color, I made sure I got one of the washable dyes. I threw on a pair of dark sunglasses and waited for the bus to start loading.

As I climbed on the bus, it was loud and crowded. I found a seat halfway back by a non-intimidating looking guy. "How'd I get so lucky to be sitting next to the hottest girl on the bus?" His eyes traced my body. Suddenly I wish I had Micah's hoody on, anything to keep from having people look at me.

I gave him a weak smile and shrugged. "Fate, I guess."

He continued to watch me as I pulled my bag closer to my chest. "What are you running from?"

"Who says I'm running? I'm not running. I'm stepping away from some bad stuff." I had to stop the rambling.

As the bus stopped midway, I climbed out and remembered my phone could be tracked. I cursed and started to drop it in the trash. Pulling it back to me, I texted Eli that I love him, before convincing myself to drop the phone into the garbage can. "Track this!" I said as I turned and walked away. I had to remain strong. *Duct tape and honey* I told myself as I wiped a stray tear away.

When I returned to the bus, I kept to myself and quiet. The lack of sleep was now making itself known. It kept trying to draw me under, but my nervous insecurities kept me up and checking over my shoulder. My thoughts were darker than the darkest starless night, this was one that even Micah's smile couldn't penetrate.

What do you do when everything you have come to love and trust manages to be a lie? What do you do when you find yourself alone, away from the one person you once thought you couldn't live without, the one person you needed most? What do you do when you get scared? I run, away from everything and everyone.

My seatmate was trying to get me to talk more. He even offered to keep an eye out while I got a little rest. Being lied to by Eli made trusting anybody close to impossible, but I really needed a few minutes of rest. As I dozed off, I had flashbacks of Eli. His smiling face caused me to jolt awake. His words running through my head, *No matter where you go, if you ever need me, always remember I will find my way back to you. Wherever you are is where I belong.* I cried when he told me that as we were cuddled up together on the small bed, I was struggling as I tried not to cry right now.

His face used to bring me joy, now it was causing nightmares and making me extra jumpy. Maybe running away wasn't the answer.

"Need something to help take the edge off? Maybe you need something to help you sleep?" the guy beside me asked.

I nodded, then rubbed my stomach absent-mindedly and shook my head no. I wouldn't do anything stupid to my unborn baby. My body was starting to get tense. When I checked my watch, I realized Eli should be back in his room about now. He will be hurt when he sees the mess I left on his bed.

"You suddenly look like your daddy ran over your puppy. You ok babe?" he asked, reaching over to touch my shoulder.

"Don't call me that!" I cringed and pulled my legs to my chest. No one called me that, except the man I'm running from.

"You are a hot little number, what do you want me to call you?"

"I don't know. Just not that, please?"

By the time the bus got to New York City, I found a cheap hotel and paid cash for the room. I didn't want to be traced, tracked, or followed. I needed a plan and a place to hide. I couldn't push my body any further, I was exhausted. Getting in the room, I quickly locked all doors before stripping and taking a quick shower in the crummy shower. By the time I crawled into bed, I was out. I was too exhausted to even have dreams or nightmares.

I woke up startled by a noise outside. *What was that noise? Was that gunfire? It was too loud to be fireworks, wasn't it?* Pulling on some clothes, I inched myself towards the window. Peeking through the small opening of the curtain, I saw a bunch of hoodlums having a confrontation right outside my room. Was that the guy from the bus? I quickly moved away from the window, suddenly I wished I had Eli to keep me safe. This is what I get for running away. I was scared shitless as my body trembled.

A loud pounding on the door caused me to jump and squeal. "Hey, little bitch, you got something we want. Let us in." His words were heavily accented. "Come on out. We know you're in there."

I started shaking and moving between the two beds. They have to be mistaken, I had nothing for them. I have no idea who they were. No one knew who I am. Do they know Eli or Micah?

Before I could think further, the door was kicked in. I was quickly found, it's hard to hide in a hotel room. Pulling me by my hair until I stood up, my hands held tightly behind my back. Then, the guy holding his hand over my mouth traded his hand for a cloth over my face.

The next thing I knew, my entire world went black.

Chapter 19
ELI

I had an amazing day! My wife, man it makes me smile every time I say or think that, and I got to see our baby on the screen. We even got to take some pictures of the speckle home. I was so excited! I took the pictures into work and showed them off to the guys. They weren't as excited as I was, oh well, their loss.

She really had changed my life around. Ever since she got out here, I've been in better spirits and focusing at work. I'm a changed man. Less time in the gym, more time in love. Her showing up at the coffee shop caused me to stop and see what was really going on. A real eye opener.

We had to work later than normal, so I tried to call Abby to let her know. The call went to voicemail. *Hmm, she's probably sleeping.* The doctor explained that she would probably need more rest for the next few weeks, so I would let her rest. Yes, I listened to every word the doctor said, I wanted to make sure I knew everything that I could to ensure I was doing it right for Abby and the baby. I've already screwed up enough in life.

A couple hours later, I got a text saying she loves me. Man that girl knows just how to make my heart soar, and my smile even bigger. Just because I'm in love with a beautiful girl does not make me less of a man. It's just the opposite; it makes me try to be a better man.

By the time I finally got off work, I hustled back to the barracks. The elevator ride was quiet. I was antsy and I wanted to get back to my girl. I hurried through the halls, anxious to see her beautiful face.

When I opened the door, I knew instantly knew something was off. Something was wrong.

I turned the corner into my side of the room, expecting to see my wife. Instead, I saw Micah's journal open on our bed. Is that her necklace on top of it? FUCK! She wasn't ever supposed to see that journal. It was our way to get some of that shit out of our heads. It was supposed to be destroyed, but I didn't find it, my beautiful, innocent wife found it. I saw his old hoody laying on the floor and realize I never checked it.

As I got closer to the bed, I noticed her rings on my pillow. No! Please tell me that she is here somewhere! I glanced in closets, the bathroom, even back in the kitchen. *Fuck! She's gone.* I wish she would have let me explain.

I tried her cell again, still no answer. I left a frantic message begging her to come back so we can fix this. Hoping she would call back, I paced the room waiting. As I got closer to my bed, I realized there was folded paper under her ring. *Oh God, please don't be a good bye letter.* I can't handle the thought of her crying. I can't handle her leaving me. She is the glue that holds me together.

I picked up the tear stained pages and began reading.

> Elijah,
>
> Is it true? Is everything in this journal true? After all this time, instead of upholding the values of the Special Forces, you guys were burning villages and stealing from some of the world's evilest men? Was everything you told me a lie?
>
> Why did you lie? Seriously, am I truly not worth the truth? My father used to be pure evil, but at least he told me the truth, I knew what to expect with him. My trust in you has been broken, maybe I have been the naïve little girl all along.
>
> You guys never stopped the interrogations, what

> happened to these 'men of honor' you talked about? In the end, I am once again the fool. I'm carrying the child of a man I thought I knew; a man who will always have a piece of my heart. No matter how hard I try, I can't unlove you.
>
> You used to be my safe place, now I am scared of you. Did you really love me, or was that another lie? Is a full bank account worth an empty heart? Where did the Eli I know and love go? As I write this, I struggle to not see you as the heartless villain described by Micah's journal. You let me see one side of you, but hid the dark side.
>
> You will always be loved by me, but never again trusted. You shattered my heart so even duct tape and honey can't fix me this time.
>
> Abigail Remlock

My heart was tearing apart. What the fuck? I have to fix this and fix it fast. I loaded the tracking app on my phone and tried to track her phone. It wasn't moving. When I zoomed into it, the app pinpointed it in a garbage can. *FUCK!* I checked the bank accounts but saw *no activity.* Of course, I didn't expect her to, but it didn't hurt to double check. I needed to know any little piece of information I could about her.

Sitting on my bed, I finished re-reading the letter. No matter how hard it was, I knew I had to finish it, absorb it all. I was going to complete the hardest task I've ever had to do, I deserved to be hurt. Secrets destroy people. *Please don't let it obliterate us.* Once I finished and folded it, I shoved it into my pocket. Grabbing my keys, I headed down the hall, stopping at Dirk's room. I pounded the shit out of his door.

"Dude! Take it easy on my door," Dirk started to tease as he was pulling his shirt on. His laughter silenced as soon as he looked at my face. "What happened?"

Words escaped me, I couldn't talk. Instead, I held up Micah's journal and Abby's letter to me. I couldn't think it was her last letter to me, it just hurt too much.

"Fuck!" He was not happy. "Where is she?" He watched me shrug.

Reaching over he grabbed the cursed journal out of my hands as he shook his head. "How'd she find this? I thought you took care of this?"

"I couldn't find it," I admitted. "I kept putting it off, it hurt too much. It was inside that fuckin' hoody. I should've known." I bowed my head and thought to myself. Micah's journal was hard, but finding this letter was ten times worse.

"We need to find her, and fast. I don't have to tell you there is a bunch of people who aren't happy with us," he paused, shaking his head in frustration. "Any ideas of where she might have gone? It's too fucking dangerous out there alone, especially for her. Too many threats are out there against us and our families."

"Her phone was left at a gas station east of here. My guess is New York City."

He searched my face for answers. "Why would she go there? Why not back home, or the safe house? How do you know?"

"Liz hasn't called me and chewed me a new ass yet, which means Abby hasn't gotten in touch with her. Yet." I ran my fingers over my head, my hands gripped the back of my neck, and pulled it towards the floor.

"Montgomery, we will find her. Have faith. Get rid of that fucking journal. NOW!" He returned the diary to my hands as he watched me struggle to get my emotions in check. "You better fucking get your head straight. She needs you. She's running scared. It's too dangerous for her out there."

"Yes sir!" I stated before I headed back to my room. I can't lose her, I won't live without her. I can't fail Micah anymore. More importantly, I can't live without my heart, I need MY Abby back.

I twisted my wedding band and silently prayed I could find her before something happens. If something happened to her, I would never forgive myself and I would never live it down. I will spend the rest of my life trying to make up for failing her. My heart is out there running scared, afraid of me, afraid of what she read. She should be more afraid of what is out there, waiting to take us down. The deals we made with the devil caused paybacks to be waiting for us every step of the way. Each mission we completed left us with more enemies than friends. She wasn't supposed to find out about our rogue vigilante activities. Ever.

She never understood just how much we focused on her safety. The house that had a coded alarm was so she was safe if we couldn't be there with her. While she was in Utah, we had our friend Gabe watching out for her. There were reasons behind all the security measures surrounding her—reasons she should have never found out.

That notebook was supposed to be burned, like mine was. I'm such a fucking failure. I shouldn't have stopped searching Micah's shit until I found it. Instead, I let pain rule me, all while telling myself I would find it eventually. Damn it, I should've just manned the fuck up and found it. I should've destroyed it. Instead, it destroyed me and it ruined Abby's trust. I could only beg it doesn't destroy the chance of a future for us. But more importantly, I hope she doesn't get into any dangerous situations because of it.

I headed to my truck, unsure of what I was going to do, I just knew I needed to get away. I sat there a few minutes debating where exactly I was going to go, which plan of action I was going to take. Running off blindly searching for her was not a very reasonable idea, especially since she ditched the phone and my ability to track her. Sure wish I were a Bloodhound, or any other scent dog, it would definitely make it much easier to find her.

Ryland knocked on the window, startling me. His hand held out, palm open, waiting for something. *Fuck! Dirk must've already alerted the boys.* I opened the door and handed him my keys. I don't fuck with any of our boys, especially Ryland. Ryland was the calm before the storm. A tornado is less deadly.

"Running off ain't gonna solve the problem. Get your ass upstairs to Dirk's room. We need all heads in the game. This is a mission I'm not letting you fuck up."

Carl was standing behind him. "Find your fucking balls Monty. We need you at your best, no more pussyfooting around. Nut the fuck up! You are the best God damned tracker in the Army, when your head is in on straight." He grabbed my arm and tugged me out of the truck. I'm a big guy, but Carl was massive. If I was a truck, he was a Peterbilt.

I followed them back to Dirk's room. His girl, Kate, held open the door, a sad smile on her face. Unable to find words, I ducked my head in greeting. She followed us into Dirk's room, finding her place wrapped in his scrawny arms. I couldn't look at them for long without jealousy boiling up. In my arms is where Abby belonged, not out in the big, bad world somewhere by herself.

Christian's voice drew me out of my head. "I was searching the scanners, when I found this," he said as he turned the laptop so I could see the screen. Some hotel in New York City had a break in, big deal its New York City. The second I saw the grainy footage of some guys hauling a lifeless, dark haired girl across a parking lot, I thought of Abby. As they dumped her into the bed of a rusted old pickup, I got an unexplainable chill that shot down my back.

"That's the wrong hair color, but her size. Something feels familiar about her," I stated.

I watched Christian pass a look to Carl before returning to me, "I got better footage. One sec." He zoomed to the unconscious girl being hauled out.

"Motherfuck!" I threw my fist towards the screen, only to be caught in Carl's viselike grip. I yelled, "Get the fuck off me! That's her!"

He kept me in his grip until I managed to take my rage down a notch. "We have even bigger problems E," Carl stated.

Dirk's girl watched me. She reached out a hand and placed it on my arm, feeling the need to reassure me of her faith in our team, "If anyone can find her, it's you guys."

Bo was asking to zoom in on one of the guys' faces. The second I focused on the face, my blood ran cold. "That's Juan Ramirez, the fucking drug king of Colombia," I stated.

"The drug raid we did? The one we took his family hostage?" Trevor asked as he got closer to the screen. Looking to me, he asked, "How would he know it's her?"

I paced back and forth as I flashed back to the night we set fire to his house, in hopes of drawing him out.

"Remlock, you got my back? Philips you go north. Evans come in tight. Reynolds go south. On three! Three!" I instructed over our headsets.

We stormed the house from all sides. Bo "Reynolds" kicked in the back door as I kicked in the front door. We even gave our trademark greeting as our feet connected to the doors, "Knock, knock Motherfucker!" Our team of eight made quick work of the main floor, Ryland "Alberts" tore off up the stairs with Carl "Carlson" on his ass.

According to intel, we were supposed to be rescuing fifteen kids and three of his spouses. As soon as we located some of them, we struggled to get them out. They were panicking, causing us to get a little more stressed out. We were trying to help them, but they couldn't understand why we were there. Ryland and Christian translated everything to them, trying to get them calmed out of their state of panic. We wanted to get in, out, and done quickly. Their panicking would have to wait till they are back at our base camp. As we got the last of our hostages out, Carl set fire to the place, the smoke billowed out every orifice of the house.

Our goal was to draw Juan and his men out, it worked. They came out, guns blazing. Making sure all my guys were out and safe, I turned my focus towards Micah. Micah and I were always the first ones in and last ones out. We were the faces no one ever wanted to fuck with. We could communicate without words, which made moments like this much easier.

Ryland and Carl helped the hostages into the back of the LMTV, giving us a countdown. As soon as they had safely gotten the hostages loaded into the LMTV, we got word to move out. We did, with me covering Micah's back as we ran, a ricocheting bullet bounced between our helmets, casting them to the ground. I was momentarily stunned before Micah grabbed mine and planted it back on my head. "Let's go E!" Micah grabbed his, quickly replacing it before jumping into the truck right before me.

It wasn't until we were back at our base camp before we realized the pictures we carry in our helmets were gone. I shrugged. "Must've lost them in the fire. It's just pictures, we can always get more." I tried to reason with him.

"What if they were on the ground and didn't get burned? She might be at risk," Micah worried. He was the worrier of the group. If something was off by a millimeter, he worried.

Honestly, I didn't think twice about it. I knew I had to find a way to calm him a notch, anything to stop him from the annoying pacing he was doing. "She's in Utah. They won't look for her there. The only Colombian in Utah is coffee. If someone dares go after her, we got their toe tag numbers."

"The only way they know her would be from the Kevlar, we lost it in the fight when the bullets ricocheted. The picture was her crowned as the prom queen," I stated as I recalled the picture in my mind. "It was our last mission together." I plopped on the edge of the bed, lost in thought. "I'm going to kill those fuckers. Mark my word. Every single one of those fuckers will die."

"The footage is six hours old now. She's probably already on a first-class flight to hell," Bo stated as he pointed at the time stamp.

The sun had already set and begun rising, but we were still busy replaying the footage, trying to figure out how to get her. Each time I saw her lifeless body, a part of me died. I feel as though I have died a thousand deaths, only to get back up and die again. That's my wife and my baby they are fucking with. Nobody fucks with what's mine and gets away with it. It won't be just me coming for her. I know I have a team that has my back no matter what. Hope that worthless piece of Colombian trash was prepared for a fight because we sure as hell would be bringing one with us.

Christian wasn't the best fighter, but he was the greatest hacker that ever lived, at least in my opinion. "Monty, I found the flight records, looks like they are heading back home. Boys, we got a mission to do. It seems we are going to get another stamp on our passports!"

A knock on the door drew our attention away from the screen. Kate was laying curled into a ball on his bed behind me, silently offering any strength she could. Occasionally she would reach out and rub a spot on my spine, then pull away afraid to overstep some boundaries. I knew she wanted to help but wasn't sure how. In a way, I felt sorry for her. I knew the feeling of helplessness all too well.

Carl went to the door only to return with Adams, the new guy, on his ass.

"What's going on? You guys missed morning formation and half a day of work."

"We've been busy trying to get a lead on where Abigail is," Bo stated. By then we had hooked the laptop to Dirk's flat screen TV. Everyone was watching the different sections of the screen that Christian had pulled up, getting into as many programs as necessary for us to get a better grasp of their plans and as many resources on our side as possible.

"No bitch is worth that much trouble," he stated matter-of-factly.

Next thing I knew, Carl's hands were around Adams' neck, his feet dangling about a foot off the ground. Ryland's face was a mere inch or so from the new guy's face. "You will take that back right now fuck face," he hissed. *Fuck!* There was only one man whose temper was worse than mine in our platoon, and that was Ryland. He was seething with anger, I had to stop him.

"That is my wife you are referring to, she also happens to be the sister of my best friend. Might I also add this platoon swore on our last breaths that she would be kept safe," I managed to hiss through my teeth, my fists clenched and unclenched to keep from attaching themselves to his neck.

"She ran away, ain't worth my time." He cocked his chin up.

This fucker did not know who he is fucking with. This wasn't the mess with the bull, get the horns. Ryland was a bull in a china shop. If he was let loose, Adams was about to have a rearranged face and taking his next breath through a tube out his asshole.

Kate touched Ryland's shoulder. "I have this. Go count to ten or something. Just do whatever it is you do to relax." She stood between Carl and Adams, her eyes darted to Carl. "Let him down."

Carl instantly relaxed his grip. One thing about these guys, our girls weren't the sissy type. No one fucked with us, and no one fucked with our women.

She stood on her tiptoes and pulled Adams' chin down so he met her eyes. "Listen new guy, I don't know who you think you are, or what you think you know. It's best to not mess with one of these guys, or you will end up with your name at the top of all of these men's shit lists. I suggest you apologize now and hold your tongue in the future. This is the only warning you will ever get," she stated. God, she reminded me of Abby so much. Damn firecrackers.

"I'm sorry." He looked at me. "I'm too used to the floozies that hung around the last unit."

"I guar-an-damn-tee you our women are nowhere near floozies." Dirk pulled Kate back into his arms. "I got this baby." His attention went back to Adams. "Just don't fuck with us unless you are trying to figure a way to breathe out your ass. Hear me?" Dirk waited until Adams nodded before he continued. "Let me just tell you a little about us." He smiled and rested his chin on Kate's shoulder. "Have you heard of Elijah Montgomery?" he asked as he pointed towards me.

"Fuck. Sorry man, I didn't realize you were Elijah. We studied your tracking methods in basics."

I shook my head, a smirk sneaking onto my face. "Yep. Call me Monty or Eli." I nodded to Dirk. "That scrawny fucker there is Dirk Stinson, he doesn't miss. Ever. Christian over there can hack any system out there. Trevor keeps to himself, but won't think twice about rearranging your vital organs, just for fun. And you've met Carl, need I say more? May I encourage you to never piss off Ry. It takes *days* for him to return anywhere near remotely calm. He will chew you up and spit your ass out, leaving you to choke on your balls."

Bo stepped forward. "I'm Bo. I'm the sweetheart of the bunch. I highly recommend you change your tune in regards to Abs. She is the sweetest, strongest girl I've ever met, no offense Kate."

She smiled. "None taken. I agree, I could learn a thing or two from her."

"She also happens to be one of the most loved. Her brother had our backs. We gave our oath that she would stay safe," Bo continued to inform the newcomer. "You want to get on our good side?" Adams nodded. "You will help us save our platoon princess."

"Yes sir." He nodded.

"Collins will not know of this either," Carl piped up. "Get dressed boys, we got work to do." He's an intimidating man, I wouldn't go against him. He was as dark as he was big. As a safety precaution, you'd be better off dead than going against any one of these guys. On their team, you were safer than the gold in Fort Knox.

Against them and they could kill you more than 27 different ways before their morning coffee.

I turned to head out of the room. Christian's voice stopped me, "E. I got radio signal! Lucky for us some dumbass made a call. Check this." Christian pointed to the screen as a red dot lit up.

I tapped the signal data into the app I created on the phone, the same app I kept tabs on Abs. "I got movement. Dirk?"

"I got it. I'm heading to get clearance." He kissed Kate's lips. "I love you, sweetheart. Boys, take care of her." He quickly threw on his uniform and started towards the door. "Adams, let's go."

Adams followed Dirk out of the room. Carl looked over my shoulder. "When we get back, I want that app."

"We get Abby home safe, I'll hook you up." I nodded. "I'm going to shower and track this shit. I'm not letting that fucker out of my sight."

Ryland snatched my phone from me. "I got watch. Get cleaned up."

I nodded and went to my room. After a quick shower, I threw on my uniform. I put Abby's ring on the same chain as my dog tags, and put her necklace in my pocket after securing it onto my belt right next to my Gerber multi-tool. Come hell or high water, I was getting my girl back.

I grabbed Micah's journal, took it outside and lit it on fire, like I should've done months ago. As I watched it burn, I prayed I wouldn't be too late to save my girl.

Please dear God, give me the strength and courage to be my girl's hero.

Chapter 20
ABBY

I started to choke on my own vomit, someone grabbed hold of me turning me onto my side as duct tape was ripped from my lips. My hair was yanked harshly away from my face as I continued to retch until nothing came up but air. My mind was in a fog. Where was I? Who is touching me? I know it's not Eli. It couldn't be. He would never be this rough with me. What happened? When the retching stopped, they placed a new piece of duct tape across my face.

"Oh! I am so glad you finally decided to join us again! Although you were quite a bit of fun while you were out of it," I heard a voice behind me, when I tried to turn my head, another round of nausea hit.

"So glad our little one is awake." My head jerked up, he wasn't my family. How'd he know that nickname? I was dry heaving with the movement.

I tried to curl in on myself, but my limbs were too heavy. Glancing towards my hand, I tried to wiggle my fingers. Were they moving? I focused on it until I managed to curl it into a fist. Why can't I move my arm? Wait, what is that shiny stuff? Is that a handcuff?

"You aren't going anywhere sweetheart." I knew that voice. Where did I hear it? Suddenly it all flashed in front of me: the guy from the bus, the hotel room, the noise, the darkness. My vision was still blurry, but I tried to focus on the faces coming closer to me.

Struggling with all my might I tried to pull my arms to my chest, only to have my wrists bitten into by the metal cuffs. If my arms won't move, maybe my legs would. *No, please don't let them be cuffed! I need to protect my baby!* They won't move either. I seemed to be shackled to whatever this hard surface is. Is this a backboard? A table? A piece of wood? My ears started popping. Where are we?

"We are going home sweetheart," the darker figure stated as if he read my mind. He placed a picture in front of my face, and asked, "Recognize this picture sweetheart?"

My eyes squeezed shut as soon as I saw it. *How did he have a picture of me being crowned prom queen? Who were these people? How do they know who I am or where to find me?* Many questions went through my head. The reoccurring answer I had was: I never should've gotten on that bus.

"Been following you for a while, it's been hard to get you alone," Mr. Tall, Dark, and Menacing stated. "Seems you are one of their pets."

The other guy touched my face, causing me to flinch. "I say we have a little fun with her, maybe make a video and send it to the one who never let her out of his sight. I knew eventually he would slip up, let down his guard. They always do. They always get too comfortable, mistakes always happen." He smiled. "What a pleasant mistake it was."

I shook my head frantically, fear paralyzing me further. *Please, let me go numb*, I begged my body. I pleaded with anyone or anything that might be listening. I need to protect myself. I needed numbness.

"Relax sweetheart. It's going to be fun, for us at least. Leon, call the boys," Mr. Tall, Dark, and Menacing bit out as he stroked over my leg. My skin began to crawl; no one has ever touched me aside from Eli. *Dear Lord, please take me now. If you can't take me, please make me numb*. His hand continued to slide up my leg. "Such lovely legs." I shivered as the panic set in, magnifying the feelings of disgust, bile rising in my throat.

"I bet she's a tight little number. I wonder if she is still a virgin," Leon mused, coming back into my line of sight.

My mind was screaming. My body was shutting down, one part at a time. It couldn't happen quickly enough. The thought of them touching me there tore me apart. Only one person has ever touched me there. That's how I'd love to live my life, only ever having my Eli. My heart broke thinking of him. I shouldn't have been so rash, I shouldn't have run off. Maybe he was trying to protect me from this world's ugliness. I should have given him a chance. Maybe there truly was a better explanation of why they hid that from me. *Why'd I run?*

"So little one, do you see this man right here?" He pulled another picture out from behind me, a surveillance camera picture of Eli with his arm around my shoulders. *Was that the airport?* I slammed my eyes shut. "At first I wasn't sure it was you, but Leon made sure it was you. You know you should never leave your bags unattended, right? I hear it's dangerous." A ruthless smile was on his face.

They tore the duct tape back off of my mouth. "Answer me this question. Will today be your first time?"

I refused to open my eyes and refused to let any part of my body give me away either. Obviously, it was the wrong answer, a fist slammed into my face. *Did it hurt? How about you run into a brick wall and let me know.* The problem for them, they hit like a girl compared to my father. Although, I had no doubt it was going to get worse.

"Oh, so we are putting on a brave face, are we? Don't worry we will break you pretty quick."

I looked up and saw the evil in his stare. Smiling, I said, "I've had years of conditioning. Pavlov's dog has nothing on me."

They tore at my clothes, ripping them all off. I was left naked and cuffed to whatever this hard surface was. I tried unsuccessfully to struggle and get free, only to have my skin bitten into by the cuffs. I was stuck.

"She is bare. Has she hit puberty yet? Oh well, if not, means I get to her before the hair does." I had no hair anywhere on my body, other than on my head, I was born that way. Suddenly my legs were being spread further and further apart, my hips protested the stretching. This was not going to be anything like it was with Eli.

My mind tried to go to a happier place. I went to the memory of Eli and I having a country night.

We climbed into the old Maverick in the garage. It was a nice night to take it out for a spin. Eli wouldn't let me sit anywhere other than the middle of the seat. He laid his arm across my thigh and settled his hand on the shifter, one of his little quirks he always did. It felt natural. I asked where we were going, only to see his smirk in place. "Just a little drive, Babe."

We drove around the countryside, enjoying kicking up the gravel from the roads. I spun so I laid my head on his lap, looking towards his broad chest. My legs sprawled across the seat. I smiled up towards his face as I started toying with his zipper. His hand moved from the shifter to the back of my head, entangling his fingers in my hair.

"You better behave! Don't make me pull this car over!" Pure temptation oozed out of him.

I worked his zipper loose, my fingernails slipped under the band of his boxer briefs. I looked up at him. "Help me get this thing loose."

A sexy smile played across his face. "This thing, huh?" He lifted his hips enough for me to get his pants and boxers out from under his hips. His erection sprang to life.

I rolled onto my stomach and folded my legs up in the air, crossing my ankles. My mouth quickly began pleasuring him. His hand slid down my back, tugging up the dress I was wearing while trying to focus on the road. He moved my veil of hair away from my face, glancing down as I continued to suck and enjoy his member.

"Babe, slow down. I'm about to lose it." A moan escaped his lips. "Come here Babe, there's a turnoff up here." He tugged my

mouth up to his as he pulled into a field entrance, the lights illuminating the growing corn. As soon as he threw the Maverick into park, Eli's mouth crashed on mine, bruising my lips. He moved away from me long enough to vent the windows and kill the engine. The darkness around us was lit up with a bright sky full of stars.

Not wanting to lose contact, I continued to stroke along his length, while my other hand palmed his balls. He slipped his arm around my shoulders, nudging the straps of my new sundress down. He spun me so I was facing away from him, his leg on either side of me holding me tight. As he planted kisses along my neck and shoulders, his fingers worked to unbutton the row of buttons that held my dress together. His length was pulsing against my backside. I needed more. "Eli, I want to feel you inside me."

"I will be there shortly." His teeth grazed my earlobe, tugging lightly before he returned the focus of his lips to my neck. His hands slipped inside the top of my dress and rolled my nipples between his fingers. Not stopping until he had me moaning, begging him to ease the pressure growing between my legs.

He turned me in his lap, so I sat astride him. He ducked down and drew one of my nipples into his mouth, my moan came louder. He kissed the space between my breasts. "That's one of my favorite sounds Babe." I slipped my hands between us and stroked him. He leaned up and kissed me. "I love the feel of your hands on me, lay back, please." He struggled to keep his breathing even as he helped me lay back. I smiled innocently at him. "Babe, you can no longer get away with the innocent act, especially with me. I bet when I lift that dress up, you are bare underneath."

"Your fault! You bring out my wild side." My legs fell apart as the dress slid up higher. Eli managed to tug them a little further apart before settling himself between them. I watched Eli peruse my body. I couldn't help but smile. "You have no idea how you make me feel when you are looking at me like that. I feel like the sexiest, most beautiful person you've ever seen."

He crawled over me and kissed me hard and passionately, pouring everything into the kiss. "Because you are the only person I've ever truly seen, and the only one I've ever let see the real me." *Leaning back on his knees, he unbuttoned the entire length of the dress. Kissing me each time just a little more skin shows. Each time he undid a button, he planted a kiss as his way of keeping me covered. I slipped my fingers under his chin, trying to drag his eyes back to mine.*

"I'm not done kissing you yet."

"Babe, I want to taste you and kiss those bare lips down there." *He quickly leaned up placing a chaste kiss on my lips before disappearing from my face and slipping his tongue into my soaked slit. His finger slid into me as his tongue flicked my clit. His fingers did a "come hither" motion, causing me to fall over the edge. My fingers ran over his hair, it was too short for me to get a grip. My legs went straight, I couldn't hold back. He sucked a bit harder on my clit, causing me to fall apart again. I tried to push him away, but he continued to lap my juices.*

"Oh My God! I'm never going to get enough of those. Sorry for getting it on your face." *I was suddenly embarrassed. All this sex was still so new to me.*

"Babe, I can't get enough of you. It was like heaven, you taste divine." *He planted a kiss on my lips, sneaking his tongue in, letting me taste a small sample of what he treasured.* "I love you more than my next breath. You are my home, you are my heaven. Where you are is where I belong."

I wiped at a stray tear. This man was the best thing to ever happen to me. He watched me as he prepared to enter. His eyes locked on mine as he nudged himself in slowly inch by inch, waiting a few moments to allow my body to adjust to his fullness. My body still wasn't used to his massive size. He worked himself in and out lazily until he was sheathed to the hilt. Kissing me deeply, he continued to work his member in and out of me. Leaning his weight onto his arms, his hands framed my face as we held eye contact. His lust filled blue-greens to my desire filled purples.

His thrusts started coming faster and harder as his body began to lose control. His breathing changed to heavy pants. I felt it coming, my body was starting to go rigid, he must've felt it too. "Babe, I'm almost there, hold on." The next handful of thrusts were hard and quick, drawing out my orgasm as I milked his from him. As the final pulse ended, he collapsed on me. He was heavy, but he was my safe. I ran my nails up and down his muscled back as our breathing worked to return to normal.

He lifted up and looked down lovingly at me. "I could stay like this forever." A kiss planted on the tip of my nose. He started to pull out. "Did I hurt you?"

"Please don't move, you belong in me." I tried to hold him closer, wrapping my legs around his waist, locking my ankles over his backside, trying to keep him from pulling out all the way. "You didn't hurt me, you saved me."

"Let's get back to the house. I will feed you and then we can do this all over again."

The man from the bus was climbing onto the hard surface trying to position his self between my thighs. I closed my eyes searching for my happy place, or somewhere I could get back to the numbness I depended on growing up. Being numb helped me overcome a lot of the stuff my father put me through. I could only hope it would help me survive this.

I felt ripped wide open when the darker man pushed himself in with one quick thrust. I screamed out in pain. "Oh yes! A tight number indeed! Either she was a virgin or her previous attempt was with a boy much smaller than I."

"That man who was in the picture, he's someone important to you, yeah?" An evil grin crawled across the man's face. "Such a big man, I wouldn't take him as lacking in the size department."

I laughed through the pain. "You are nothing compared to him. He's at least twice your size asshole."

That earned me a hard boot to the ribcage. The bus guy was still attempting to thrust hard into me. Luckily he was much smaller than Eli; otherwise it would have hurt me much more. I finally understood why Eli took his time getting started with me, slowly stretching me, he was well endowed and he never wanted to hurt me. Eli was my first and only, so I was suddenly finding out the way it happens when it's done out of hate and spite.

My vision was blurred. I felt warmth spread over my cheek as well as around my ribs. My body was no longer mine. My heart still beat strongly for Eli. No matter how much they take from me they can't take the love I have for him out of my heart. Would he even want me after all of this? Could he ever stand to look at me again?

My heart ached, my body ached, but most of all, my head ached. I wish I could take back the hate I wrote in that letter. I wish I would have just talked about it with Eli instead of running. What if that journal was never supposed to be seen by anyone but them? Maybe he was trying to protect me from the struggles they went through. I shouldn't have run away. Hindsight—20/20.

Now, I have to remain strong, or remain numb. I can't give up hope. He has to come for me. But, how will he even know where I am? My dumb ass left the phone in a trash can. I thought it would be safer for me to be away from him. He is a tracker, I pray he can follow the tracks I left on his heart and find me. My heart hurt but was still full of hope.

"He took something that was mine. It's only fair to take something of his." The eyes of Mr. Tall, Dark, and Menacing ran across the length of my body, his fingers trailing along the same path. "He seems very possessive of you."

My eyes darted down to my stomach. *Are they going to hurt my baby?* I closed my eyes and prayed to God we would get through this. I looked towards the one who seemed to be the leader. "Where are you taking me?"

"Somewhere far away from lover boy and his band of rejects. I am going to enjoy our time together, probably much more than you will." His yellowed teeth showed. "When we get through with you, no one will want you, much less look at you." Reaching out, he firmly grasped one of my breasts, squeezing tighter than a vice grip. I couldn't hide the wince of pain as tears welled up in my eyes.

"Boss, I have the guys waiting for us at the compound." I heard from somewhere behind me.

"Fabulous! This shall make for an excellent day." The evil gleamed in his eyes as he finally let go. "Seems we will have something for you to write home to lover boy about."

I listened as they plotted and planned. Begging to be let free, I tried to struggle against the restraints. "No use struggling sweetheart. No place to go but down. We're 35,000 feet in the air. Might as well relax, it's going to be a long week for you."

Please, Eli come save me. Don't get hurt, I couldn't handle the thought of someone hurting you because of me. If he ever comes after me, *please let him have backup.* I had to keep hope. He promised me he would always come for me; he would always find me and destroy anything in his way. *Will that promise mean nothing when he reads that letter?*

I slowly turned my emotions off, I needed to be numb. Repeating my thoughts again, it was my new mantra. I turned off my racing thoughts; I needed to focus on my numbness. I either had to be strong or I had to be numb, I couldn't bounce back and forth between them. It would only amplify the pain if I let my emotions swap between strength and numbness. After silently telling my family and friends that I loved them and never meant to hurt them or cause them pain, I never wanted to let them down. A little prayer went to Micah and Mom. *Please forgive me for giving up, if possible, could you show me the silent strength to make it through this.* It was time to close down my heart. *If there is no love coming out of it, no one I love can get hurt.*

Battered. Beaten. Discouraged. Alone. I won't be defeated. Somehow I will make it through. I will end up on top, stronger than ever. *I hope.*

Chapter 21
ELI

As I walked into the office, my mind was stuck on replay. I sat in my chair staring at the clock. My nerves intensified knowing each minute that passed was another minute those fuckers got to live. My wife, my life, was out there at risk, while I was stuck sitting here with a thumb up my ass. My beautiful girl was under the control of a monster far worse than I am.

My eyes glanced at Micah's picture next to the clock, returning my thoughts to him. He would be so disappointed in me right now, I let him down. The one person he spent his life trying to get safe and keep safe was the one person I was now trying to find. The one person he made me swear my last breath that I would protect and love. The one he begged for me to always give happiness. Do anything to keep that bright smile on her beautiful face. He depended on me, and I fucked it all up.

"Montgomery, we have a problem," Dirk stated as he sat on the corner of my desk, pulling me from my thoughts.

"I don't want to hear problems. I need solutions," I stated as I leaned back in my chair. "Please tell me we got clearance."

"That's the problem. We got clearance. We just can't head out for a week. That's the first I could get us out of here."

"Fuck! Every fucking minute is a minute too long. Abby is in fucking danger. Who doesn't get that?" I pounded my fist on my desk.

Ryland sat down. "E. They stopped moving." He handed my phone to me. "According to that app, they are 38 hours away from us."

I glanced at the coordinates that were flashing on the screen. "Let me see what that looks like." I typed in the coordinates into my tracking app that showed what was around, including the layout of the land and any building structures. Pulling up a view of the location, I smiled. The house that popped up on the screen looked almost identical to the one we burned down.

Christian glanced at my screen, and then pulled a couple more screens up on his laptop. "Well, I got some good news boys!" He rotated his laptop. "They made it home. This security system they have is easy to maneuver around, for us at least."

"How is that good news?" I asked as I watched him hack into another system, pulling up a couple more screens.

"She's still alive," Christian stated. Suddenly the surveillance cameras came alive on our screen. Christian managed to rewind the footage a little, turning the laptop back so he could fiddle with the settings. I tried to look over his shoulder, only to have him hunker down, blocking the screen. He warned me, "Back off E! Let me work for a couple minutes."

I sighed but nodded and found myself pacing around the concrete box we considered our office. "You have anything yet?" I asked after each revolution around the office. "How about now?" Another revolution began.

"Promise me you won't hit any of us, or our equipment, this shit is expensive," Carl stated as his glance kept going between the screen and me.

Bile rose in my throat, they wouldn't tell me that if it were something pleasant. I nodded and walked towards the screen. They stilled the footage, zoomed in on Abby. She was stripped bare.

Her face and body were battered and bruised. Her beautiful lips were swollen and busted. My breath was knocked out of me. I dropped to my knees, unashamed of the tears streaking down my face. That's my girl right there, so close yet so far away and so broken.

I felt hands on my shoulders, Bo's reassuring voice sliced through my misery, "E. We will get her."

Juan's face turned towards the camera, his evil smile in place. "So nice of you to join us. I saved a little extra show just for you and your buddies."

Christian pounded the desk. "I knew that was too fucking easy. They let us in on purpose."

"Such a smart one! Give the man a cookie!" His assistant clapped and rubbed his hands together.

My beautiful wife was being held by one of our worst enemies. She was cuffed to the table. She lay there limply taking a beating. I've never seen her look so defeated; she seemed so cold and distant. Her face was bloody and bruised, her legs, her arms, her ribs were bruised. *Oh God, is the baby all right?*

Why am I worried about the baby? She could lose the baby, I just couldn't lose her. *Lord please save my wife, the rest of this life isn't worth living if she isn't beside me.* We could always make more babies. Even if we can't, as long as I have my girl I will have my whole world. I would die without my Abby. Her life was more important than my own.

Juan looked straight at me. "How's it feel seeing us take pleasure in her? She's so beautiful, so easy. You want to make a deal? You have exactly one week. Otherwise, we keep her." He seemed to pause and think. "Until she becomes of no use for us."

"Please don't hurt her anymore! I will do whatever it is you ask of me!" I cried out, watching Abby. She shook her head no. Fuck! She was ready to quit, ready to die. My heart ached for her, my beautiful angel was now broken. Her wings are no longer holding her up. Her smile was gone. The fight in her was no longer present.

"I thought you'd say that. You are also to bring one million when you come. One minute late and there will be nothing left to come after."

"Don't hurt her anymore! Baby I will move heaven and hell, I promised you. I will save you, hold on please sweetheart, just hold on. No matter where you are, I will find you!" I begged her. Her eyes looked into mine, her lips moved to say something, but I couldn't hear her.

Suddenly the screen went blank. "Christian, get her back up there! Hurry! I need to see her!" I was in full blown panic mode. "What's taking so long?" I raised my voice as I paced the floor.

Dirk stood between me and the laptop. "We can't get back into it. They disconnected the system." He sighed. "I should've guessed there was a reason it was so easy to hack into."

"Tell me what she said in the end. I saw her mouth move, what'd she say?" I stood, stuck in the same spot, staring at where she just disappeared from.

Trevor looked at me. "She said '*I love you. You are my first, my last, my everything, my forever.*' At least I'm pretty sure that was what it was or something very close. Then she said something like *duct tape and honey.*" He shrugged.

I nodded, that cut me deep. I remember uttering those same words to her over and over again. *Damn I thought I hurt when I lost Micah, this was much worse.* Is there a word beyond devastated? Is it possible to have pain worse than cutting out my own heart and eating it for breakfast?

"I need to go talk to Collins. We need to get there yesterday," Dirk stated as Carl followed him towards the door.

"Don't let him out of your sight Ryland," Carl stated before ducking out of the room.

I saw Ryland out of the corner of my eye, stalking towards me. "Dude, that fucker is going down. I plan on drawing out his death."

My phone rang, who the hell was calling me? *Unknown number?* I put it on speaker as I answered, "Hello, Eli Montgomery speaking."

"I see you are taking real good care of my worthless daughter. Care to explain why I am getting a video in *MY* email?" It was Ed; my blood stopped cold in my chest.

"She's been kidnapped. We are going to get her back." *Fuck! Why'd they send him a video? It was bad enough we had to witness it, why would they share it with Ed, the uncaring?*

"I wouldn't waste my next breath on that worthless wench." He pissed me off beyond the point of spitting nails.

I slammed my phone onto the desk. Bo frowned and shook his head. "I say we swing by and give old Mr. Remlock a piece of our minds, just as soon as we save Princess Abby."

"That man just took one of his last breaths." Ryland started pacing, he seemed to be plotting something. "The world won't miss him."

"We are going to take turns," Bo mused. "We can't kill him, but we sure can put a damper on his day."

"He's been asking questions, stirring up trouble. I think he found out about the accounts Micah left for her today," Christian stated, pausing to look back to me. "Someone was checking in to the bank, trying to get through the system. Luckily we managed to get an extra round of security codes attached. He can't get into anything without her present."

"How do you know all of this?"

He pointed to the screen. "Bank cameras and stalking computer systems. I'm doing my job." He focused on a small square in the corner, a hint of a smile on his face. "Yep! There is the man trying to get her info." Pointing to the man in view, the man that deserved to stop breathing, it was definitely Ed.

I glanced closer. "That fucking bastard, check her savings account, please?"

Nodding, Christian's fingers sailed across the keyboard. Damn, that man knew what he was doing. "It was emptied yesterday, here's her father's signature."

Ryland swore a string of curse words as he pumped his fists open and closed. Normally, someone would be trying to calm him down at this stage, but we were all too stunned by everything else happening. "I will be back in a few minutes." He turned and headed out of the room.

"Somebody should stop him," I stated.

"The only one that can keep him in his place at this stage is Carl and he isn't here right now," Bo reminded us. "Give him a moment to cool off."

We refocused our attention to the screen, which is where we spent the rest of our work day. Dirk managed to get clearance for us to leave out in three days.

Hold on Babe, we are coming for you! I sent up a silent prayer. *Dear God don't let me fail her.*

As we headed to the barracks, Carl looked around. "Where'd Ry go?"

Chapter 22
RYLAND

*T*here comes a time in your life when it's either fight or lie down and surrender, yet in my life there was no option of surrendering. I have spent the last two days watching one of my buddies enter hell time and time again. My switch finally flipped, it was time to fight.

I never had a fight I couldn't win. Before I joined the military, I had no one who cared about me, no one who cared if I was still breathing. Now, I have my brothers. I'd give my shirt off my back to help them out, they were the same with me. The place in my chest burned with pain, it wasn't my heart though, I don't have one of those. I didn't fight with that spot, or for it, the only thing that helped when I fought was my fists.

Someone took a critical piece of our puzzle. Someone hurt the girl that only deserved happiness. Someone was going to pay dearly. When someone should've been protecting sweet Abby, he chose to beat her instead. Now, he is going to get a small dose of his own medicine. My size 11 boots had his name written all over them.

As far as the guys knew, I'd decided to go for a little walk to clear my mind. What was I really doing? After changing clothes, I hitched the first plane to Salt Lake. I was seeking revenge. They say paybacks are a bitch. Well, guess what, this bitch just had puppies.

I used the flight to mentally prepare myself for what I was about to do. I smiled and cracked my knuckles as I imagined the panic and surprise on that face of his. My phone was off, I needed no distractions. I needed to get where I was going, and do what I needed to do as quickly as possible. Get in. Get done. Get gone. A mission was ready for me as soon as I returned.

I rented a car shortly after landing and drove straight towards Abby's childhood hell. I pulled into the driveway taking a moment to imagine what it felt like to be Abby as she pulled into this driveway day after day. "It's time to turn off your brain Ry, it's time to do this." *Yep, I talk to myself.* Twisting my neck from side to side, as it cracked, my brain shut down, and shifted into autopilot. Following the washed out brick pathway to the front porch, I knocked on the door. Reciting the words we always used when we met a door, "Knock knock motherfucker!"

The front door opened, but before Ed got his first word out, my fist connected to his face. The sound of his nose cracking was music to my ears. Adding a few more blows, he fell to the ground. A couple kicks had me connecting my foot to his ribs and stomach.

From the ground, he started to yell at me, "What the fuck? Who the fuck are you?"

"A nightmare." I smirked. "So I hear you have a little extra cash in your pockets?" I pulled him back to his feet so I could stare him in the eyes.

"That bitch owes me every penny of it!" he growled. "The money we used to save her life was supposed to be for my retirement."

"Parents make sacrifices for their children," I stated, though I was unsure of where it came from. My parents dumped me on the streets, they sure as hell didn't sacrifice anything. "It's not Abby's fault."

"You couldn't even begin to understand what she put us through," he spat at me.

"Try me." I raised an eyebrow, daring him.

"That pregnancy should've been terminated! It would've saved money, pain and suffering. Instead, all our money went to helping Karen through the pregnancy. I almost lost her early on when she hemorrhaged. Gail tried killing her from the inside."

"Still not seeing how this is her fault."

"Every penny was drained from us after she nearly killed Karen again during childbirth. She came 13 weeks early with so many issues she spent two months in the NICU. The only reason I put up with it was because Karen wanted it. I should've just pulled the damn plug, like I wanted to," he stated. There was no remorse in his voice.

I said, "No sir. That girl is something special." I shook my head in disgust, how can someone talk like that about her?

"She ruined Pauline's chance at a future. I needed the extra help with Gail, so she dropped out of school."

"Her choice, not Abby's." I had heard enough. I was so fed up with the whole thing. Everything is Abby's fault. If it weren't for her, he'd have money. *Fuck money and fuck him!*

I swept his legs out from under him, dropping his ass onto the porch. I started raining blows down on him. Each blow I issued had a reason. Each explanation was silently added in my head. A nice, hard punch to the gut for all the gut wrenching pain he caused Abby. This kick is for kicking the shit out of Micah when he tried to protect her. Another couple of kicks for trying to kick Eli out of her life, unsuccessfully I might add. The one-two punch to the face was for the soft spot I have for Abby and the anger he sparked within me. I opened my fly and pissed on him. And that is for pissing off the platoon. My boot pushed pressure against his skull, holding him to the ground, for all the pressure he put on Abby growing up.

Never before have I stopped issuing a punishment until I was done. This time I did. The moment Abby's worried face passed through my head, I stopped. As much as I wanted to, I couldn't kill him, it would hurt Abby. I remember Eli telling us over the years that if it didn't Abby pain, he would've killed the fucker, and now I totally understood.

He was sputtering, blood spitting out his mouth, "You worthless piece of shit, you will pay for this."

I stepped down just a little harder. "Let's make a deal. You stay out of her life. We'll stay out of yours."

Once he finally agreed, I tucked a slip of paper in his pocket. I then turned and walked back to the rental car, feeling proud of myself. As much as I wanted to kill him, I didn't. Tugging my old cap down a little further, I headed back the same way I came.

Glad to be back in New York and in my old beater of a car. I headed back to the barracks. A sense of calm washed over me, I felt accomplished.

"Where the fuck have you been Ry?" Carl greeted me as I entered our room.

"Just taking care of some business," I stated as I tossed my hat on the counter.

"You do a booty call?"

"Something like that. A boot was involved," I responded as a Cheshire grin snuck across my face.

He whipped around facing me. "You did it, didn't you?"

"If you mean I made a house call, yep I sure as hell did." Cracking open a beer, I took a long pull. I needed a distraction to keep from giving everything I just did away.

"We need to work on your problem solving skills. I thought you were working on compromise?" he asked.

"I tried to give him a high five, but forgot to open my fist and somehow mistook his face for his hand. Accidents happen. I solved a problem where compromise was not necessary." I sighed and plopped on my bed. "Something happened though. Normally after my brain shuts down, it takes a few days to regain the right frame of mind, as you know. I was about to shove my boot through his face, but her face flashed through my head. She gave me peace and stopped me from killing that fucker."

Carl's face fell. "Wait? You are telling me the switch just flipped back that quickly?"

I nodded.

"You said her face, which *her* you referring to? Ashley? Kate? Abby?"

I felt my teeth grind as my jaw clenched, just hearing Ashley, my ex-fiancée's name, the lying cheater that I wasted two long years with. "Abby. Honestly it's never switched that rapidly. I saw her face and I felt her strength. All I know is that the fucker won't be calling or talking anytime soon."

Someone pounded on our door, so Carl answered the door. Eli walked straight in the room and gave me a hug. "I just got the pictures."

"What pictures? How do you know it was me?" I stepped away from him, trying to act shocked.

"Your trademark boot print is on his face. Nice job Ry." He handed his phone to Carl showing off the pictures. "Wait. What's going on? You aren't all jacked up on some adrenaline high?"

"She brought me back. The second her face flashed in my head, I was strong enough to stop." I sighed as I scrubbed my hands over my face. I was getting tired, I really didn't want to sit and clarify anything else tonight. "I can't explain it. The only thing I know is we need to get her back, she is the strength I need, the love you need. I promise we will get her back home, come fire or holy water that girl will be found. She needs us and we need her."

"You are saying my wife's face stopped you from doing it?" he asked with a dumbfounded look on his face. It didn't make much sense to me either. I couldn't explain it.

I nodded. "What happened? What did I miss?" I needed the attention off of me and what I did.

"We leave Thursday. Tomorrow we need to analyze the floor plans, search those cameras and see what we can get," Carl stated.

Eli looked at me. *"My* Abby flipped your switch?" He was still trying to grasp it.

"Let's go get your girl. You aren't the only one that needs her." I smiled one of the first real smiles in a long time. I hope he didn't take it as I wanted her in the same way he did, I just needed her strength.

Revenge is so sweet it made my teeth hurt.

Chapter 23
ABBY

I saw Eli, I started to smile, but it quickly faded when I saw him fall to his knees on the concrete floor. My strong angel has fallen, he looked destroyed. My rock. *My Eli*. I was supposed to save him, now I am dragging him through the gates of hell with me.

I was being moved somewhere darker. I was so weak I couldn't even lift my head. Seeing Eli caused me to momentarily forget my numbness. Once I started to feel again, I couldn't stop. The pain and panic took over. Suddenly, blinding pain shot from places I never knew existed. When I looked at the males coming towards me, I cringed, this was going to hurt. He saw them beat me up. Eli saw them take advantage of me, he watched them steal another part of me. He cried. *My brave soldier was crying, for me*. He broke because of me. I broke him.

"Little bitch, I have something for you," Leon stated as he ran his hand along my leg. I knew this routine by now. They sure as hell wouldn't be offering me food, romantic getaway for two, or even a puppy.

I lolled my head towards him. "Leave me alone." I tried to be brave, put up a little bit of a fight. It turned out to be useless, I was still strapped down, fighting only caused the cuffs to tighten and dig deeper into my skin.

"Lay still and take what I have to give you." He smelled of booze and old cigarettes. Climbing onto the surface I was attached to, he thrust his length all the way in. It felt like I was being ripped apart. It felt like sandpaper being shoved inside me, shredding everything he touched.

I couldn't fight against him, I couldn't protect the baby that may or may not still be in my stomach. They started asking questions yesterday, and rewarded me with a punch in the gut for any wrong answer or a slap to my face for any answer I didn't give. Cigarette burns were singed sporadically along my body. When I answered the question, I tried to think how they think. I wasn't as successful as I hoped I could be. I took more hits than a joint at a rave party.

As soon as he finished, I asked if there was a bathroom or shower. I'd laid in my own filth for too long. One of them felt sorry enough for me that he unhooked the cuffs. Before they picked me up off the table, they moved my arms behind my back, reattaching the cuffs. My ankles stayed cuffed together. I felt like a murderer in prison with all the shackles keeping my hands and feet from attacking someone. "I promise to behave. Please, just let me free of these cuffs," I begged and pleaded.

"Boss says you are to be cuffed. Means you better get used to those," Leon stated. "I want you to shower first, then we might let you soak in the tub. If you behave, we might let you walk around for a little bit."

God that sounded like something wonderful, I've been strapped on the same hard surface for so long, I forgot what it felt to be able to walk. Unsure if I could even walk with the atrophy of my muscles from not using them like I always have. It hurt so much to move, I could really use a big stretch right now.

They carried me to the bathroom, and sat me on the edge of the dirty tub. "Let me start the water, then we will rinse you off. Hang tight sweetheart," it was one of the new guys talking. I wasn't sure of his name, but he really seemed like a nice guy. Honestly, how nice could a guy be if he was part of keeping me hostage?

I kept my eyes downcast. My right eye was swollen leaving just a little sliver I could barely see out of. My left eye looked me over, taking inventory of my injuries. Bruises covered my chest, my ribs, my stomach, and all down my legs. A few gashes left by the leader's knife marred my skin. Mr. Nice Guy turned the faucet on. Using the detachable shower head, he let the water trail over my legs. It was a little cooler than normal, but it felt so good.

"Is it too hot sweetheart?" he asked. I shook my head no, reveling in the feel of filth falling off of me. "Can you stand up for a second? Let me rinse you all the way off." He helped me stand, offering support when I teetered slightly. "Easy."

I stood there trying to regain my bearings. My body was stiff and sore from being held in one position for too long. I stretched my legs as far out as possible while holding onto the railing in the tub to keep from falling.

He stepped away to shut and lock the bathroom door. When he returned his focus to me, he whispered, "I'm going to take those nasty cuffs off you, but please stay still. I'm begging you to not fight me. I can get in a ton of trouble if they find out."

I nodded, opening my mouth to speak, but nothing came out. After trying to wet my mouth, I leaned forward and drank from the shower head. "Thank you. What do I call you?" I asked as he removed the cuffs from my wrists.

"Jaime," he answered as he moved the shower head around to different parts of my body. It felt so good to get cleaned up, who knew how long this niceness would last? I had to enjoy it while it lasted.

I watched as the blood trailed down my body, my hands immediately went to my stomach. Was the little one all right? There was a lot of blood coming from my body. I know I'd been stabbed several times, was it from the stab wounds? Or was it coming from inside of me? With all the cramps going on, am I losing the baby? Was it from not eating? "Where's that blood coming from?" I managed to squeak out as I steadied myself from falling.

"You have a lot of cuts and bruises, some of those might need some stitches," he stated. "You have your monthly girly stuff yet?" his cheeks reddened as he asked.

I shook my head. "I shouldn't, I'm pregnant. Or at least I was." I bit my tongue as soon as that came out. *Crap!* They didn't need to know that, now they can use it against me.

He must've caught the concern on my face when I spoke. He reassured me I was okay with him. "How far along? It's ok your secret is safe with me."

I looked him over. Maybe, I could make a friend while I was stuck here. Could I trust him? No. I cannot trust anyone anymore. Eli ruined the idea of trust. "How long have I been here?"

"Four days." He handed me the sprayer head and reached for some soap, creating a rich lather and running it over my body.

"I'm 13 weeks," I whispered. "But my stomach has been doing a lot of cramping, and I see the blood, I'm scared."

His hand replaced mine. "There is a good chance you have already lost it. I can stitch your wounds, but I can't fix that if you are already losing the baby." He seemed lost in thought for a moment before he returned to washing my body.

"You can't tell them. Please don't tell them," I pleaded as I searched his face for a response.

He nodded his head. "I won't say anything." He planted a soft kiss on my forehead. "You are the same size as my wife. That's why I can't find it in me to hurt you. Those men they had on the video earlier, they love you, no?"

I nodded. "I think so. I think they loved my brother more though," I admitted as I met his chocolate brown eyes.

"They love you, especially that guy on his knees. He's a good one. I remember him," he said a small smile. Plugging the tub, he urged me to sit down. As I sat down, he turned up the water temperature before he continued talking, "He was at the raid that happened six months ago. I asked him to help me get her somewhere safe. He carried her to safety."

A sad smile ghosted my face. *My man saved his loved one, could he save me?* A knock on the door quickly pulled me out of my thoughts. Jaime frowned as he clicked the cuffs closed around me again. The door burst open just as Jaime removed his hands from my wrists.

Leon looked at us. "Get her out of the water, boss wants her hooked up to the table."

"She needs some of these wounds stitched up," Jaime stated as he helped me stand up. He wrapped a towel gently around me and lifted me up as if I were a feather. As Leon stepped out of the room, Jaime leaned down and kissed my forehead. "I will do what I can to help you. Just try not to fight them. I don't want to see you hurt more. I can't fight against them. They hold the key to my freedom, just as they hold the key to yours. I can't do much, but I can try to help where I can." He squeezed me just a little tighter.

I nodded as he carried me back to the table that had been my bed for the past four days. He started to reattach my cuffs to the table when the boss came in. "Get those wounds stitched up, Ruiz. I'm fucking her first, then you can have your turn," he directed.

Jaime nodded and left the room as Leon finished the cuffing. I focused more on the cuffs than the man crawling over me. I couldn't return to my numbness, my mind was still reeling over the bits of conversation I had with Jaime. *He wasn't free? He wasn't evil? My boys saved his wife?* For the first time since I was taken, I didn't feel alone. I wasn't safe, but I wasn't alone.

My body was broken, beaten, bloody, and no longer mine. As I cried and begged to be let go from the rape in progress, I felt another part of me die. When he was finally done with me, he pulled up his pants and walked away. He discarded me like the trash I was.

Jaime returned with a small first-aid kit. He focused on the open wounds on my face. As Jaime's hands worked to close the wounds, I felt the last of the evil leave the room. My eyes focused on the tenderness of his face. It was just him and me. "Tell me about her, please." I needed a distraction.

His brown eyes lit up as he started talking about his love, "Her name is Sofia Maria. She is tiny, but she packs a huge punch. Her heart is pure gold. I have never seen or heard her say a mean word about or to anyone. She is an amazing cook! We always wanted to have our own restaurant when we were free."

"I'd really love to meet her sometime." I gave my first genuine smile since I've been away from Eli.

"You will love her. Your smile is as big and beautiful as hers." He smiled and kissed the freshly closed wound as he trailed his fingers along a previous scar from my painful past. "Your Eli is almost as lucky as I am. I bet he promised to never let this happen again."

"I ran away from him, how lucky could he be?" A tear slipped down my cheek.

"Sweetheart, we all get scared from time to time. He's lucky to have someone who loves him as much as you do." He kissed my forehead. "Trust me, I can tell you would give your last breath to see him again."

Chapter 24
ELI

As I headed back to my room to get a little rest, I couldn't help but smile each time I thought of those photos of Ed. That fucker deserved worse, but at least he got a small taste of what it was like to fuck with what is ours. My mind was still reeling over what Ryland was telling me. I knew he wasn't interested in Abby like me, but his admission of needing her strength caught me off guard. She did something the rest of us couldn't. She helped him flip that nasty switch in his brain. Carl worked hard with him from day one. His main goal was to lessen the time it took to turn his brain back on. Who knew that all he needed was one thought of Abby to regress?

One of my buddies, Gabe, from back home, was a paramedic. He was the one who sent me those pictures. The only thing he did to help Ed was drop an ice pack on the ground beside him along with a couple ibuprofen. "Now you can feel the way she did all those times," that's what he said, I knew him well enough to know that's what he said.

He was one of the guys that stitched up Abby's wounds over the years, thanks to him, Abby stayed under the radars and out of the hospitals. Gabe also reported every bruise as well as each stitch to Micah and me, we kept a running record. She had long since hit the 2,000th stitch, and we lost count of the bruises.

"E. I need to talk to you," Gabe informed me over the phone.

"What's up?" My body instantly set to alert.

"It's Abby." His voice barely over a whisper as though he was avoiding letting someone near him listen in.

"What's going on? Why are you whispering?"

"She's in the other room. He did it again."

"I'm on my way." I put the pedal to the metal and got there as quickly as I could. Already in town, it only took me ten minutes to get to Gabe's. If I hadn't got to town earlier this morning, hoping to see her tomorrow at her swim meet, it would've taken me at least four hours by plane. It was supposed to be a surprise, yet once again Ed fucked that up.

I got out of my truck and headed inside of Gabe's house without knocking.

"We are in the living room," Gabe yelled down the hall.

I dropped my jacket onto a bar stool next to the center island and took a deep breath before I walked into the living room. Abby was curled into a ball crying uncontrollably. It put my feet into motion as I fell to my knees beside the couch.

"Babe, I'm here. What happened?" I pulled her hand into mine, trying to get her to look at me. "Babe?" I put my fingers under her chin, drawing her eyes to my face.

"Eli? Am I dreaming?" she asked as she touched my face. "Please don't let me wake up if it is."

I kissed her forehead. "I'm real Babe. What happened?"

She searched my face. "Why are you here?"

"You have a big swim meet tomorrow. I wanted to be here watching. Micah couldn't make this trip, he's still rehabilitating the family we just brought back." I smiled at her. "You know he would've been here for you too."

"She shouldn't go if I'm being honest," Gabe stated as he started setting up some sterile needles and thread, alcohol wipes, gauze and everything else he may need.

"What do you mean?" Abby asked, trying to sit up.

"Show Eli," Gabe instructed her as he leaned over the back of the couch and helped her sit up.

Abby cringed and struggled to catch her breath. Tears streamed down her cheeks. She met my eyes, looking for strength and comfort. I nodded and held her knee tightly. Slowly she lifted her sleeve while

Gabe helped steady her. Under the sleeve of her t-shirt, was a six-inch gash that started near the outer part of her shoulder and ended on the backside of her arm as if she tried to turn away from whatever it was that he used to cut her. It was almost identical from the previous scar he gave her.

"How'd it happen? What did he use?" I asked as I ran my eyes and fingers down the length of her freshly opened wound. Bruises stuck out against her pale complexion.

Abby buried her face in her hands. For some unknown reason, she seemed embarrassed.

"Babe, look at me. Please look at me. How'd he do this? Why?" I pried her hands from her face. "It's not your fault. I'm sure you didn't do this to yourself. It's not like you ran into something sharp."

"I got home late from practice. I wanted to break my time on the 200 butterfly. He met me at the door, without a drink in his hand." She paused a second trying to regain her composure. "He waited until I sat down at my spot at the bar before he grabbed me and threw me into the fridge."

"Where was Liam?" I asked as I rubbed her shoulder.

"He was working the late shift, Mom was at work too," she responded quietly.

"Let me get this stitched up while she tells the rest of the story," Gabe suggested as Abby laid down with her injured arm up. "I'm going to numb this area and give you an injection for pain. Relax as much as you can, let me know if the pain starts getting too bad." Gabe talked to her like she was an injured or scared animal.

She nodded and held my hand while he started sewing the long gash back together. Every once in a while she would squeeze a little harder. I whispered sweet nothings to her. I was unsure what to say to get her to relax so I hoped the sweet words would ease her pain.

"He said I was worthless and caused too much trouble. He pulled me to my feet and slapped me across the face. I crumpled to the floor and didn't see him coming. It was too late. I felt a stab of pain and tried to get away from him."

"What did he use?"

"A glass shard from his broken beer bottle, again," she answered as she held tight to my hand. "Gabe, can I please swim tomorrow? I have my long sleeve suit."

"Abs. you need to relax. Too much movement is going to tear the stitches and take longer to heal. This is the deepest he's ever cut you Abs, it needs time to heal."

"It's the last swim meet of the season. I've been training so hard, I can't miss it," she whined, reminding me she was still only sixteen. She still had so much innocence left, even though her father kept gradually pecking away at it.

"There is always next week Abs," I reminded her.

"All the scouts will be there. If I impress them, I can get scholarships or maybe a free ride."

"We will figure this out in the morning." I kissed her forehead and stood up. "I will be right back, Babe." I needed to get away for a little bit and calm myself down. I jumped in my truck and headed over to the Remlock house. I couldn't let this fucker get away this time.

I shut the engine off and walked the worn footpath up to the shoddy porch that needed some boards replaced years ago, as well as a couple coats of paint. Without knocking, I walked right in. Ed was in his old recliner, still drinking. I crossed the room and hauled him up by his shirt. Face to face, I met his eyes.

"What the fuck are you doing in my home, threatening me?" Ed slurred and slobbered.

"What the fuck are you doing beating up an innocent child?" I replied.

"She was two minutes late, I demand punctuality from all my children," he spat at me. I reared my left arm back before my fist hit him square in the face. I followed that with a few more punches. I truthfully wanted to kill the fucker, but settled for a beat down.

"You worthless piece of shit! You are no better than she is! I should get the police involved. Assault and battery will wreck your career," he threatened me.

"Go ahead, press charges. Don't fucking threaten me! You file charges, so do I. Every last cut, bruise, broken bone. ALL her scars will be turned over to the state of Utah. Tell me how good that will make you look. We have enough evidence to lock you away for a while. You would make a good bitch to your cell mate." I didn't back down, there was no way I was letting this slide.

"You wouldn't dare!"

"Try me motherfucker! I dare you!" My words dripped with venom as I let him drop to the floor. My boots echoed across the wood floor, reminding Ed I was still here. Needing to check on Abby, I got in my truck and headed back to Gabe's.

"Eli? Is it you?" Abby's voice sounded weak.

Gabe was still stitching her arm, I took her hand and knelt down on the floor in front of her. "I'm back. You still doing all right?"

"Gabe just gave me some more lidocaine to numb it. I'm tired. Where'd you go?" she asked as she searched my face for answers.

"I cleaned up a little misunderstanding." I kissed her forehead. "You aren't going home tonight. We'll get a room. I need to protect you."

My phone rang. It was Micah. As soon as I answered, Micah tore into me asking what was going on. Fuck! Ed must've said something.

I gave him a rundown of the night and sent a couple pics of her wound.

"How the fuck did that happen?" Micah was livid.

"A broken glass piece from his beer, that's what Abby told me. I gave him a little bit of what he deserved. He threatened me with assault and battery charges, so I threatened to release all the pics of every last injury to the state of Utah."

"How's she holding up?"

"She's tough, hanging in there, still in a bit of shock. She is more concerned about missing the swim meet than her injury. Gabe doesn't want to let her even if she wears her long sleeve suit."

"Take her to a hotel room. Do not let her go home."

"I already planned to," I responded. "How's the mission going? They still being difficult?"

"Yeah. Ry is about to blow a gasket and kill all of them. They are very needy and argue every step of the way. I gotta go E. Tell Abs I love her." He hung up before I could even respond.

"Was it Mikey?" Abby inquired, looking towards my phone.

"Yes, and he told me he loves you and wishes he were here." I kissed her cheek.

"What'd you do to Dad?"

"Don't worry your pretty little head. It's not worth it." I tried to avoid telling her what I really did.

"We are done with the stitches, let me just wrap it up so she can get some rest," Gabe said as he stood and fetched the roll of gauze. He slowly and very carefully wrapped her arm, trying to avoid causing any unnecessary pain.

"You bring anything with you, Babe?" I stood looking around the room for anything that looked remotely feminine.

"My backpack has everything in it. It's by the front door," she answered as she headed towards the front door to retrieve it.

I took it from her. She followed me to my truck once we thanked Gabe for everything and said our goodnights. I helped her into the truck, asking her what she wanted to eat.

"I'm not hungry." She stilled her hands in her lap.

"You need to eat, Babe," I reminded her as I took her hand in mine. "What do you want to eat? How about we grab some burgers and head to the hotel?"

She nodded and leaned her head back, closing her eyes.

"Don't fall asleep over there." I squeezed her hand, reminding her I was still here with her. "You need anything for the pain, Babe?"

"Gabe gave me a couple V's. I have to eat something before I can take one," she answered and shook her head, disagreeing with some internal battle going on in her head.

"What's going on in that pretty head?"

"I want to swim tomorrow, but my arm hurts. Maybe I can channel the pain into drive?"

"Let's discuss this in the morning, K?"

She nodded and stared out the window. Her mind was still off in the distance. I knew her enough to know she was still bound and determined to swim tomorrow. Maybe I need to get Micah on my side and have him talk some sense into her.

Through the night, we ate and I held her close.

Guess what she decided to do the following morning? She swam. She swam hard and fast. Abby won every event she swam.

"Hey E! I found a note in his pocket," Gabe stated as soon as I picked up the phone.

"What did it say?" I asked.

"7.2m in 72h."

"K." A smile broke across my face. "Thanks man. I got to get going, I will chat with you later."

"What's the note mean?" he asked.

"Nothing you want to get involved with. Trust me on that one." I hung up and headed for the shower.

I tried to sleep a little, but had no luck. My bed smelled like Abby, making me crave her more. I also knew I couldn't keep this from Liz any longer. It had already eaten me enough.

"Where has Abby been? She hasn't called lately," Liz asked.

"Are you sitting down? Let me explain before you jump down my throat and leave me choking on my balls."

"What happened Eli? Did she lose the baby?" her response was etched with panic and concern.

"No. Yes. I'm not sure. Maybe?" I stumbled over my words, "It's actually worse than that. She found Micah's battle journal and left me."

"She will come back as soon as she calms down. She loves you too much."

"That's the problem, Liz. She's been kidnapped."

"How the fuck? What the? Who?" her questions poured out of her mouth. The final ones struck too close to home. "Why are you talking to me instead of saving her? After all she has done to save you, you are just going to sit there and not save her? I would have thought by now your balls would've dropped, grab hold of them and man up."

"We can't get clearance to leave until Thursday. We know where she is at, but we can't go there until then." I sighed. "I would if I could. That's not the worst part of all of this Liz."

"What could be worse than having my best friend kidnapped? Let me rephrase that question, what could be worse than having my *pregnant* best friend kidnapped?"

"We managed to breach their security feed." I paused to gain strength, knowing she wouldn't like what came next any more than I did. "We stood there shocked as she was being raped and beaten on camera. She's never looked so lifeless and destroyed."

"Go. Get. Her. Now!" she stated and hung up.

Fuck! That was much harder than I thought it would be. Tears fell as I looked at our wedding picture. We were so happy and in love; my decision was made. Tossing on my civvies, I laced my tan boots up. My dog tags still hanging on the chain next to Abby's ring around my neck, I was ready to get there and save her. Attached to my belt, next to her necklace, was my Gerber multi-tool. Instead of alerting the boys or grabbing weapons of choice, I hopped in my truck, with my trusty old backpack.

The first flight out of the airport was in three hours, it would eventually lead me to Colombia after several layovers. Liz was right I needed to get my ass in gear. Technically in about 24 hours, I would be considered AWOL. But that no longer mattered. My flights were only covering about 2500 miles, then it would take another couple hours by car to get where I needed to be. According to my tracking system, they were about another half hour to an hour walk outside of Tunja. Yep, those fuckers have gotten on the wrong man's radar.

"Where are you at E? They found our flight plans, they are planning to be there waiting for us," Christian asked.

"I'm out for a bit."

"Got it. Track it down and get us all the intel you can. We will see you in a couple days," he stated. "I love the tracking app." I could hear the laughter in his voice as he hung up on me. The hacker has once again hacked into my shit. I closed down my phone and paced a section of the terminal. I have been doing a lot of pacing lately; sitting down was completely out of the question. About the time I begin to calm down, her beautiful face popped up right in the front of my brain, those cuts and bruises reignited my pain and hatred.

As I buckled myself into the plane, I cleared my mind as much as I could. I knew enough of Colombia's terrain from the last time we stopped in. This time, it wasn't much different and less than an hour from the old place. When they allowed us into their security system to show us how they were treating my beautiful Abby, they weren't paying attention to Christian as he hacked the rest of the cameras, giving us the entire layout of the house. If there was a silver lining to watching my wife getting beaten and raped on the live video feed, it was finding out we had complete layout of the building.

I needed to clear my mind and focus on getting my girl back. As the plane hit the air; my brain switched into hunting mode. No longer was I worried about my personal safety, I was worried about getting the mission completed successfully. I turned my common sense off, my animal instincts kicked in.

My fingers flexed and relaxed as I thought of those men stealing my girl. My legs bounced up and down, I was anxious to give them a small taste of their own medicine. By the time the plane touched down in Bogota, I had a plan of action. I passed through customs swiftly, using a fake passport, I needed the element of surprise on my side. With my bag thrown over my shoulder, I found a car rental counter. Thankful we took the extra language courses, I was able to communicate.

Grabbing a rental, I swung through a local gas station. After I put a few dollars into the tank, I stepped inside in search of a few missing items. I picked up some brake fluid, motor oil, and some baking soda, among other things, things I couldn't risk getting caught with. Throwing it in my bag, I continued down the road to Tunja. I couldn't really drive all the way to the compound; that was asking for trouble as well as alerting them a pissed off American was on his way. After leaving the car on the side of the road, I took off on foot heading north of town. I probably could have driven closer, but a little extra caution never hurt.

As I got closer, I double checked the coordinates. Looking ahead, I reached down and tugged my dog tags to my lips, kissing them and sending up a silent prayer. I didn't pray for safety, I prayed I would find her swiftly and get her back home. After tucking my dog tags back in my shirt, I hit the row of trees I was planning to use as my cover to get closer. I sat down hidden in the trees, waiting to make my move, it was almost dark.

While I wished I could send out a message, I knew there was a good chance someone was monitoring the radio waves. The only way I could get a message to them without giving away my position was pinging the map on Christian's phone using my app. It would only stay pinged for five minutes, but it was the best shot I had to get them my location and stay off of Juan's radar. I knew he caught it when he pinged me back. Turning off my devices, I switched into survival mode.

I kept to the shadows, weaving around the lights. The wall had Constantine wire coils across the top. I've had my fair share of interactions with the razor sharp wire. I have my battle scars, I wasn't afraid to add a few more to the mix. Especially if that meant I find Abby. My heart rate picked up a little just knowing Abby was close.

In case you were not sure on the protocol, here's a hint: never show up to the encampment with only a Gerber multi-tool and no backup. I am just that crazy to attempt it. Nothing to gain, nothing to lose. Lucky for me, I also have a bag of goodies stocked with stuff I brought as well as some of the little things I picked up before I left Bogota. This goody bag would make MacGyver jealous.

As I approached the wall, it was then that I realized I hadn't really gotten to this part of my plan. I was banking on armored guards patrolling the area, which seemed to be missing from the equation. It wasn't like I could just knock on the front door and they would let me in. It's not like there is the chance of a pizza delivery this far out. I depended on taking one of the guards out in order to get access and possibly a firearm.

I retreated back to the tree line, squatting over my bag, I rifled through it in search of what I really needed. Pulling out my K-bar, my knife of choice, I attached it to my left thigh. I tugged my hoody on over my head to keep the chill off, and made use of the inner pocket, I tossed in a few throwing knives. There in the bottom of my bag was what I was looking for. A travel set of shampoo and conditioner bottles, what's inside won't make my hair all soft and shiny, but it will make for a makeshift smoke bomb. It was great having hands on knowledge.

Normally, I would have already cleared the wall and got straight to my girl, but this is something I have to be careful with. My decisions could really affect Abby's treatment. As I sat and planned out my plan of attack, I prayed Abby wouldn't get hurt in the process. I knew the guys were still waiting for their clearance, I had less than 48 hours until backup arrived. Maybe by then I would have saved my girl and be halfway home. I could hope.

Popping open one of the little bottles, I threw it against the outside of the far side of the wall. Opening the container of brake fluid, I repeated the process, adding it to the mix near the wall and watched as smoke hit the air, the smell was atrocious. I quickly made my way around the corners to the opposite wall. As the smoke went higher, alarms started going off inside the building. Climbing the brick wall, laying down flat on the top, I watched as three men fled the house and looked for the fire. Dirk would've had a hay day sniping them off one by one. Slipping into the shadows, I edged my way closer.

One male began heading towards where I was lurking, *here's my chance.* I waited quietly, with my K-bar in my left hand, until he passed me. The knife went to his throat as I pulled him back against me. "You scream and I will cut out your tongue," I hissed through my teeth.

The man struggled. A small sound came out of his mouth, but quickly stopped when I increased the pressure of the knife against his jugular. My right hand snaked around his hand, snatching the gun from his grip. After placing the gun into the waistband of my jeans, I turned the man so we were face to face.

"Where is she?" I asked. "Where is the girl you stole?"

He shook his head and attempted to shrug. "I tell you nothing," he spat at me.

Without a moment's hesitation, I slit his neck, watching him collapse to the ground. Looking at him, I knew he would fail to give me any answers I needed. I felt no remorse, I gave him a chance. Answers were what I wanted, I was not here to beat around the bush. Two choices were given—either answer my question or meet your demise. More noise was coming from behind me. I had to get out of there. There wasn't a clear enough chance to get inside the building undetected. I quickly scaled the fence, adrenaline pushing me as the wire ripped through my hoody and my skin. Silently I retreated back to the shadows of the trees.

If I calculated right, I had about five hours until sunrise. Sleep was not an option this close. The enemy was too close yet Abby felt too far away. I could either retreat to town or I could find cover nearby.

If I retreated, I could get a fresh start in the morning, but then I would be further away from Abby. If I stick around this place, I can't get close enough to her. I'd basically be a sitting duck. I headed further north, away from the encampment, away from Abby, away from everything. Collapsing against the trunk of the nearest tree, I dozed off for a few minutes. My eyelids felt weighted down, I could no longer fight to keep them open.

The sun coming over the trees had me alert and ready to take on the day. I had to get close and stay close. They were planning on meeting my boys at the airport, it was an ideal time for me to sneak in and find her. I doubt they would take her with them, so this was my only hope.

Chapter 25
LIZ

Hearing Eli say Abby had been kidnapped tore my breath out of me. I lost it. I slid down the wall until my butt hit the hardwood floor. Questions poured out of me, I couldn't stop them if I tried. None of this made sense.

Sweet little Abby was stolen.

The news just kept getting worse. Not only has someone taken her, they are doing evil and disgusting things to my best friend. Anger boiled in my veins. Before I could stop myself, I tore into Eli, letting him feel the depth of my pain and anger.

I swiped angrily at the tears cascading down my cheeks. After hanging up on him, I stood and staggered to the doorway of our office, in search of Liam.

I was supposed to start school tomorrow, but it was going on hold. "Lee!" I yelled down the hall. My strength had been zapped by the emotional trip I was still on. I feel as though the rug had been yanked from under my feet. "Liam!" I yelled again, struggling to keep the tears out of my voice.

Liam came charging in from the living room like my knight in shining armor. He opened his mouth to speak but stopped dead in his tracks, mouth gaping like a fish. "Liz? Sweetheart, what's wrong?" Words finally formed as he stepped closer to me.

I couldn't tell him yet. My mind was still trying to process words. "Hold me," I managed to squeak out.

Liam pulled me into his arms, consoling me from the anguish coursing through my body.

"Liz, talk to me, please? You are killing me sweetheart. Tell me what's going on." He had tears in his eyes as he kissed away a few of mine.

Looking down at my trembling hands, I opened my mouth to speak, "Abby. They took her."

Liam sat up ramrod straight. "Who took her? What are you talking about, love?" He pulled back as his eyes searched my face for answers.

"They took her," I managed to mumble.

"Who took her? Liz you are scaring the hell out of me." He continued studying my face. "Sweetheart, who took her? Eli?"

I shook my head and shrugged my shoulders. "Lee, they took her. They are hurting her."

"Who?" he asked, fear creeping across his face, as the color drained.

"I don't know Lee. Eli told me they took her."

"Someone took her from Eli?" his concern was etched deeply on his pale face.

"They are hurting her Lee. I'm scared. What if they hurt the baby?" I shivered as the words poured out of my mouth, not because of cold, but out of fear.

"Baby?" Liam's eyes popped open as the word came out. "What baby? Liz what are you saying?"

"She's supposed to be happy. What if they hurt her baby?" The words poured just like my tears, "They are taking her happy away."

Liam interrupted me, "She's pregnant?"

I shrugged, "Maybe not anymore. They took her and raped her and beat her. Eli saw. Oh God, what if he can't save her?" Panic rose in my chest.

"They took her from Eli? They hurt her? He will find her. If he doesn't, I will," Liam stated. He seemed to be trying to convince himself more than me.

"What about the baby? What if they take away her happy?" I pulled away from Liam so I could pace. I was no longer able to sit and do nothing. Pacing didn't solve the problem, but helped calm my tears. "That's my best friend Lee, I'm so scared."

"We've already lost Mom and Micah. We won't lose Abby too." Liam pulled me back into his arms. "We won't lose her. We can't."

He held me for hours as I went from tears to smiles, even back to tears again. The vicious emotional cycle started over and over. That night we did something we normally never did, aside from Christmas Eve service; we went to church and prayed. We spent a couple hours talking to God, begging him, even tried bargaining with him. We were willing to do anything to ensure Abby came back safely.

After we had left the church, Liam called the family. As soon as Wes heard, he went on a rant that made the devil seem tame, before he went dead silent. Wes and silence were not a good combination, we knew he would be on the first flight to New York ready to fight whoever it took to get more answers. Rob asked us to update him as soon as we knew anything as he choked back his tears, as did Lynn. The normally happy-go-lucky Colt was wrecked with anger. We heard Missy trying to console and calm him down as we hung up. He didn't waste his time calling Pauline, she wouldn't give two shits one way, her hatred towards Abby was permanent.

Liam held me tight throughout our first of what may be many sleepless nights. I wouldn't rest until she was safe again. Even then, I wouldn't sleep until I saw her with my own eyes.

Lynn called me as the sun was coming up, "Liz. Please tell me it was a nightmare."

I bit my quivering lip and shook my head, willing my tears away. "I prayed all night it was someone's idea of a sick joke," I sobbed. "I prayed that maybe it was just someone who looked like her, and really she was hiding out somewhere. It was a nightmare Lynn, and we are still living it."

"He will find her. Micah said he was the best damn tracker the Army has to offer. That's his heart out there. He won't stop until he brings her home," Lynn tried to reassure me.

"I need her. We need her," I whispered through a sob.

"We all need her, Liz, especially Eli," Lynn reminded me.

Chapter 26
ABBY

I was pulled from my dreams of dancing with Eli in the rain by a lot of commotion and shouting. Leon darted out of my room with his gun drawn. For the first time since I've been here, I was left totally alone. Why they felt the need to have extra guards on me while I remained cuffed to the table, I had no idea. It's not like I could just get up and walk away, right now I really doubted I could even walk if I were given a chance. My legs felt heavy. The throbbing pain was blinding.

Jaime came in to check on me. "Sweetheart, you all right?" he asked, his hand squeezed mine.

"What's going on out there? I heard a lot of noise going on," I asked. My anxiety was heightened as the panic coursed through my body.

"Someone set a fire along the wall. One of our guys didn't make it," he informed me, "I think someone is coming for you." A smile crossed his face. "I checked the video feed but didn't see him, but I think it's someone for you."

"He said he would *always* come for me. Maybe it is him." I let the fantasy settle in my head for a couple seconds.

"Whoever it was; was one hell of a sneaky bastard," Jaime stated as he sat on the chair next to where I was cuffed.

The boss man peaked into the room. "Ruiz, it's time for our meeting. Grab Leon and meet in my office." He turned his attention to me. "Don't worry we will get you moved in a few minutes too. Seems we have some company. Got to protect my latest prized possession." He winked my direction before leaving the entry way.

I stretched my fingers, reaching for Jaime's hand. He glanced out of the corner of his eye while still keeping an eye on the boss. As soon as the boss turned and headed out of the room, Jaime returned his focus to me. "What's going on sweetheart?"

I looked down at myself and realized I had nothing I could give him to pass to Eli. Our phrase hit me. "Stronger than duct tape, sweeter than honey."

"What?" He gave me a confused look.

"It's something we say to each other. If it's one of my boys, all you will have to say: *duct tape and honey*. I guess it would work as a safe word. It's something my brother always told me. If you tell them *duct tape and honey*, they will know I trust you enough to pass it on. They will know I am alive."

"*Duct tape and honey*, is it? Such a strange combination. Promise me you will tell me the story behind it when we are both safe again?" I could see the smile reaching his eyes. He repeated duct tape and honey to himself a few times.

"Yes." I smiled weakly. "I promise."

"Ok. I will be back as soon as I can." He planted a kiss on my forehead, giving my hand another quick squeeze. He also let me know he would find out as much as possible and hurry back.

Once again I was alone, but something was different. I had hope that someone was coming for me. It could very easily have been a random hoodlum, but I felt like Eli was closer. Perhaps he had come for me after all. Maybe he was holding true to his word that he would always come for me.

I was unsure how long I was alone, time seemed to drag on. I had no windows to tell if it was light or dark out, and I stopped counting in my head long ago.

When they finally returned, Leon clapped happily. "Yay! We get to have more fun with our beautiful roommate." He quickly began unbuckling his belt.

Jaime put his hand on his chest. "Boss said we move her first. That's gonna have to wait." He waited until Leon fixed his belt before turning to me. "Sweetheart, we are moving you deeper down." He leaned down and started removing my cuffs. I silently thanked him for stopping Leon from mounting me again. Once I was undone, Jaime picked me up and carried me down the hall, through a couple large rooms, and then down a long set of stairs where the darkness continued to get darker.

It was completely dark and smelled like a freshly dug hole. I shivered from the chill in the air. Jaime ran his fingers along my spine in an attempt to ease my fears, but it didn't seem to help much. Leon tossed an old woolen blanket on the ground.

"Put her there. We are cuffing her wrists to her ankles. Let the little bitch sit up." He dragged me out of Jaime's arms dropping me down to the ground. I landed hard, feeling the pain in my hip and ribs. I couldn't keep from gasping in pain as my body crumbled to the floor.

Glancing toward Jaime, I saw the deep grimace taking over his face. It seemed he felt as much pain as I did. His eyes shifted down, as Leon knelt before me reattaching the cuffs, clicking the cuffs extra tight, digging into the open wounds around my wrists. My wrists were once again bleeding as were my ankles. My eyes welled up in pain, I couldn't let the tears fall. I couldn't let them know they were stronger than me.

I met Leon's cold empty eyes. "Oh sweetheart, we can't forget this little added piece of your costume." He shoved a hard rubber ball into my mouth, tightening the straps around my head. "Don't want anyone to hear that voice of yours. A gagged woman makes me a happy man."

Once he finished tightening everything to his satisfaction, he threw another itchy wool blanket on me. I waited until they left before I let my tears fall. Silently, I begged to God he would let me die.

They broke me, the tears streamed down my face. I was unable to be heard, the last of my fight had been taken from me.

Chapter 27
ELI

*I*t made for a really long day waiting for the sun to start setting. I had to wait to make another attempt at drawing the guys out. I needed to know how many I was dealing with. I knew I was dealing with more than the three from last night. A better idea was what I needed.

Most of the day was spent between pacing, planning, and pacing some more. It sucked not having my guys here to have them help in a diversion plan. I couldn't start a fire or do anything drastic that could risk the chance my girl could get hurt worse.

I watched the wall waiting for someone to come out and play with me. Seems I have managed to keep off the radar and stay undetected. I would still be able to catch them off guard when the chance arises. Every once in a while a new guy started patrolling, must be a change in guard shift. I knew I could easily take him, and I could probably hit him from here with one of my throwing knives, but it would draw attention to my shadowed hiding place.

As I watched him pass by, I knew the next one would probably be around again, give it about ten minutes. Even though they weren't on a clear cut schedule, they seemed to roam around every ten to twenty minutes. I quickly made my way up to a small patch of branches, being sure to stick close to the shadows. I broke down a couple branches as quietly as I could, using the backside of my K-bar.

It was time to make a trap, lure those dumb fucks away from that damn wall. Starting up a small brush fire, I snuck further down into the brush, repeating it another spot on the opposite side. I then ran as fast as I could to the other side of the compound to stay undetected knowing that they would all come check out the fire.

This pulled five guys out of the house. The gate suddenly swung open, beckoning me to it. I quickly darted in the gate, looking at the front door hanging wide open, I couldn't resist going towards it. My heart is somewhere in the building. As I got closer, a man came out, blocking my way. His gun was trained on my chest. I had no time to panic and I did what came most natural. I knew I couldn't outrun a bullet, nor was I able to dodge one. Adrenaline took over, dropping down, I full forced charged him when most would run the opposite direction. His face was struck with fear and confusion. At that moment, the hunter became the hunted as I took him by surprise in one swift swipe of my arm. I had gained the upper hand. I had him down on the ground before he knew what was going on. He had the fear of God in his eyes, the wind knocked from his chest, and his life in my hands. He was too shocked to let out a sound.

My hand covered his mouth as I jerked him to his feet, my K-bar attached to his neck, daring him to move. I had to get out of the open. Half shoving, half dragging him, I retreated to the shadows alongside the house. I yanked him out of the front gate into the shadows of my hiding spot.

"Let me make this clear, I am going to ask you a few questions and you will answer them, if not, you won't make it far," I whispered into his ear. "You got it?"

He nodded. I turned to face him, staring directly into those God fearing eyes of his. He tried to reach down, I quickly caught his hands.

"I wouldn't try that stupid fucker. Keep your hands still." My eyes stopped him in his tracks. "Where is she?"

"I can't tell you." He flinched even before my fist met his face.

"Let's try this again. Where is she?" I bit out.

"Inside," he stated.

I backed him so his back was flush with the broad tree offering us its shadow. "Try again fuckface." My forearm putting pressure across his throat, as I asked again, "Where is she?"

"She's in a hole inside." He struggled to catch his breath. "You can't get to her."

No one ever told me what I can and cannot do, especially when it concerned Abby. My knee came up, rearranging his man junk, he tried to crumple down upon himself except my arm never moved. "Let me try this again. Where is she?"

His hands went up in surrender. "We moved her to the hole of hell after the first smoke bomb." My K-bar was now pushing against his jugular. He helped move her, he touched her, and he deserved to die. "I have a message from Abby. You are Eli, right?"

The instant he said my name, I relaxed the pressure against his neck, waiting to hear whatever else he knew about my beautiful wife.

His hands rose in surrender, he began to stammer, "Honey." He tried to take a breath. I reared my fist back and aimed at his face, I wasn't a patient man. He didn't try to stop me. Finally, he figured out what he was attempting to say, coming out more like a stutter, "Du… duct tttt..tape and honey."

My fist instantly dropped as I heard those words. No one else would know about that, she wouldn't freely give out that information. "You?" It was now my turn to stutter, "She trr..trusts you?"

"She knows I don't want to hurt her. She knows I remember you saving my Sofia. Last time you were here, you protected her," he whispered, his hand reaching out to touch his neck where my K-bar was, rubbing it, checking to see if he was bleeding. Luckily, I didn't break the skin.

"Sorry man, I needed information. I can't trust anyone around here. I need her back," I stated, trying to make him understand where I was coming from.

"I understand. She told me she loves you more than yesterday," he stated. "You are her forever. She has fought against everyone in there. I want to save her the way you saved my Sofia. They catch me helping you and I'm a dead man. I'd rather be dead than hurt her though. She is such a strong woman, reminds me of my Sofia."

My heart filled with hope again, Abby was still fighting to survive. "Help me get to her."

"I can't get to her right now. Boss is watching my every move. He knows I haven't had my way with her, he knows I don't hit her or hurt her. I think he figured out I have a soft spot for her." He seemed to be telling the truth. "There are too many guys inside there."

"How many are we talking about?" I was willing to make a deal with the devil if that meant I was going to get my girl back in my arms. Information, that's what I needed the most right now.

"There has to be at least thirty right now. Some of them are planning on meeting the plane your friends are on. Might be able to get in there then," he reasoned. "Their flight should be landing soon. You came fast once you saw my call?"

I wanted to get to my girl as soon as possible. It wasn't like I could go in all Rambo and gun them all down. I had no firearms, aside from the one I stole off the fallen guard, the one holding a single bullet. "Thank you for the signal. Definitely helped. Get back in there and keep her safe as you can." I met his eyes. "You get her safe, and I will do my best to get you back with her, Sofia was it?"

"Yes sir." He nodded. "I will do my best."

"Tell her she is my first, my last, my everything, and my forever. I will always come for her." I wiped a tear that managed to slip out. "My life means nothing without her."

I let him go, believing there was still good even in all the evil of this world. I watched him go through the main gates, my heart filled with hope, my head filled with conflict. What if he turns out to be a good-for-nothing liar? What if my instincts were wrong or I was blindsided with hope? What if I didn't see the true him? I regretted hurting him after finding out he was on our side and could only hope he understood.

I remained in the shadows, watching and waiting for them to head out. A prayer was sent up. *Please let him be telling the truth.*

Chapter 28
RYLAND

*O*ur bags were stored properly in the overhead compartments, aside from our goody bags stored under the plane, our research has been done, it's now time to sit back and enjoy the ride. My brain was preparing for the shut down, just like the mandatory shutdown of our electronics. I listened to the guys replay their plan of action over and over all the while playing out my plan of attack in my head. Just as the flight attendant showed us the exit options, I thought through many different exit strategies and possible outcomes of this mission.

Who might get injured? Would we be too late? What if something goes wrong? What did Eli find out on all his recon work? Did we have enough weapons? Was Trevor's bag stocked with everything we would need for Abby? Did we get to torch this place like we did the last one? Will Abby be alive?

These guys weren't going to like my plan, but I was following through with it. Was my plan the smartest idea? Nope. But I am doing it anyway; I never claimed to be a brilliant man. Did I give a fuck? That was a better question. However, the answer was still no. The guys would tell you I'm a reckless dumbass, and they would be right.

"Ry, what's going through your head over there?" Carl looked over at me, pulling me from my thoughts.

"Preparing for the fun we are about to have." A smile turned up my lips. If he only knew what was really going on inside this head of mine. My hat remained tugged down tightly over my eyes. They were the gateway to my dark plans. Avoiding eye contact was the key to this successful *foolproof* plan.

"We land in about an hour, I'm pretty sure we will be under fire." Dirk was smirking, cracking his knuckles. "Even though we are coming in a few hours earlier than planned, it seems someone is watching us closely."

"Any word from E?" I asked, glancing toward Christian.

He shrugged. "Not since he pinged my map. I'm sure he is around there making a few friends."

Oh yeah, that sounded just like Eli, perfect gentleman looking to make a few new friends to go out with for a cup of coffee. The only time Eli has ever been a perfect gentleman was when it came to Abby, and even that was questionable. The chance he was making new friends with her kidnappers; was about as likely as me being considered the sweet and innocent one of the group.

As the plane got closer to landing, my legs were bouncing nervously, my fingers drumming restlessly on my leg. I had my eye on the prize, and was actually looking forward to what was about to go down. I adjusted my hat, tugged it down even lower, to further shield my eyes. Carl kept looking over at me. I couldn't let him know what was going on inside this head of mine. One look at my eyes and he would know I'm about to do something reckless. As the plane touched down, I bounded out of my seat.

My brain had officially gone into action. Sitting on my ass was no longer an option. Leaning down, I looked out our little windows, yep that beautiful black SUV with the blacked out windows definitely made me smile. It called to me, like a hooker to a two-dollar bill. I smirked, "Looks like we have company boys, are you ready for a little fun?"

"Let me go first," Christian stated. "Nobody wants to hurt the nerd." He squeezed in front of me, opening the bin to grab out his bag of goodies. I didn't even reach for mine; it wasn't part of my plan. I watched the rest of the guys snatch up their bags, loading their bodies with weapons. Normally I would be attaching my K-bar to my thigh, my shoulder holsters would usually have a matching pair of nines, and inside my boot, I would slip in an extra four-inch blade.

As Carl finished attaching his toys, he smacked Christian on the shoulder. "Let's go man. We got this."

We opened the plane door, I watched as Juan's men started to climb out of the SUV, weapons drawn. It was about to get fun. Slipping in front of Christian, I stepped out first, hands in the air. I told the guys to stand back, I had this under control. "Are you out of your fucking mind?" Dirk asked his face dumbstruck.

I nodded. "Of course, we've known this." I nudged Christian back.

Carl raised his eyebrows and shook his head. "No, Ry, don't do this shit."

I stepped forward. "Trust me on this. I have a plan. Just stand back," I begged as they nodded. They knew there was no point in arguing with me, I had made up my mind.

Juan's men held guns pointed at my head, obviously not trusting me or what may be waiting behind me on the plane. I glanced back once more, giving my boys a smirk of knowing this shit was about to get real. With my arms up, I continued walking down the stairs and away from the plane. Once I was far enough away from the plane two men quickly rushed over and pulled me into their custody. I willingly gave myself over to them, letting them trap my arms behind my back. I could have taken them all, but it would have hindered me getting to Abby.

Someone stepped out of the plane and a shot was fired, I was pretty sure it was Christian. The stupid fucker should have stayed on the plane where he was told. He really was lacking in common sense. He was proof that someone so smart could be so dumb. I couldn't pay much attention to what else was going on, because they were busy tying me up after checking my body for weapons. As gunfire ensued, I struggled to play the weak, submissive hostage. My hands were yanked behind my back with impressive force, although they could learn a thing or two from us. Duct tape was used to hold them together. They even added a strip of the silver adhesive across my face to keep my lips from moving. A dark pillow case was thrown over my head for good measures.

My body was shoved into the rear end of the SUV. Now, I had to rely on the training exercises we had. When they turned off one sense, it heightened the other senses. As much as I hated the rolling around the back end of the vehicle, I was able to zone in on which direction we were going.

After the vehicle had started moving, I begged that they would take me straight to Abby. I was really banking on them taking me into the compound and throwing me in the same room as Abby. They seemed to be just dumb enough to do something like that. I wanted to check on her, ensure she was still alive and well. Then, I would fight our way out of the building, her in tow. The rest of the guys were going to fight their way in as we fought our way out. It was the quickest way I could think of to get her to safety.

I was able to keep track of the route we took, benefits of blindfolded exercises. I could tell which direction we were heading, keeping my thoughts empty except to follow the path. When the vehicle pulled to a stop, I knew we should be about there. Fourteen right turns, three left turns, mostly moving Northwest over a span of a couple hours. Wait, we are moving again? Phew, only a couple hundred feet, must've been a gate or something. My fingers moved restlessly, another sign I was about to lose control over my actions. I told myself I needed to calm down. I was supposed to wait until I was inside before I lost control. This wasn't something I could count to ten and magically fix. I had to dig down deep and picture Abby's smiling face. Her beautiful image reminded me of why I was here preparing to get my ass beaten. Her innocent face did wonders in bringing me down off my high. As they opened the trunk, they hauled me out and dragged me to the house. *Lazy fuckers! They are scuffing up my boots.* What do I do? I go limp, complete dead weight for them to try to maneuver me wherever it was they were taking me.

They retaliated by hitting my head with something hard, the butt of a gun maybe? That'll leave a mark, but it was well worth it.

I smirked to myself, welcoming the pain; it's going to take more than that to change me. It was fun feeling them struggle under my weight, I could only imagine them trying to haul Carl's massive weight around. Going up the stairs took a toll on my dangling legs, it's all right, pain is temporary. I felt the chair I was thrown into. Oh, it was a hard wooden one. I think maybe I could break it if I did it right, but I have to wait until I'm alone in the room which was probably not happening anytime soon.

My pillowcase was removed; Juan's face was two inches from mine. "Welcome to my home." His breath smelled of cheap whiskey, his teeth yellowed from cigars or cigarettes, the cologne he was wearing seemed to be a combination of everything and its mother. The duct tape was ripped from my lips, ripping a moan with it.

I met Juan's eyes. A smile formed on my lips. "We meet again."

The fucker hauled off and bitch slapped me with his pinky ring wearing hand. "I talk, you listen. My house, my rules."

I nodded, not looking away from his eyes, no longer the weak submissive. I had a score to settle with this asshole. "Where is she?"

"Safe from you." He hauled off and left another imprint of that damn pinky ring on my cheek.

"You hit like a fucking girl. I bet your mom hits harder." Remember how I said I'm not the brightest?

I was greeted with a closed fist. "Throw him in the room." With that, Juan turned and started to leave the room.

"Sir, I would like to see if I can get some answers out of him," one of his guys spoke up. Holding up a taser, he looked at his boss. "Please?"

Juan nodded and continued out of the room.

"My name is Leon, and I would love you to meet my little friend." He lit up the taser and came closer to me. Internally I was groaning, this was going to hurt like hell. My shirt was ripped open and the taser sent volts straight into my chest. I bit back my scream. I'm not going to break.

Another man stepped forward. "So let's play a game of twenty questions, how does that sound?" He nodded and Leon took the taser away from my chest. "Give us the truth, and we will save you the pain. If not, well you will accept the consequences." He paused. "All right, first question. What is your name?"

I shrugged as my answer. The taser hit my neck.

"Let's try this one, how many are there outside?"

I shrugged and groaned as I got tasered once again. "Don't know how to count." I let it slip from my lips before I knew it. That comment ensured another healthy dose of electrical volts. Surprising me, they shoved their fist into my chest. I'd applaud their change of technique if it weren't going against me.

"Why are you here?" The male started pacing around the room.

"You bastards brought me here," I spat out. *Really? They couldn't answer that question on their own?* Leon shoved his fist into my face. Fuck that will leave a mark. I focused on the idea of paybacks.

"Who are you?" The pacing male paused to face me.

I looked up at him and smiled. "Your worst nightmare." As that left my mouth, I was rewarded with another unhealthy voltage of electricity through me.

Leon smiled. "Maybe he is so dumb he doesn't understand how this works."

"Maybe I'm just a sucker for pain?" I faced him, my eyebrow raised.

"How many people are outside?" Leon asked.

"No se," I smirked as I answered in Spanish. My chair was kicked so I was on my back staring at the ceiling. A foot came to rest on my chest.

"How many people are outside on your team?"

"No se," I responded, instantly feeling the pressure increase on my ribs. He's using the same pressure building technique I used on Abby's father.

"How did you figure out where we were located?"

"We are rocket scientists. Mother fuckin' geniuses!" I smiled. Of course, that was not the answer they were looking for, so I got another round from the taser as well as pressure increased on my chest. Catching my breath was getting a little harder. I'm going to break more than this fucker's foot for touching me, wait and see.

"Last time I ask you this question. How many of your friends are waiting for us outside?" Leon's face was right in mine.

I rolled my eyes. "Je ne sais pas," I answered in French. Leon removed his foot from my chest, only to rear it up and drop it through my chest. The tell-tale snaps had me cursing in agony. That fucker broke a rib or two.

"Where are they?" the pacing man asked.

"How the fuck do I know? I'm in here getting my ass tore up," I lashed out.

Leon kicked me in the side, causing me to let out a snarl. "When will you answer with truths?" The pacer stopped near my head.

"Truth? You can't handle the truth!" I couldn't resist. "Take what your pansy asses get! Get what you get, don't throw a fit, didn't your mama ever tell you that?" I responded between breaths.

Once he got through beating me and felt I was roughed up enough, they moved me to another room. They must've realized I'm not the friendliest since they called in another guy to help move me.

Even though my face felt like it was used as a punching bag, my chest felt like there was hope I was getting closer to Abby. I didn't make it easy for the three goons moving to the next room. I threw my weight around, causing them to lose their grip on me. I may not be as big as Eli or Carl, but I can still make a scene, especially when I'm pissed off. My arms may be laced together with duct tape behind me, my legs may be duct taped together at the ankles, but just like Abby I am stronger than duct tape.

You know if you manage to get a small tear in that silver shit, you can shred it, right? Throwing myself around knocking the guys off of me and somehow I managed to rip it, at least a small tear on the part around my ankles. A flex of my calves and done, the tape was ripped apart, my legs were freed. My arms however were still laced together with the gray tape. Right about now, I was wishing I would've worn long sleeves. This is going to hurt, yet pale in comparison to the taser action I received. Looking down, I realized somewhere along the way I must've pissed myself during the interrogation. No time for embarrassment, I have an important mission that required my full attention.

As soon as I was all alone and free, digging the earpiece out of my boot, I managed to light up my in-ear radio. I popped it to our radio channel and heard the other guys over the radio too. They had caught up to Eli. I whispered, "It's a great day to be a hostage, they are so pleasant and accommodating. They could learn a thing or two from us with their *persuasive questioning*. Who got hurt at the plane?"

Dirk came through my ear. "Christian got nicked but is all right. Everyone else made it safely to Eli."

"Do you see her?" Eli's anxious voice nearly deafened me.

"Not yet. Hell will erupt when they check on me though. They left me in a room without a view." I smiled and touched my swollen cheek. "I told your dumbass to stay back Christian, for such a smart guy you can be so dumb sometimes."

"Look for a guy about your size. Brown hair. Brown eyes," Eli continued to rattle off descriptions, agitation evident. I could tell he would rather be the one on the inside searching for her himself.

"Dude we are in Colombia, everyone has brown hair and brown eyes." I rolled my eyes and looked at the bruises covering my arms, raising my shirt I saw a couple large spots beginning to purple with bruises. "I need more to go off of E." I could picture him pacing like an expectant father.

Trying to reassure him I would find her was easier said than done. Thankfully the guys were out there to hold him back. They were waiting for me to give them a go. Just as soon as I found Abby, they would tear through hell to get to us.

Eli's voice came over the channel, "He doesn't really fit in, and he seems too gentle."

As I was sitting here in this room waiting for company to come give me another welcome beat down, I pondered what Eli had just told me. *He thinks there is a man on the inside that will be helpful. How is it that he trusts a man that is in cahoots with the enemy? There has to be a reason Eli feels he can trust the guy. If Eli can trust him, so can I. I hope.*

He doesn't fit in? He's too gentle looking? How the fuck does someone look too gentle? Did he have more sugar in his pants than in the canister on some grandmother's counter? Or maybe his hands were softer and smoother than a baby's bottom? This really made me wonder what words they use to describe me as well as what accommodations this guy really did offer.

I definitely don't look too gentle.

Chapter 29
RYLAND

I paced around the room, as I tried to remain calm while waiting for the welcome committee to come back for another round. We turned off radio chat once Eli was settled enough to realize I was going to do everything in my power to find her. To avoid getting caught with a communication device, I quickly stored the ear piece carefully back to the spot in my boot. Another lap around the room, my mind was still bouncing through all the different ways I could get through this with Abby safely in tow. From Eli's intel, I knew there were around thirty guys in here, so I couldn't exactly do it all alone.

I heard movement outside my room, so I quickly squatted down in the far corner, using the darkness to my advantage. My breath left me, the pain was blinding. The door knob was tested, then the sound of a key sliding home in the lock. The door opened and two guys walked in, one carrying a tray of food, if you could call it that, it looked more like a pile of leftover table scraps that even a starving dog wouldn't take. They made a menacing team as they stalked towards me. Evil was smeared across both their faces.

I stayed in the corner letting them come closer to me, meeting their eyes effectively sending a challenge. The male carrying the tray dumped it on the floor less than a foot from me. Using his broad booted foot, he ground the tray into the floor squishing the food into the cracks. Any hopes of getting fed quickly vanished as he muttered, "Oops."

I stood up and charged towards the man taking him down. The other guy crashed down over the two of us, dragging me off and tossing me into the wall like I was a ragdoll. Yanking me off the ground, he held me against the wall. His forearm pushed against my throat stealing my breath with it. "Wrong move ese," he growled.

While he held me against the wall, his buddy regained his footing and began using my body as a punching bag. He slammed fist after fist into my ribs, causing me to flinch each time. The lack of oxygen had me gasping for breath as much as the fists that continued to rearrange my vital organs. My body was betraying me from the lack of food and oxygen. I was losing the energy it took to maintain my inner fight. There was no way for me to fight back.

When they were sure I wouldn't fight back, he moved his forearm from my neck, letting me drop to the floor in a heap. My lungs struggled to take in a breath. It's never hurt this much before to breathe. I started to wheeze before I broke out in a coughing fit. Fuck! Maybe I'm not going to be able to do what I had in mind, seems I forgot to factor weakness from lack of food. Maybe the plan wasn't foolproof, but proof that I am indeed a fool.

They left me to suffer alone in the room, quickly exiting and locking up behind them. By the time I was able to catch my breath, I was exhausted. Holding my head up took too much effort, so I stared down at the floor and tried to refocus. It was pitch black in my room, except the small stream of light coming under the door. I kept an eye on that patch of light, watching shadows walk by. Focusing on that eased my pain just a smidgen.

A shadow stopped in front of the door. I heard the key slide into the lock and cowered down onto myself. The door opened and a guy walked in carrying a glass of clear liquid.

He shut the door behind him and flipped on a light switch. I didn't fear him. A closer look at him had Eli's description flashing in my head. This was the guy that he was talking about, had to be. He didn't have the hard lines and menacing demeanor like the other ones did.

He crept towards me as one might an injured animal. "It's ok, I am here to help."

"How can I be sure?" I asked as I eased my legs straight out in front of me, letting my butt land on the hardwood floor.

"Duct tape and honey." As soon as those words left his mouth, I let out a painful sigh of relief. "I'm Jaime." He offered as he held out the glass of liquid, "Here is some water."

I eyed him carefully as I reached out to take the glass. "I'm Ryland. Where is she?"

He reached his hand out again, holding two tablets. "They aren't much, just ibuprofen."

I took them and swallowed them down with the water, after I smelled it cautiously. "Thanks. Where is she?" I asked anxiously.

"Down below, there are between four and ten guys patrolling her cave. Give it a couple hours. There should be less of them. They are still on high alert from Eli's attacks outside," Jaime told me as his eyes scanned my body. "I can maybe stitch up a couple of those cuts, but looks like you need a real doctor."

"Thanks, Captain Obvious." I managed to give him a smirk. "But don't worry about me. I'll be fine once we are out of here with Abby. How bad off is she?"

"They haven't let me back down there since I came back inside. She wasn't good when I left her though. She seemed to be losing her fight. I don't know for sure, she was bleeding and bruised." Concern shadowed his face. I could easily see that he felt sorry for her. So this is what a guy that seemed too gentle looked like? I could see this guy fitting in with our group more than the guys he was with.

I must've let a growl slip out because he jumped back eyeing me warily. "Sorry. I'm pissed. I need to get to her yesterday."

"I have to go, or they will get suspicious. I will come back when they go lax on the guard duty," he stated.

I simply nodded and handed him back his empty glass. More time to wait. I hooked up my ear piece again, figured I should check in with the guys. "What's it looking like on the outside?"

"You sound like shit. What is going on?" Carl's voice sounded in my ear.

"Pretty sure I am sitting here with a couple busted ribs, maybe a punctured lung. The welcoming committee came in and gave me another round. I found the guy, Jaime, he does stick out a bit. He gave me something for the pain and shared the status of guards. Right now there are anywhere between four and ten guys watching her cell, he promised to come back when they started to relax. Seems they are still on high alert from the smoke bombs someone was making." I let them know.

"Give us the word and we will knock down the doors, create a distraction," Carl stated. He was itching for a confrontation.

Eli interrupted, "He say anything about her?"

I took a breath, letting out a sigh. "He hasn't seen her since he's been back, says she wasn't in very good shape when he saw her last."

"I shouldn't have waited to get in there...." Eli started.

"They are packed deep in there; you wouldn't have made it all the way in there without being beat to hell. Get your head in the game, I know this is Abby and you are worried about her, but you need us as backup," Dirk could be heard talking Eli off the ledge.

I began pacing my room again; I'm not a patient man. I need to get to Abby and fast. My mind needed to get off my pain and onto the mission. We carried on with a little more conversation. They were disappointed they couldn't get in as fast as they'd like, and I was frustrated with being locked in a room unable to search for her.

I settled back onto the floor, realizing the pacing wasn't helping with my pain. My fingers tapped my legs restlessly as my feet bounced. The pain was kicking my ass, but I know I need to relax as much as possible. When Jaime comes back, I knew I had to get on my feet and act fast. Pain would have to take a back seat.

Chapter 30
ELI

I was going crazy being this close, yet still so far away from my girl. When I heard Ryland talk about how many people are on guard near Abby, I couldn't stop cursing. Now we knew it wouldn't be nearly as easy as we thought, but it would definitely be worth it. I was ready for a fight, as were the rest of the guys. As brave as Ryland tried to sound over the radio, I knew he was really hurting. He would need medical care as soon as we could get him out of there.

I began pacing again. Needing something to do to bide my time until we could do anything, I started going through my weapons. Both of my holsters held matching glocks, my K-bar was firmly hooked to my left thigh, inside my other pockets I had multiple throwing knives at the ready, and of course, I had extra ammo on hand thanks to the goody bags the guys brought with them. Glancing down I double checked the extra blade in my boot. I was ready for action and I knew the other guys out here with me were too.

"Ry, what weapons you have on you?" I decided to check in.

"Two fists and one hundred and eighty pounds of pissed off motherfucker!" he responded.

"Damn it. No actual weapons?"

"Where the fuck would I have put them to keep them hidden? They would have taken any weapons on me and used them against me. It was pointless," he growled. "If I were to die by someone using one of my own weapons against me, they'd use that as a training exercise of what not to do. I'm pretty sure that Jaime will help make sure I have a weapon of some sort." He sighed.

I knew he hated depending on people, especially people he didn't know.

Now we had to figure out how to get Ryland more weapons. The plan was to wait for the signal. As soon as we got the signal, the boys and I on the outside would be breaking down doors as Ryland and Jaime went to get Abby safely out of there. We would fight our way in and clear a path so they could get Abby out of this hellhole. As soon as everyone was out, we were heading to town and then flying back to New York.

I worried about Abby. Hearing that Jaime hadn't been in there since he got back was nerve-wracking. Finding out that she wasn't in good shape before I had my little interrogation with Jaime, had me praying and pacing, and praying some more.

I continued to quiz Ryland about what he saw, what happened, and how many people he has seen. He let out a small, humorless chuckle. "Leon and his buddy are mine. Those fuckers tased me one time too many. Incidentally, they asked me some of the same questions."

"I want Leon. He was the guy from the bus stop," I called dibs. "He gets to feel a little bit of the torture he has put me through. Hell maybe we should double team that sorry S.O.B."

"Sounds like a plan my man," he agreed with me. "Shit! someone is coming, going offline." I heard a little shuffle as he must've been taking his ear piece out to return it back to his boot. Now I was nervous as all hell, maybe it would be Jaime giving us a go.

"Eli, we need to prepare just in case it's our chance to storm the building." Dirk pulled me from my thoughts. "This is your mission. You tell us who is going where."

I nodded and stood before my buddies. I recalled the map in my head. "This place has three entrances. Dirk and Bo take the front; Carl, Adams and Christian take the side. Trevor you have my back as we go in the front door."

They each nodded their head as they got their positions called out. "Do we have any idea exactly where Ryland is at?" Adams asked as he checked his pistols to make sure they were fully loaded.

Bo pulled out the map we had of the location, then from Ryland's description I showed the place he would probably be at. "If he's not at this one, he will be here." I pointed again at the map. "Carl, I'm sure you will get to him first. You have the extra weaponry, right?"

He nodded and gave a smirk, "Of course. Any idea of how many we are looking forward to playing with?"

I shrugged, "Maybe thirty or so? Just make sure you have extra ammo."

"I have Christian on my team, of course I have extra ammo." Carl let a small laugh out. Christian sighed and looked down at the ground, Carl answered, "Suck it up cupcake! You sit around and play with computers all day instead of hitting the ranges with the rest of us."

Christian pulled out his little tablet from his cargo pocket. "I will be able to scramble the security system as soon as we get ready to go."

I nodded and took another look at the rest of my guys. "This place is very similar to Juan's last place. Just like last time, our goal is to get in there and rescue our hostages, and get the hell out of there."

We heard noise from behind us, all of us turned on heel towards the sound, guns aimed and ready. "Duct tape and honey" was called out from the guy. We instantly let our weapons down to our sides as the male continued to approach us. When he was close enough, we realized it was Commander Collins. "Sorry I'm late, couldn't let you guys have all the fun." Collins smiled.

Once he was within our group, we laid out the mission. I placed him with Trevor and myself, in case of something went wrong and we needed to carry Abby or Ryland out, we could use the extra team member. "Thank you for coming."

"You think I was going to let you boys do this on your own?" Collins asked as he double checked his weapons, he was ready.

I nodded as Ryland's voice came in through my ear, "False alarm. Jaime came to check on me, said there are about five guys leaning against Abby's holding area. I was given a nice shiny little gun, along with news. We are moving into action in about a half hour."

"Ten four. Are you in the west room or the east one?" I asked.

"West. How are you guys coming?"

Collins butted in, "Eli, Trev and I will be coming in the front door. Bo and Dirk are taking the back, and Carl, Adams, and Christian will be coming in the side."

"Wait, hold up. Was that Collins?"

"I wouldn't let you have all the fun without me." Collins jested, "See your dumbass inside. We will discuss this later."

"E, I don't want you to come towards me. You need to hit the staircase heading to the basement. Intel says she is down there, behind a door that looks more like a storm cellar than a room. It's a freshly dug hole in the ground." Ryland gave off as many details as he could.

I swore to myself, cursing me out for letting her go through this hell for this long. Collins patted my shoulder. "We will get her to safety. You need your head on straight to get to her. We know there are multiple targets inside gunning for us. When we get back, we will discuss why you let Ryland pull off his dumbass plan and your decision to disobey direct orders."

Carl shook his head. "That will be between you and him. He told us to stand down and let him do what he was going to do. Eli used his heart instead of his head."

Ryland let out a burst of laughter. "This is on me Collins. I knew we needed to know what we were looking at on the inside."

"You willingly put yourself in danger in hopes you might find out something? Why?"

"She's important to us," Ryland stated. "I made an oath to Remlock, and I am damn sure going to live up to it."

Collins simply shook his head, muttering under his breath. I could see he was pissed off by the emotions that played across his face. But more than pissed off, he was frustrated. He glanced my direction and nodded his head. "Let's get in position boys."

As we gathered in our three separate groups, the other two groups heading to position themselves around the house, near where they were planning on entering. Before we headed towards the front door, Collins turned towards me and patted my shoulder. "We will bring her home. We got this."

Chapter 31
RYLAND

Jaime had just handed me a shiny yet powerful weapon before he headed back down the hall to take care of some of his tasks required of him by Juan. Even though I hurt every single time I moved, I took a few deep painful cleansing breaths and prepared myself for action.

Holding my breath, I took a tour of the room. I needed to get my feet moving and clear my brain of everything aside from taking care of the business at hand. This pain would be my motivation to find her faster. The faster we rescue her, the faster my pain could be taken care of. I wouldn't rest until she was safe again.

A knock on the door had me sliding back down to the floor. I wasn't sure who it could be. Jaime snuck into the door, barely opening it enough to squeeze his small frame through.

"What's going on outside?" Jaime asked as he brought me a bottle of what appeared to be dirty water. "Don't drink it, I learned from your buddy Eli. Inside is something that will make one hell of a smoke bomb."

"They are ready, just waiting for us to give it a go," I stated and placed the bottle into my cargo pocket. "Boys, we are a go here."

One by one they let us know they were ready. We were to give them about two minutes to clear the wall as soon as Christian fucked with their security system.

"Scrambling in ten. You guys in position?" Christian asked.

As he counted down, I could hear the guys moving around, their breaths and small conversations were carrying through their mics. As Christian said "one," I heard grunts as I guessed them to be scaling the walls. I heard a lot of cursing as they got through the Constantine wire, that shit is brutal and will definitely leave a mark. We all carried our fair share of scars from interaction with the shit over the years.

"That is going to leave a fucking mark, I hate this fucking wire!" Trevor mumbled.

"She better be fucking worth it. That bitch better be fucking worth all this. These were my favorite jeans," I heard Adams grumble.

Next thing I heard was a loud 'humph.'

"Sorry, just trying to help your sorry ass down, didn't want you tearing up that nice-looking face of yours," I heard a smile in Carl's voice. I could only bet that he gave him a shove off the top of the wall.

"Seems we need another team building exercise boys," I heard Collins muse. "We ready? Team one is at the front door."

"Team two in position," Bo stated.

"Team three is a go," Carl added.

"Knock knock motherfucker," Eli stated as the doors were simultaneously kicked in.

Jaime looked at me as I stood up. "It's go time," I informed him.

He smirked and cocked his weapon, a sawed-off shotgun. "Ready? Follow me." He opened the door as our guys stormed the entry ways.

I met Eli's eyes, giving him a stiff nod. I followed behind him as we took a left and hit the basement stairs. Punching a couple holes in the bottle Jaime gave me, I tossed it down first, effectively drawing out four males with their weaponry aimed our direction. Guess this was the unwelcoming committee? "Wrong move ese," the one we knew as Leon stated.

"Looking for something boys?" the one who was responsible for tasing and questioning me asked.

Without looking at Eli, I knew the plan. He went left, I went right. Those two boys were held high against the walls. Jaime and

Collins met the two remaining guys with their guns trained between their eyes. "Move and you have taken your last breath. Drop your weapons motherfuckers." Collins took a step closer and cocked his weapon, proving he was speaking the truth. They dropped their weapons to the floor. Collins stowed the weapons away from them and Jaime helped zip tie their hands behind their backs. They hauled the two males up a couple stairs before zip tying their ankles together. "You move, you die."

"I knew you were a traitorous son of a bitch," The taser guy spouted off as he saw Jaime. I pulled the guy a little closer to me and then shoved his head, and back, hard against the wall. If he had any brains in there, they would've been rattled and useless.

He started to lash out against me, but Collins quickly helped me subdue the douche bag. "I got this one. You go find her."

Trevor stood quietly by the two zip tied guys. One male started to move, only to have Trevor's glock meet his temple. "Go ahead, move. Try me."

There was a lot of loud noises and gunfire happening above us, but I didn't have time to check if our boys were holding their own, I had to find Abby and fast. I knew our guys enough to know they weren't about to do anything stupid, because let's face it I was the reckless and stupid one of the group. I glanced towards Eli; he nodded towards me. "Find her for me." He continued using Leon's face as a punching bag.

Jaime led me towards the darkest corner of the basement. He turned on his flashlight, looking for the door. "Looking for something?" A male stood in front of the door with a gun pointed directly at my chest. A shot was fired off as I strafed at last minute. The smell of freshly singed flesh had wafted towards me before I realized I was hit. I aimed the nine I was carrying and shot off a shot, right in the chest of the guy. He dropped like a sack of potatoes, actually more closely resembling a ten pound pile of shit in a five pound bag.

"Ryland, talk to me, what's going on down there?" I heard Collins call out.

"Need a tourniquet," I responded and headed back towards the group.

Trevor shook his head when he saw the wound, being our medic, "It's barely more than a flesh wound. I will put a tourniquet in place for now, yet when we get back, I want to personally dig in that wound to retrieve the bullet."

I shook my head. "Yeah I know you are pissed."

He tightened the tourniquet above my wound. "Just as I know you are a dumbass," he responded. "Give me a sec. Watch these two." He pointed to the two guys still zip tied together before turning to dig in his cargo pocket.

As I watched the two guys, Eli turned towards me. "Want to throw in a few swings Ry?" I nodded.

I watched the two males sitting on the stairs. "Ouch, what the fuck was that?" I yelped when I felt a stab of a needle in my ass cheek.

Trevor smiled. "Its ok nut lick, just a little morphine to take the edge off. And I couldn't resist jabbing you with a needle."

I cocked my head to the side. "Thanks."

Eli let Leon drop to the ground, so I gave him a good hard couple of kicks. Reaching down, I snatched up the taser that fell from his pocket. A smile crossed my face. "Time for a little fun. A little payback if you will." Pushing the button, I ensured there was still juice in it. I looked at Collins. "That one gets some of this too."

Collins nodded. "Have at 'em." He stepped back, yet kept his arm across the man's neck, allowing him only to take small breaths. "Think of it as a little get well soon gift."

I stuck the taser to Leon's jugular and gave him a nice long jolt. The smell filled the room, he had shat himself. "How's it feel man? Not feeling so big anymore, are you?" I took the taser away, but couldn't resist shoving the taser to his balls.

His string of curses brought a smile to my face. After giving a few shocks to the other guy, I turned and headed back to where Jaime was waiting. "You ok man?" he asked.

I nodded but said nothing. Instead, I focused on the door. Looking closer, I realized there were four padlocks holding it closed. As much as I wanted to just pull out the nine and aim at each lock, I didn't want to scare Abby. Gunfire in an enclosed area was loud as fuck. She has been through enough. I didn't want to traumatize her further.

Digging through the guard's pockets, I got lucky and found a set of keys. "What the fuck? Why are there so many damn keys? There has to be close to fifty keys on this thing," I complained before I started trying each of the keys. As I tried each key, I prayed silently that she would be ok by the time we got in there to her.

After trying many keys and failing, Eli took the keys from me. "Watch my back. I will get these locks opened." I slid down the wall, landing on my ass waiting for Eli to get the key and lock combination figured out. "Babe? You in there Babe? We are coming, hang on a little longer. I promised we would always come for you."

He continued to talk to her through the door. I could see it was his way of trying to remain calm and focused on what he was doing. Even in the dark, I could see the pain on his face, and wished I could take away some of it.

Finally, after trying ten keys, he got one lock off. One down, three to go. His fingers began shaking as he tried key after key. At last, all the locks were off and the two halves of the cellar-like doors were yanked open. It was pitch black. I was at his side as we entered the tiny room. Jaime joined us, using a flashlight to scan the room.

In the corner, was a heap of what could only be Abby.

She wasn't moving, no noise came from her. Within moments, we both hit the floor beside her. "Abby, baby, we're here," Eli whispered as he pulled her into his arms. She was limp.

I left the room to go get Trevor. "She needs help, we might've been too late," I told him as I got closer.

Collins and Jaime watched our zip tied friends while Trevor grabbed his bag and followed me. When we returned to the room, Eli was still talking low to Abby, trying to rouse her, "Baby, come back."

"We need to get out of here, there's not enough light. Carry her out to the hall so I can check her out, Eli," Trevor stated.

Eli picked her up and hauled her to the hall, laying her down gently on the blanket that was used to cover her in the hole. She didn't move. Not even the slow rise and fall of breathing was evident.

Chapter 32
ELI

We got to her, but it was too late. I wiped tears away from my face as I watched Trevor do his magic. I couldn't stand there helplessly any longer, so I tore off up the stairs to see how things were going up there. *Keep busy, Trevor knows what he is doing, just get the area cleared so we can evac quickly,* I told myself over and over.

There was blood and bodies everywhere. Christian was sitting on the floor next to three zip tied guys. "What's the situation?" I asked.

"We've shot six, not life threatening, yet. A couple of them won't be walking, figured we'd let them suffer a little bit. Carl and Bo went upstairs to find Juan; Dirk is down the hall. I'm not sure what he is doing. You find her? How's Abby?" He looked at me hopefully.

"We're too late," I stated and looked at the worn wooden floor.

"Oh no. We can't think like that. Is Trevor taking care of her?"

I nodded. Avoidance, that's what I am good at. "I'm going to check on the rest of the guys. You good here?"

"Yep." He nodded and gave me a weak smile. "Have faith."

I checked the hall and found Dirk tying two guys together. "Find her?"

"I think we are too late. She wasn't moving at all," I let him know. "You need help here?"

"Nah, I'm good man. You should get back there with her."

"I can't do shit. I'm just in the way. I need to help get everyone taken care of here. Lead the mission. Follow directions. Keep moving," I began rambling as I darted up the stairs, and found Carl and Bo in position with guns aimed at Juan's head. Moving up between the two, I pulled out one of my little throwing knives. With a quick flick of my wrist, the knife was impaled into his leg, just above the knee.

"What the fuck?" Juan attempted to pull the knife out of his leg, with no luck. I made sure I hit him deep.

Without a single word, I flicked my wrist, landing another blade in his other leg, causing him to fall down. "I wouldn't do that if I were you," a guy said as he came out of the room holding a gun trained on my chest.

"Do what? This?" Raising an eyebrow, I let another knife fly out of my hand, hitting the male just to the left of his sternum. He collapsed to the ground without another word.

Juan's eyes flashed with fear before he managed to get his emotions under control. I smiled and withdrew another blade from my pocket, and flipped it over and over through my fingers, taunting him. "I'm not scared of death," Juan spat at me.

"Oh, but I wouldn't let you go that easily." I smiled as I let the blade fly and hit his gut. He curled into a fetal position, trying to protect himself. "Let's call this blade karma, a little get what you give." I stepped closer to him with my K-bar in hand. Juan was unable to hide the fear that seeped out of his pores. Closer yet, I knelt down beside him and debated where I wanted to hit him. The decision was made. I rolled him onto his back and stabbed my K-bar down deep into his groin, slowly withdrawing it. Standing back up, I turned and walked away. "Finish him."

I took the steps back down to the main floor, looking through all the rooms, making sure we didn't miss anybody. *Keep going*, I told myself, *Trevor is doing his job, just keep going.*

Talking into my headset, "We need a count. How many?"

"Three dead, two tied," Dirk called his off.

"Three tied, six injured," Christian informed me. I added them together. So far we were up to fourteen.

"Four dead, four immobilized," Carl gave his count.

"One dead, four tied and crying," Collins gave me a head count from the basement.

"I'm tracking 27, right?" I asked as I traveled back into the basement.

"Yep. Let's get Abby and get out of here," Dirk stated. "Put all these people on the main floor. We torching this joint?"

"Yes. I don't want there to be a chance in the world for any of these guys to ever come in contact with her again," I stated as I traveled down the last couple of stairs.

Somewhere between the time I was upstairs and the time I made it back down, the cuffs were removed from her ankles and wrists. She was flat on her back, not moving. Never in my entire life have I been so scared.

Trevor's face was grim when he turned to look at me.

Fuck! We really were too late? I dropped to my knees beside her and begged and pleaded for her to come back to me. I told her over and over that I love her and need her, "Baby, please don't leave me. I won't last without you. I love you. You are my forever."

Acknowledgements:

I would like to take the time and give you, the reader, a special thank you. Thank you for the time you took to read and hopefully enjoy my book. If you enjoyed it, won't you please take a moment to leave me a review at your favorite retailer?

A special thanks also goes to my husband, Cory, the king of the common senselessness. Thank you for all the little tidbits you gave me! You have earned your very own teddy bear.

To the rest of my family, thank you for your support and love! I wouldn't be where I am today if it weren't for you! I love you and feel blessed to call you mine!

For my amazing friends, thank you for chasing after me while I followed my dreams. The bigger the stick, the stronger the motivation. Some of you peeps have crazy BIG sticks!

To all my WoW Freaks, thanks for listening to my incessant rambling! Thanks for keeping me off task during editing!

About the Author

I am a mom of two truly amazing daughters, Cadence and Cailee, and the wife of my very own camo angel. Writing has always been my way to escape reality and live in my very own imaginary world. I love to entice the imagination of others with my words, allowing them to escape as I do.

My love for animals led me down my education path. Not only do I have a bachelor's degree in biology, I am also a certified veterinary assistant and dog trainer. Being a part of the animal rescue in my hometown and a therapy dog team lets me share my love of animals with the rest of the world.

Although my life hasn't always been sunshine and rainbows, I have always been a very generous and nurturing person.

Outside of my house growing up, I had to be the sweetest little girl to hide the struggles going on inside our house. Inside the house, I had to be stronger than any child should ever have to be. Making it through it all has molded me to be the person I am today. I am:

"Stronger than duct tape. Sweeter than honey."

Contact Me:

Follow me on Facebook:
https://www.facebook.com/Cassandra.Kirkpatrick.Author

Join me on Goodreads:
https://www.goodreads.com/CassandraKirkpatrickAuthor

E-mail:
C_kirk001@live.com

Made in the USA
San Bernardino, CA
20 September 2014